The boy wa...  God.

Richard turned Jamie over. To his surprise, he found, instead of broken and bleeding skin, thick bandages covering most of the boy's back.

Without further thought, Richard crossed to his desk for some scissors. Then he cut through the bandages from waist to shoulder. He was more than a little relieved to find that a few fine red lines were the only sign of the beating Jamie had received.

Gently he turned him on to his back to make him more comfortable. The bandages fell away. To Richard's astonishment, he found that his hands were cradling, not the body of a thirteen-year-old boy, but the delectable breasts of a fully-formed girl.

Richard's head was spinning. He was remembering everything that had happened since Jamie had come into his life and discovering new perspectives on both her reactions and his own. All the strange attractions he had felt towards a simpleton boy... As he tried to gather his tumbling thoughts, his hands continued to cup her breasts.

And at that moment, Jamie's eyes opened and she looked up into his.

Joanna Maitland was born and educated in Scotland though she has spent most of her adult life in England or abroad. She has been a systems analyst, an accountant, a civil servant, and director of a charity. She started to write for her children when they were very small, and progressed from there into historical fiction which she used to write while commuting daily to London. Joanna now works as a part-time consultant so that she can devote more time to her writing, her husband and two children, and their acre of untamed garden in Hampshire.

A PENNILESS PROSPECT

Joanna Maitland

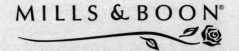

MILLS & BOON®

For Frances

First published in Great Britain 2001
Harlequin Mills & Boon Limited,
Eton House, 18-24 Paradise Road, Richmond, Surrey TW9 1SR

© Joanna Maitland 2001

ISBN 0 263 82730 5

Set in Times Roman 10½ on 12½ pt.
04-0501-73085

Printed and bound in Spain
by Litografía Rosés S.A., Barcelona

Chapter One

'It's Cinderella, all over again. Who says fairy tales don't come true? The only difference is, I'm a mite short of fairy godmothers.' With a heartfelt sigh, Jessamyne sank into a hard, straight-backed chair, the only one in her spartan bedroom.

'Oh, miss, you mustn't take on so. If my lady should hear you—'

'The wicked stepmother? Come now, Biddy dear, she knows precisely what I think of her, as you are well aware. But she also knows there is nothing I can do about it, since she has my father's ear as well as control of the purse-strings. Papa will not help me. And without money, I cannot help myself. Now, if you were but a fairy godmother, Biddy…'

'Oh, give over, Miss Jamie, do. Them things only happen in fairy stories. There ain't no Prince Charmings in the real world. P'raps if you was to make more of an effort to please her ladyship—'

'I've tried that, Biddy. You know I have. It doesn't work. She simply walks all over me. But if I stand up to her, she has to acknowledge I exist, however little good it may do me.' She glanced at the empty grate and the layer of crazed ice on the inside of the window pane. Drawing her threadbare shawl more closely round her shoulders, she smiled bravely at her old nurse. 'At least she doesn't make me scrub floors and sweep cinders.'

'No,' agreed Biddy, 'but it would make little difference if she did. Your hands are little better than a scullery maid's, with all that gardening you do. In the depths of winter, too! If only you would—'

She was interrupted by a scratching at the door— a maid with a message summoning Miss Jessamyne to her stepmother's dressing-room.

Jamie swallowed hard. Such a summons always boded ill. Sometimes she would simply be berated, belittled for her looks or her behaviour. Sometimes she would hear of punishments to come, for real or imagined transgressions. And sometimes both. Never, in all Lady Calderwood's time in the house, had she spoken a single kind or loving word to her stepdaughter. There was no reason to suppose that this summons would be any different.

Although Jamie entered those stern precincts with head held high, she could not wholly conceal the uncertainty she felt. Lady Calderwood was seated at her dressing table while her abigail put the finishing touches to her hair. Jamie was left standing by the door, unacknowledged, for several minutes. Her uncertainty was soon replaced by indignation. How dared that woman treat her so?

At length, her ladyship was satisfied, and her woman was dismissed. She turned slowly to look at her stepdaughter, scrutinising her from head to toe with ill-concealed dislike. Her lip curled slightly. 'Well, Jessamyne, you may guess why I have sent for you.'

'No, ma'am,' replied Jamie evenly, 'I have not the least idea.' She noted, without surprise, that she was not invited to sit. She was deliberately being left to stand like a disobedient child awaiting punishment. Well, she would not help her stepmother to play her little games. Jamie lifted her chin a fraction. She would not say anything more.

After a moment, Lady Calderwood continued grimly, 'Very well, I shall tell you, since you do not wish to venture an opinion.' She gave a very nasty smile at which Jamie shivered a little, in spite of all her efforts at self-control. She felt so helpless when she was in the power of this woman.

Her ladyship's smile broadened. 'You are past twenty already, Jessamyne. It is high time you were married and ceased to be such a charge on your poor papa.'

Jamie bit her lip in frustration. She was precious little charge on 'poor papa', considering how little was spent on her. She could not remember when she had last had a new gown or anything becoming to wear, even at second hand. But marriage—did that mean a season in London, *at last*? And perhaps even a few new gowns? For if they did not garb her becomingly, who would be found to offer for her?

'Of course, there can be no question of a season for you,' announced her ladyship sharply, watching her stepdaughter's face fall. 'Your papa could not countenance the expense. And it would be a waste of money, for who would choose to offer for a girl like you? No looks and no portion? No. Even *I* could not fire you off successfully.'

Jamie could feel the colour draining from her face. She clamped her lips tightly together in an effort to control their trembling. No doubt her ladyship was pleased with the effect.

'I see you have grasped my meaning. There is only one solution for a girl like you. And you should be grateful to your papa for all the trouble he has taken to find you a husband who is prepared to have you, in spite of all your shortcomings. What have you to say to that, my girl?'

She smiles like a snake, thought Jamie, a snake who is about to swallow me up. Oh, God! What am I to do? She is waiting for me to ask who has been found to take me off their hands.

She compressed her lips even more tightly and stared brazenly at her stepmother, refusing to give her the satisfaction of a response. She was pleased to see her stepmother's frown. Jamie's defiance had turned self-satisfaction to anger. Good—even if it did turn on her.

'You think to defy me, girl? But not for long, I assure you, not for long.' Lady Calderwood paused to rearrange the generous folds of her amber silk gown. 'You will be married within the month. And I shall warn your husband about the need to curb your rebellious nature, be sure of that. He will see that you abide by your vows of obedience.'

Jamie remained motionless, but her brain was

churning. Who was this man who had agreed to marry her, a plain girl with no dowry? And why? She shivered again, but then she forced herself to straighten her back and stiffen her wobbly knees. Clearly her stepmother was determined not to give her a name until she asked for it. So be it. There would be a battle of wills.

For long moments, the two women stared at each other—one young, shabbily dressed but proud, the other somewhat past her prime and indulged in every way. The older woman broke first. 'Insolent chit!' she hissed. 'Go to your room. I shall deal with you later.'

Head held high, Jamie left the room and returned to her own freezing chamber, where she threw herself on to the bed and thumped her clenched fists into the pillow. 'The old witch,' she muttered. 'May she rot in hell!'

Much as she tried, Jamie was not able to prevent a few tears from squeezing their way out on to her cheeks. She despised her own weakness. But the thought of marriage to some unknown man—chosen by her stepmother, so bound to be utterly hateful—was horrifying. She would be completely in his power, forced to submit to his will in everything—until the day she died.

Not for the first time, Jamie was left alone in her room for hours with neither food nor company. She had known it would be so. However frightened she might be of the fate which awaited her, she refused to yield to her stepmother's petty tortures. Dumb insolence was her only weapon and she was quite prepared to use it, at whatever personal cost. In this case, she knew she would win eventually, for she would have to be given the name of the lucky bridegroom sooner or later, even if only on the day of her wedding.

She huddled herself into a ball on the bed, wrapping every scrap of blanket around her in an effort to stop herself from freezing. Eventually, in spite of cold and hunger, she fell into a troubled sleep.

It must have been the sound of the door which woke her. Biddy was standing in the centre of the room with a gown draped over her plump arm. She looked uncomfortable. 'Her ladyship sent me to warn you that your betrothed is arriving later today. You are to be ready to receive him.'

Jamie sat up immediately, her eyes wide with shock. She was still freezing cold, in spite of the blankets, but at least she was not shivering. She refused to appear as a quivering wreck in front of her old nurse.

But she was not too proud to ask Biddy for the man's name.

'I'm sorry, miss, but I'm afraid I don't know. Nobody does—except her ladyship, and your papa.' Biddy moved towards the bed. 'Her ladyship sent this gown for you to wear to dinner this evening.' Biddy sounded more confident now, moving on to practical matters.

It was a plain white muslin gown such as might be worn by a debutante from a family of modest means. 'White,' breathed Jamie bitterly, 'as becomes the virgin sacrifice. How very appropriate. With my colouring, I shall certainly look the part.'

Her irony was lost on old Biddy. 'White is the proper colour for a young girl such as you, miss. I'll admit you do look better in colours, being as you're so pale-complexioned, but you have no choice tonight. You have no other decent gown to your name. It'll have to be this white muslin.'

Jamie got up, pulling the blankets from the bed and wrapping them round her shoulders. 'When is he due to arrive, Biddy?'

'Nobody is sure. He may be delayed by the weather, o' course. It's difficult travelling at this time of year.' Biddy seemed to be trying to avoid the subject of Jamie's future.

Jamie was not really surprised. Old Biddy had served the family for over twenty years as, first, Jamie's nurse, then as her half-brother's, and now Jamie's three half-sisters'. Biddy would not dare to risk her place with the Calderwood family by taking Jamie's part against the formidable mistress of the house.

Jamie forced a smile. She still had her pride. 'Thank you, Biddy. I shan't need you this evening. Go back to your little ones. They'll be fretting for you.' Biddy hurried away to the nursery where it was warm and cosy.

As Jamie began to change into the thin muslin gown, she heard the sound of wheels crunching across the drive. He was here! The ice on the window blurred her view, but she could just make out a gentleman's travelling carriage and four horses. Her betrothed travelled in style to acquire his reluctant bride, it seemed. He must be wealthy—which might explain how he could afford to marry a girl with no dowry. What else might it mean?

She felt an overpowering desire to see what this man was like. Would she recognise him? Would he be one of her father's gambling cronies? Hastily throwing her shawl around her bare shoulders, she crept down the stairs to find a safe vantage point on the landing. Kneeling behind the balusters, she peered through to get a glimpse of her fate when he was admitted through the great doors of Calderwood Hall.

But the gentleman who stood in the entrance hall to be relieved of his travelling coat was like no man she had ever met. Although he was dressed in deep mourning, to Jamie's untutored eye he was tall, dark and unbelievably handsome.

She drew in a sharp breath and held it, waiting for him to speak.

'My name is Hardinge,' he said, in a deep, well-modulated voice that sent a shiver all the way down to her toes. She was transfixed by the sound. It set her mind spinning so much that, for several moments, she could not make out a word that was being said.

She came to her senses as the gentleman stopped speaking. The butler was glancing surreptitiously at the card in his hand. 'Certainly, my lord. If you would kindly step into the saloon.'

Jamie watched as the noble visitor was bowed into the crimson saloon. The door closed on him, but his image remained before her. How could it be that such a man—a man whose mere presence could make her skin tingle and her heart race—should arrive at Calderwood now? He could not be her betrothed.

Could he?

Chapter Two

'My name is Hardinge.' Richard, Earl Hardinge, proffered his card to the butler. 'Be so good as to take my card up to your master and beg him for the favour of a few minutes of his time, with my apologies for having arrived unannounced. It is a matter of some importance.'

Richard was content to wait in the saloon while his message was delivered. He looked carefully at his surroundings. So much for the rumour that the family was deep in debt. This elegant room was fairly recently refurbished, as far as he could judge from the sumptuous hangings. A pity the family's extravagance did not extend to more than a tiny fire—the room was absolutely freezing. He was not altogether surprised, for he had heard nothing but ill about this family of wastrels. He would be glad when his business was concluded—provided, of course, that he was successful. He could not afford to fail.

Richard stood with his back to the fireplace, trying to get some warmth into his limbs after the long journey. He hoped his servants were receiving better hospitality in the kitchen than he was, for they must by now be frozen to the marrow.

Barely five minutes after the door had closed behind the butler, Lady Calderwood entered the saloon and extended her hand politely to her visitor. 'Lord Hardinge,' she said, with a hint of enquiry in her voice, 'you have come on a matter of some urgency?'

'Lady Calderwood.' Damn the woman! The last thing he wanted was to discuss his business with Calderwood's wife. Surely the man was not too cowardly to meet him? Richard managed to conceal his annoyance as he bowed over her immaculate white hand. 'How kind of you to receive me, ma'am. I hope Sir John is not indisposed? I shall not take up much of his time, I assure you.'

Lady Calderwood took her seat in a wing chair near the fire and motioned her guest to sit opposite. 'I am afraid my husband is suffering from a severe chill,' she said silkily. 'His doctor has forbidden him to leave his room—or to receive visitors. It seems you have had a wasted journey.' She smiled. 'But you must be cold after your hours on the road. Perhaps I can offer you some refreshment before you leave?'

Richard shook his head, returning her false smile. He had not the least intention of leaving empty-handed. If Calderwood did not dare to face him, then he would have no choice but to get to the man via his wife. She was just one more calculating society woman—he would put the fear of God into her, if he had to. By the looks of her—he could tell at a glance exactly how much had been spent on her lavish attire—she was deeply involved in her husband's spendthrift habits. He was going to enjoy putting her in her place.

He relaxed slightly into his chair and lifted his chin. The smile still played around his firm mouth. 'You must be wondering about my errand, ma'am,' he began. 'It is a matter of business, you understand.' He paused. 'Normally, I would not dream of discussing business matters with a lady...so few men confide in their wives. And yet...yet I feel somehow certain that Sir John is one of those rare men who knows how to value a shrewd and intelligent helpmeet. I cannot doubt that you are in your husband's confidence.' Lady Calderwood was smiling broadly now. Excellent. Just a little flattery and she had given herself away. Her husband would have been more on his guard, Richard was sure. Perhaps it was as well that the man was indisposed, after all. 'It is a matter of some delicacy, I fear, ma'am, but I am sure I may rely on your discretion.'

Lady Calderwood inclined her head graciously.

Good. Now he had her. 'I should explain, ma'am, knowing that I may speak in complete confidence to you, that I am in the process of settling my father's affairs following his recent death.'

Lady Calderwood murmured condolences.

'Thank you, ma'am.' Richard looked innocently at Lady Calderwood, keeping his expression unreadable. 'You will be aware that my late father lent a very large sum of money to your husband,' he said bluntly. 'I have come to collect that debt.' Lady Calderwood had become suddenly paler. He bent forward so that his face was near hers. In a low voice, but with every syllable absolutely clear, he said, 'The debt is repayable on demand.'

Lady Calderwood flushed. 'How can you possibly know that? Your father had no—' She stopped and bit her lip.

He held her gaze for several seconds without speaking. 'No papers?' he said gently.

He gave her time to speak, but she did not. He found he was not really surprised. 'The debt is, none the less, due. And I intend to collect. Every last penny. You may tell your husband that he has fourteen days, otherwise...' He let the threat hang in the air. Without written evidence of the debt, Richard had very few legal avenues open to him, but the Calderwoods might not be aware of that. And there were other ways.

Lady Calderwood had been outmanoeuvred and she probably knew it—but if she felt any chagrin, she did not allow it to show. 'My dear sir, I shall naturally convey your message to my husband, though I am not sure... I cannot say what his reaction will be. He has never mentioned to me any financial transactions with the Hardinge family. Indeed,' she added with a titter, 'as far as I am aware, the only dealings we have had were in the matter of references for my present abigail. She was previously employed by your lady mother, I collect.'

'Ah, yes,' said Richard vaguely. He was not surprised by her ladyship's attempt to turn the conversation. 'A tall woman, I recall, though I do not remember her name.'

'Smithers,' said Lady Calderwood.

'Ah, yes,' said Richard again. 'I believe she was
with my mother for some years. A first-class dresser,
I think my mother said, but really only suitable for a
lady who is prepared to spend a fortune on her back
every season.' He looked her up and down apprais-
ingly. It was a studied insult. 'No doubt Sir John
makes you a very handsome allowance, ma'am.' He
was being incredibly rude, but he was determined to
shock this woman into some kind of action which
might prove useful to him. Otherwise he might indeed
leave empty-handed.

Lady Calderwood's eyes flashed dangerously as
she rose abruptly and started for the door. 'I do not
think my financial arrangements can be of any interest
to a stranger, sir,' she said icily. 'If you will excuse
me, I shall go and tell my husband of your visit—and
give him your message.' With the faintest bow, she
passed through the door he was holding for her.

Richard smiled faintly as he closed it on her. He
had struck a spark, right enough, but would the tinder
catch?

The butler soon returned with a decanter of madeira
and some biscuits. Richard was glad to see that he
added some wood to the pitifully small fire in the
grate, but it was still far from generous. Her ladyship
obviously practised strict economy in her household—especially on unwelcome visitors. Richard was
still pondering the inconsistency between the mean
fire and her ladyship's extravagant attire, when the
door opened once more. It was the abigail, Smithers.
Now, why on earth…?

Richard took a few moments to scrutinise the

young woman. He had barely noticed her when she had been part of his mother's household. She was about thirty, tall and slightly angular, with rather wiry, dark red hair and a host of freckles across her nose and cheeks, but she was dressed with the quiet elegance of a top-class lady's maid.

Smithers returned his gaze for a moment before making a quick curtsy. Richard fancied she looked uncomfortable. 'Her ladyship's compliments, my lord. She…she has asked me to tell you that, since Sir John is likely to be convalescing from his illness for some time, it would not be…advisable for you to make another visit. She will write to you when Sir John is recovered enough to receive visitors.'

So neither of the Calderwoods would dare to face him now. Damn them! Richard fixed the abigail with a hard stare. She coloured slightly. Obviously she was embarrassed at having to tell such downright lies, especially to the son of a previous employer. He should feel sorry for her. It was not her fault, after all. 'My mother will be glad to know that I have seen you, Smithers,' he said, adopting an affable tone. 'I hope you are well?'

The abigail visibly relaxed. 'Yes, my lord—and thank you for your enquiry. Her ladyship was kind enough to write that she hopes I am well settled here. I admit I did not expect to receive such a mark of attention.'

Richard refrained from asking whether the woman was happy in her new position. It was none of his concern. On the other hand, she might be a useful source of information about this appalling household.

She might even know some detail of her master's financial dealings. With an engaging smile, Richard deliberately set about exercising his charm on the abigail.

He did not succeed. It seemed that Smithers was too clever to let fall anything really helpful. Eventually, he gave up.

'I am keeping you from your duties, Smithers. My apologies to your mistress—and my thanks for her hospitality.'

Smithers curtsied herself out, looking somewhat relieved to escape.

Richard sat quietly sipping his madeira while he reviewed his meagre store of information. Precious little so far. In fact, almost a wasted journey. Almost.

Chapter Three

Watching the comings and goings had been more than a little confusing for Jamie. Her stepmother's speedy arrival, and smug smile, had led Jamie to believe for a few minutes that this was indeed the man who had been chosen for her. Perhaps he was not as stern as he looked. Perhaps he might eventually come to value her, especially if she made every effort to be a good wife. Perhaps…

Doubts were sown by Lady Calderwood's sudden departure. It was obvious from the set of her shoulders that she was in a boiling rage. And Jamie's father did not appear at all. Jamie knew then. Whoever the visitor was, he was not for her. What a simpleton she was, to imagine for a moment that her betrothed would be young, or handsome. It was time to go back to her attic.

Just as Jamie made to rise, her stepmother's abigail appeared in the hall and went into the crimson saloon. No doubt she must be delivering some message from Lady Calderwood. But as the minutes passed and Smithers did not reappear, Jamie began to wonder what on earth the visitor and a mere servant could be talking about for so long. It was very strange. Jamie resolved to stay where she was.

The sound of Lady Calderwood's door opening made Jamie shrink down behind the polished balusters. But her precautions were unnecessary. Her ladyship strode downstairs without a sideways glance, reaching the hall just as her abigail came out of the saloon.

From her vantage point above, Jamie could hear every venomous word. 'And just what, pray, have you been discussing with his lordship all this time?'

The abigail blushed. 'Why, nothing, my lady. His lordship was merely asking how I did and…and telling me about the Countess.'

Lady Calderwood's eyebrows rose. 'Was he, indeed? How very…how very kind of him, to be sure.' She turned away and put her hand on the doorknob. 'Wait for me in my dressing-room.'

Jamie recognised that voice. Lady Calderwood always used it when she planned to inflict some kind of punishment on her underlings. And, judging by the way the abigail hurried off, she knew it too. Poor woman.

Barely five minutes later, her stepmother re-emerged and marched up the stairs towards her dressing-room. She looked even angrier than before. And the deep frown and tight lips suggested that she might have been bested in her discussion with her visitor. Heaven help them all if that were so.

Jamie was freezing now—and so stiff that she could hardly move. She needed to return to her room before someone noticed her. But in spite of the risk, she found she could not resist waiting for one last look at what might have been—even if only in her imaginings. It would give her something to dream about, something to cling on to, when she was faced with the reality of the man her parents had chosen.

The butler had returned as soon as Lady Calderwood was out of sight, but it was nearly fifteen minutes before the visitor was back in the hall, preparing to don his travelling coat. His lordship stood frowning into the middle distance, apparently oblivious of the service being rendered by the butler. But then he turned to smile his thanks, and Jamie saw that his face was transformed. The butler was flattered by the attention. Jamie was thunderstruck.

Then the door closed on the visitor with an ominous thud, bringing Jamie back to earth and to the reality of her situation. The dream was over. Her true betrothed might arrive at any moment. Faced with the prospect of her parents' choice, she now found she wanted to postpone any sight of him for as long as possible. She rose, shivering, to return to her room.

'Why, Miss Jessamyne, you have dirt on the hem of your gown.'

'What? Oh, Smithers, I did not see you. What did you…? Oh, dear. Mama will be furious.' Although such fury would be nothing new, Jamie felt a moment of hopelessness. Who would help her now?

'Let me help you, miss,' said Smithers briskly, taking Jamie's arm and guiding her up the stairs and into her room. Smithers surveyed the extent of the damage, then whisked the dress over Jamie's head. 'You had best put something round you, miss, while I sponge this, or you'll be half-frozen before I've done.'

Huddled in her shawl, Jamie sat silently on the edge of her bed, watching Smithers' expert hands at work on the soiled dress. In next to no time, the marks had disappeared.

As she helped Jamie into the gown once more, Smithers commented, 'Have you a coloured sash, or shawl, or perhaps some flowers to wear with this, miss? Unrelieved white is very difficult to bring off, especially for someone so fair-skinned.'

Jamie grimaced. 'I have nothing of that kind, I'm afraid. Mama might be able to lend me something, since she has so many. But I don't think she would be likely to agree if I were to ask her myself. I don't suppose… Could you perhaps ask her?'

Smithers' face became suddenly hard, her expression set. 'I am sorry, I am unable to help you there, miss,' she began tightly. 'Lady Calderwood has turned me off.' Jamie gasped. 'I leave in the morning.'

'Oh, Smithers, how dreadful for you. Why has she done it? Will she give you a character?' Jamie's concern was real. She knew her own position was desperate, but, whatever happened, she would not starve. A lady's maid dismissed without a reference might never find employment again.

Smiling weakly, Smithers explained that the situation, though difficult, was not quite as catastrophic as that. Lady Calderwood would give her a character, of sorts, since she had no direct evidence of wrongdoing. Her ladyship had, however, made it clear that, should any potential employer apply to her for additional information, she would feel obliged to hint at something unsavoury in the abigail's past.

'And is there?' burst out Jamie, without stopping to think.

Smithers looked at her severely, and Jamie could feel the beginnings of a flush of embarrassment. Why could she never think before she spoke?

Smithers forestalled Jamie's apology by saying, 'You know you should not have asked such a thing, miss. But it's understandable, perhaps, with her ladyship's fine manners as an example to follow.' By now, Jamie was almost scarlet. 'Don't worry, I haven't taken offence. And, no, there is no murky past. Nor have I betrayed the confidences of this house to my previous employer. Her ladyship has been misinformed.'

'By that gentleman who just left?'

'Possibly.'

'How wicked of him! Why should he do such a thing? It is monstrous!' Jamie was quite ready to do battle on the abigail's behalf. For the moment, her own troubles were forgotten in her concern to right this manifest injustice.

Smithers shrugged. 'It is water under the bridge now, miss. You must get ready to meet your betrothed. And I must go and pack my things. Her ladyship has ordered the gig at first light to take me to the inn for the stage to Bath.' If she felt bitter, she was managing to conceal it well.

'What will you do there?'

'Bath has a number of reputable agencies for the placing of domestic servants, like abigails and governesses. If I am not successful there, I shall try again in London. Now, if you will excuse me, miss, I'll say goodbye. And good luck.'

Jamie did not hear those final generous words. She was too much struck by what had just been said about agencies for governesses and the possible escape route which they might provide. No such post, she firmly believed, could be worse than her present situation with Lady Calderwood and the prospect of a forced marriage. If she could become a governess, or a companion (under an assumed name, naturally) she could at least choose her own tormentors. But first she would have to get away from Calderwood Hall.

Jamie sat down on the bed, gazing abstractedly into the middle distance. The shawl fell unnoticed from her shoulders. She was no longer conscious of the cold as she concentrated on planning her escape, exploring and then dismissing various options—the prospect of freedom had given her back all her normal courage and resolve.

Then she was summoned to her father's study.

'Ah, come in, child, come in.' His voice was tired, prematurely aged like the rest of him. Though he was not beyond middle age, his hair was thin and white, and his hands shook slightly. In spite of his neglect of her, Jamie found she pitied him, even though she had long ago lost all trace of love for him. He was just a poor old man, broken by a strong-willed second wife and by his own addiction to the gaming tables.

'Mama has told you about the marriage which has

been arranged for you, I understand? Good, good,' he finished, without giving Jamie time to reply. 'I hope you realise how lucky you are, my child. It is not every man who would take you, you know, but luckily, Cousin Ralph is rich enough not to object to your lack of dowry.'

Jamie's blood seemed to stop in her veins. Ralph Graves—a distant relation of Lady Calderwood—was old enough to be her grandfather. She went cold all over at the very thought of him, with his twisted and wizened body, and his tiny black eyes. She remembered how those leering eyes had followed her round the room, how he had sought every opportunity to touch her, how clammy was the feel of his hand. Everything about him had made her flesh crawl.

'No!' Her protest burst out before she could think what she was saying.

Her father slowly raised his eyes to meet hers. Under his increasingly stern gaze, she flushed but held her ground. 'What did you say?' he asked ominously.

Jamie took a deep breath. 'I said I will not marry Ralph Graves, Papa.'

Her father ignored her protests. She should have known he would. 'Your betrothed is due to arrive at any moment. You will receive him graciously and accept his formal proposal when he makes it tomorrow. And then you will be wed as soon as the banns have been read.'

'No, Papa,' said Jamie again, in the most reasonable tones she could muster, 'I will not marry Ralph Graves.'

He looked sharply at her then. 'You are my daughter and you will obey me. Graves and I have settled on this arrangement, and I will not permit you to undermine my position with him. I say you will marry him.' She could see that her obstinacy was fuelling his rising anger. His face and neck were turning an alarming shade of purple. 'No other man would take you, plain and penniless as you are. Take him, or by God, I'll disown you and cast you out!' His hands were shaking even more now.

Play for time, said Jamie's inner voice. Let him calm down a little or he will throw you out this very day.

Jamie forced a tiny smile. 'Papa, please, do not be angry with me! I do not mean to vex you. I know you mean to do what is best for me and I *am* grateful, truly I am.' Behind her back, she crossed her fingers. 'But Cousin Ralph is so much older than me, besides having buried two wives already. I just...I need a little time to accustom myself to the idea of marriage to him. All I ask is a little time. Please, Papa!'

She could see not the slightest sign of softening in his face. Nothing she could say would ever sway him. He expected her to submit without a murmur—to become Ralph Graves' property, his dumb, downtrodden chattel. She refused to contemplate being so completely in the power of such a man.

'You have until this evening,' her father said flatly, without looking at her. 'Cousin Ralph is expected for dinner. And you will comport yourself as you have been taught. Or else.'

She was dismissed. There was nothing more to be

said. Slowly she climbed the stairs to her freezing refuge. Inside, she leaned thankfully against the door, closing her eyes in an effort to shut out the image of Ralph Graves. It all felt like a wicked joke. Ralph Graves might be rich, but generous he most certainly was not. From what little Jamie knew of him, he was rich because he was a miser, a miser who grudged every penny he spent. If she married him, Jamie would be exchanging one freezing garret for another—and, in addition…

No! She had never allowed herself to dwell on her sufferings. Now was definitely not the time to start.

She found herself wondering why Graves would agree to wed her without a dowry. It hardly seemed in character for such a miserly old man. She could not understand how her father could have persuaded Graves to offer for her without some kind of financial incentive. Yet she was penniless.

Jamie shook her head impatiently. She had picked a strange moment to worry over impossible riddles. She had been prepared to escape before, when she did not know who had been chosen for her.

Now, she had far more reason to flee.

Chapter Four

When Jamie entered the drawing-room, the shrivelled figure of Ralph Graves uncoiled itself from the chair by the blazing fire and came to greet her. Taking both her icy hands in his, he leaned forward to place a kiss on her cheek. Jamie was enveloped in the musty smell of his clothes. Then, at the touch of his wet mouth on her skin, she could no longer stop the nausea from rising in her throat. She closed her eyes and willed herself to conquer it.

'I knew you should not mind a betrothal kiss, my dear,' he said in a rather high-pitched voice which cracked occasionally in the most disconcerting way. He turned her to face him so that he could view her properly.

He needs to examine the goods, Jamie concluded, conscious of his bright little eyes and his damp hand on hers. And he thinks he owns me already. She bore his scrutiny with dignity for a moment, then said, 'Ah, but you are a little previous, Cousin Ralph, I believe.' She forced herself to smile flirtatiously at him, subduing the temptation to pull her hand away and rub it clean on the muslin dress. 'Papa told me that we should meet this evening and I might then expect your formal proposal tomorrow. Do you tell me you do not intend to make one?' she teased, trying to hide her disgust behind a mask of archness.

It worked. Cousin Ralph laughed, an odd croaking sound. 'By Gad, she has grown up, as you said, Sir John. I think I may yet have the best of our bargain.' He turned back to Jamie. 'Very well. Tomorrow it shall be.'

With as genuine a smile as she could manage, Jamie enquired about their guest's journey. She was rewarded with a detailed recital of the horrors between Bathinghurst and Calderwood, where the roads alternated between slush and sticky mud.

Cousin Ralph had, he affirmed, put up with the cold and discomfort quite willingly. The warm welcome which awaited him at Calderwood—and here he paused to look meaningfully at Jamie and to pat her trapped hand again—was compensation for any hardships.

Jamie suddenly knew she had conquered all her fears—for she wanted to laugh. If Cousin Ralph had been plagued by cold and draughts, he ought to spend more of his hidden wealth on improving the comfort of his carriage. He probably even begrudged the cost of a hot brick for his feet! No real gentleman would travel in such a way. The gentleman who had called earlier, for example…

Jamie was nodding absently, apparently in agreement with what Graves was saying, and he beamed at her. But her thoughts were dangerously far away, with an elegant gentleman dressed in black. If only—

Jamie was saved by the announcement of dinner.

Graves naturally offered his arm to escort Lady Calderwood to the dining-room, where he took his seat in the place of honour on her immediate right. Jamie breathed a sigh of relief to find that she had been placed on her father's right, at the opposite end of the long mahogany dining table.

The dinner which her ladyship had ordered, though not lavish by the standards of the *ton*, was much more extravagant than the normal fare at Calderwood Hall. As the dishes of the first course were being served, Lady Calderwood turned brightly to her guest. 'Do have a little of this buttered crab, cousin. It is difficult to come by crab at this season, of course, but I recalled that it was a favourite with you.'

Graves helped himself liberally. There would be little or none left for the host or his daughter, but Jamie had been denied food for so long that she did not care. Indeed, if she partook of too many unaccustomed dishes, her stomach might rebel at the unwonted richness. She must guard against that at all costs. So, she ate a little soup and some plainly cooked fish and vegetables, refusing the beef. If Cousin Ralph noted how abstemious she was, he would be congratulating himself. His wife-to-be would not cost much to feed.

During the first course, Sir John addressed barely a word to his daughter. He preferred to address himself to his wine, consuming copious amounts with every dish. The second course included several deli-

cacies, together with a Rhenish cream, another of
Cousin Ralph's favourites. But Jamie's eyes were
fixed on a dish of gleaming oranges, piled high on a
nest of green leaves. It was many years since she had
been permitted to taste one, and her mouth watered
at the thought of their delicious juices.

As the butler moved to offer the dish to Jamie,
Lady Calderwood intervened. 'Leave them here, if
you please,' she said sharply, adding, as the butler
replaced the dish in front of her, 'Sir John never
touches oranges at dinner, cousin. He maintains that
they spoil the wine.'

Graves cast a shrewd glance at his host who was
now well into his third bottle. 'There may be something in that, cousin, indeed. I do not grow oranges
myself. A very ordinary fruit, in my opinion, given
the shocking cost of maintaining an orangery. Do you
not find it so?'

Lady Calderwood tittered. 'Oh, these were not
grown here, cousin, certainly not. The expense, as you
say, is not to be thought of. No, these were procured
from town for your visit. I should not have done it
else, I do assure you.'

Graves smiled smugly and helped himself to the
finest specimen on the plate.

The knot of tension in Jamie's stomach grew
tighter once more as she looked down the table at the
odious cousins. She tried to concentrate on her apple
but could not. Eyes fixed on her plate, she heard her
father signal to the butler to refill his glass yet again.
Sir John was, as usual, becoming very much the
worse for his wine. By the time Lady Calderwood

rose to signal the ladies' departure, her husband's occasional words had become noticeably slurred.

As soon as the gentlemen rejoined them, Lady Calderwood moved rapidly to the bell-pull by the fireplace to order the tea tray. A great wave of relief flowed over Jamie as the butler received his instructions. Not long now, surely? She bent almost eagerly to her stitchery, trying to shut out the sound of Cousin Ralph's voice.

'Jessamyne.' Jamie raised her head at the sharp voice. 'What are you about? Come and help me to serve tea to our guest.'

Jamie rose obediently from her place. She took the teacup to Graves, who was sitting in the best chair by the fire. 'Cream and sugar, cousin?' she asked politely, trying to avoid his sharp little eyes.

He took the cup awkwardly from her, trying to touch her fingers as he did so, but only succeeding in spilling the tea into the saucer.

Jamie's sharp intake of breath was drowned by a gasp of outrage from her stepmother. 'Jessamyne! How can you be so clumsy? Fetch a clean cup for Cousin Ralph. At once!' she commanded sharply.

Holding grimly to the thought that this ordeal must soon be over, Jamie did as she was bid without uttering a single word and then retreated to her dark corner once more.

Some fifteen minutes later, Lady Calderwood rose, glancing anxiously at her husband, who seemed to be half-asleep in his chair. 'If you will forgive us, cousin, I think we shall retire now. I am sure you agree that it is wise to keep early hours, especially in winter. The cost of candles is quite outrageous these days.'

Cousin Ralph rose to take his hostess's hand. 'You are only too right, dear lady. A very wise proceeding, which I also adhere to in my own establishments, particularly in the servants' hall. They are quite profligate with candles if one does not supervise them most strictly. As I am sure you do, cousin,' he added, relinquishing her hand and turning to Jamie.

He took Jamie's hand in both of his, pressing it with his clammy fingers. 'Good night, my dear Jessamyne. Sleep well. I shall see you tomorrow, as we agreed. After breakfast, do you not think?' He raised her hand to his lips.

She managed to overcome the urge to pull away from him, but she could not suppress a shiver of loathing as his lips touched her skin once more. He looked up sharply into her face.

Jamie's mind was racing. She must find a way of reassuring him. Oh, why did her body insist on betraying her so? She forced a rather wobbly smile. Maidenly modesty, she prayed, would be blamed for a little quiver of excitement at the thought of his proposal on the morrow.

'Until tomorrow, then, my dear,' he said again, letting go of her hand at last.

Jamie succeeded in waiting until she was back in her own chamber before rubbing the offended hand vigorously on the white muslin gown. She did not stop to wash. She had far more important things to do.

*   *   *

Jamie's preparations were swift and methodical.
First, she collected together her pitifully small store
of money and a bare minimum of clothes and other
necessities, which she stowed under her bed. Next,
she removed the awful muslin dress and her petti-
coats, replacing them with her nightgown over her
underthings. Finally, she lay down on her bed, extin-
guished her candle and drew the bedclothes up to her
chin.

Then, in the darkness, she waited.

She had known that waiting would be the worst
part. It seemed the threat was all around her, hovering
in the gloom like an evil spirit. She closed her eyes,
forcing herself to focus on practical, positive things.
In her mind's eye, she began to design a wondrous
garden…

It seemed to take hours before the house was finally
quiet. Lying on her bed, Jamie watched the moon
flood the landscape with ethereal light. She breathed
a silent prayer of thanks to some ancient virgin god-
dess for the help it would provide. Surely this was a
sign that her plan would succeed?

Cautiously she slipped out of bed and across to the
door. She listened carefully—there was no sound of
life in the house. A quick peep into the corridor confirmed that everyone must be in bed, for no lights
were to be seen.

Without lighting her candle, Jamie crept downstairs
to her half-brother's room.

Less than ten minutes later she was back with her
booty, completing her preparations. The bundle was
retrieved from under the bed and tied up for travel-

ling. Her nightgown was cast aside and replaced by
outdoor clothes. Wrapping Edmund's worn cloak
over the whole, she made her way down the back
stairs and out, by the garden door, to the stables.

Her mare greeted her with a soft whinny and allowed herself to be led quietly out of the yard with
only a rope halter.

'Bless you, Cara,' whispered Jamie, stroking the
velvet muzzle as they reached the shadow of the outside wall. 'I hope we can both remember the way of
this. It's been a very long time.' Without further ado,
Jamie jumped up on to a convenient outcrop and
mounted, tying her bundle into the small of her back
with the strings which bound it. Edmund's old cloak
covered her almost to her feet, hiding both the bundle
and the fact that she rode bareback.

Holding lightly to Cara's black mane, Jamie
walked her quietly away from Calderwood Hall.

Jamie was in no hurry, since she had all the hours
of night to complete less than five miles. Besides, she
would not for all the world have risked her beloved
old mare by travelling too fast at night.

They made good speed until they came to the edge
of the wood and the end of Calderwood land. Now
Jamie was grateful for the moonlight, since she had
to follow less familiar paths and bridleways, some of
them perilously ill-kept. 'Only another mile down the
lane, my Cara,' she whispered. 'Not long now.' The
mare's ears twitched at the sound of her mistress's
voice, but she did not pause in her gentle walk.

When Jamie reached her destination, she slid down
from the bay's back and led her through the hedge

and into the shelter of a belt of trees. 'Oh, I shall miss you so much, Cara,' she whispered, wrapping her arms round the mare's neck. Cara whickered softly in response, nuzzling Jamie's shoulder, then stood calmly watching her mistress as she made her final preparations.

Jamie extracted a small spade from her bundle and dug a hole under a leafless beech tree. Then she used a pair of shears to hack off much of her curly titian hair, cursing softly when she realised she had forgotten to bring anything to serve as a mirror. The hanks of hair went into the hole, followed by the shears and the spade.

As she was tying back her shoulder-length hair with a piece of black ribbon from her pack, she was surprised into a giggle by the look of interest on her mare's face. 'Well, Cara, what do you think of your new master?' Cara blinked slowly. 'Not very complimentary, are you? I admit I've probably made a poor fist of the haircut, but I can tidy it up later, if I can find a mirror and some scissors.' She patted her hair self-consciously. 'But, at least, Edmund's clothes are a reasonable fit. Don't you think I make a fine boy?' She twirled. Cara edged uneasily as the cloak billowed.

'Now we must wait.'

Dawn came slowly, a half-hearted winter light.

Still they waited.

After what seemed a very long time, the sound of hooves was heard in the nearby lane. Jamie crept forward to crouch behind the hedge. Yes, it was the Calderwood gig, driven by the old groom, with

Smithers sitting very upright in her place, staring
straight in front of her.

Jamie returned to her mare. 'Now, the only risk is
that old Timothy will decide to stop to wet his whistle
at the inn instead of going straight back to
Calderwood, as he ought.' She continued to wait, listening intently. Some fifteen minutes later, she was
rewarded by the sound of the returning gig. If
Timothy had slaked his thirst, he had not stayed long
to do it. Jamie watched with satisfaction as the gig
passed out of sight.

'And now it really is goodbye, Cara,' whispered
Jamie, releasing the mare, removing the rope halter
and throwing it into the hole which she then filled in
with her bare hands, allowing the dirt to get under
her fingernails and into her skin.

She turned to stroke the mare once more. 'Go
home, Cara. Back to your warm stable.' Then she
picked up her bundle and made her way down to the
lane. Behind her, the horse pulled idly at a few tufts
of thin grass. There was almost nothing to eat at this
time of year. Soon she would be hungry enough to
find her way back to Calderwood.

Jamie did not look back. Adopting the easy stride
of a boy, she walked on to the village, whistling.

At the inn, all was bustle. No one took any notice
of a slightly grubby boy, anxiously looking around as
if in search of something. Jamie ventured into the inn,
keeping her hat pulled low over her face. In the taproom, she found Smithers alone, seated primly on a
bench by the wall. Jamie sat down beside her.

'What, may I ask, do you want, young man?' asked Smithers crisply, though her voice was not hostile.

'I need your help, Smithers,' pleaded Jamie softly, looking up at her. 'Please don't give me away.'

'Good God! Miss Jessamyne! What on earth are you about?' Luckily, Smithers did not have a carrying voice.

'Please, Smithers! Help me! I need to escape. I cannot marry that terrible man. All I need is a few weeks. Then I shall be safe.'

'What do you mean about "a few weeks", miss?' the abigail asked, in a low voice.

'Don't call me that. Someone will hear. Just call me "Jamie".' Jamie searched the maid's face for a sign that she might relent, but there was none. Jamie swallowed hard. 'In a few weeks, I shall be twenty-one. Then, no one can force me into marriage with him. All I have to do is stay in hiding until I come of age. Please help me, Smithers!'

Jamie felt the woman's slow scrutiny. Surely the proposed bridegroom made even Smithers' flesh creep?

The abigail lifted one of Jamie's grubby hands and brushed it across Jamie's cheek so that it left a dirty streak. 'You'd better start calling me "Annie", don't you think?' she smiled.

'Oh, bless you!' cried Jamie, hugging the older woman impetuously.

'Hey! That's enough of that,' cried Smithers, pushing her away. 'I haven't said I'll help you yet.' She paused. 'It will depend on precisely what you want from me. Well?'

Jamie launched into her prepared speech. 'You said you were going to Bath on the stage…er…Annie. I only want you to help me to get a seat too. I have the money to pay, don't worry. And, once we reach Bath, I can look after myself.'

'Oh?'

'Yes. I plan to… But perhaps it would be better for both of us if I kept my plans to myself. Then, if anyone should ask, you can truthfully say you don't know, can't you?' She beamed innocently at the abigail.

'It sounds pretty rum to me, I must say. And, if I help you to get on the stage, I *will* be involved, whatever you choose to do about telling me your plans. How am I to explain that away?'

'No one will be looking for a *boy*, Annie, I promise you. These clothes belong to Edmund. He won't be back from Harrow for weeks and weeks, so nobody will notice they are missing. And all the clothes in my pack are my own, so when they discover I am gone, they will be searching for a girl.'

'Hmph. And what if they discover that the lady's maid from Calderwood Hall was suddenly to be found in the company of a young lad?'

'They won't. I don't want us to be *together*. I just want you to tell me how I go about obtaining a seat on the Bath stage. Then I'll do it myself.'

Annie Smithers seemed to be wavering. 'It won't do, Miss Jamie, I'm afraid. A young lad travelling by himself and buying his own seat at the last minute would be bound to attract attention. They'd wonder if you were running away from school.' Jamie's suddenly despondent expression must have shocked her. 'Don't take on so, miss. Look, I can help a little. I'll go and see if I can buy an extra seat on the stage for you. Give me the money. Right. Now, you stay here. I don't want them to know it's for you.' Pocketing Jamie's coins, Smithers left the taproom.

In five minutes, she was back. 'I'm sorry, Miss Jamie. It can't be done. Mine was the last place on the stage. There's no way he'll take you, I'm afraid.'

Jamie sat down heavily on the wooden bench. She had tried to plan for every eventuality, but she had not foreseen this. She dared not hang around the inn waiting for the next stage in hopes of getting a seat. Too many people from Calderwood and the nearby villages used the Boar's Head. She would very likely be recognised by someone.

Jamie groaned in anguish, clenching her fists. Then she slumped dejectedly against the wall. It had all been for nothing.

A cool voice from the doorway interrupted them. 'Why, it's Smithers, is it not? And in some difficulty, if I am not mistaken. How tiresome!'

Chapter Five

At the sound of that deep authoritative voice, Jamie felt a shudder run through her body. She knew exactly who had uttered those deceptively simple words. But, now that she was finally to meet the man whose image had been haunting her, she did not dare to turn round to look at him. What if he saw through her disguise? What if…? She shrank further into her boy's clothes, trying to make herself as inconspicuous as possible. Why did his arrival affect her so? He could not recognise her, for he had never set eyes on her, but somehow there was something incredibly threatening about his very presence. She sat staring at the floor, her hands clasped tightly together, as if in supplication.

Smithers, by contrast, was facing up to this unexpected arrival who seemed to find their presence so tiresome. She dropped a quick curtsy and then, without any kind of warning, cuffed Jamie lightly round the ear. 'Stand up at once, Jamie, and make your bow to Lord Hardinge.'

Jamie rapidly obeyed, trying her best to bow as

Edmund did and to conceal her dismay as she did so. What on earth was Smithers going to say? And do?

'I beg your pardon for my brother's want of manners, my lord,' continued Smithers quickly. 'He's worried, you see, because there's no room for him on the stage. They must have made a mistake up at the Hall and booked only one seat instead of two.' She shrugged. 'We'll just have to wait, I suppose.'

Lord Hardinge looked inquiringly at the abigail. 'A sudden departure, I collect?'

Smithers swallowed. 'Urgent family business, my lord. I have to get Jamie to Bath quickly. He's been...er...with me more or less since Mother died, you see, and now there's a chance of a situation for him in Bath. But I need to be sure he's settled. I promised my mother I would.'

'Ah yes, very laudable, Smithers, very.' He looked hard at Jamie. 'And how old are you, my lad?'

Jamie found she could not speak. She looked appealingly at Smithers.

'He don't talk much, I'm afraid, my lord. He's a little...well...backward. But he understands everything you say to him, I assure you, and he has the sweetest nature, too.'

Jamie gulped. Smithers was getting carried away. 'I be thirteen,' she croaked. 'Gardener I be, sir.'

His lordship laughed, but not unkindly. 'I could have guessed that from the state of your hands, Jamie, though not perhaps from your fine clothes. Are you a good gardener?'

Jamie nodded vigorously.

'He has a wonderful way with growing things, to

be sure,' added Smithers, 'though he's not been a gardener, in the ordinary way.'

Lord Hardinge raised an eyebrow.

'What I mean,' continued Smithers hastily, improvising around the truth, 'is that Jamie wasn't exactly *employed* at Calderwood, just allowed to stay there. Charitable of her ladyship, really, to give him bed and board. The gardening was his attempt to pay his way. He's not much good at household duties, I'm afraid.'

Jamie kept her head down, trying to hide her face from his lordship's penetrating gaze. She knew she was blushing. That did not seem appropriate for a thirteen-year-old boy, even a backward one.

'So, you have found him a proper situation as a gardener's boy, have you, Smithers? That sounds hopeful.'

Jamie groaned inwardly. Smithers was beginning to struggle in the complications of her own story. If she claimed there was a position for Jamie, his lordship would probably enquire as to the employer's name, and then what could Smithers say? Jamie held her breath.

'No, not precisely, my lord.' Smithers started to move towards the far end of the room. 'Sit down there, Jamie,' she called back. 'Would you mind, my lord?' she continued in a low voice. 'I don't like to discuss this in front of Jamie.'

Jamie swallowed a gasp. She wanted to stop them, but she could not step out of the part she was playing. No backward boy would understand what was being discussed, far less insist on being part of it. She must just put her trust in Annie Smithers. At least it would

give her time to school her features into blankness—
and a chance to strain her ears to hear what was being
said.

'I thank you kindly for your interest in my brother,
my lord. In fact, there is no definite situation for him
yet, but I am most hopeful. One of the Bath agencies
believes he can be placed. There are many openings
for bootboys and the like.'

'But you said he has no bent for indoor work,' he
returned sharply.

Jamie saw that Smithers was flushing, caught by
the twists of her own tale. 'Not *real* indoor work, like
a page boy,' the abigail said hurriedly, 'but even he
can black boots.'

His lordship smiled coldly. 'You would not say that
to my valet, Smithers,' he said caustically. 'However,
we are wandering from the point. Now, the stage is
due in about ten minutes. Do you take your seat on
it, and I will take the boy on the box of my carriage.
You may find him at the coach office when you reach
Bath.'

Smithers' reply came out in a rush. 'How very kind
you are, my lord. But, no, I'm afraid I cannot accept
your offer. Jamie's never been on his own, you see,
especially in a big city. I couldn't think of letting him
travel all that way by himself or having him wait at
the coach station for such a long time on his own.'
She lowered her voice a little. 'People sometimes take
advantage, make fun of him. They can be very cruel.'

Fixing the abigail with a hard glare, his lordship
pronounced on her fate. 'Your sisterly concern does
you credit, Smithers. Very well. Since you will not

leave him to me, you had better come along as well. Get the lad to load your bags into my carriage. I am leaving immediately. I hope you do not object to travelling forward?' He walked out with an indifferent nod, not waiting for her reply.

Smithers hurried back to Jamie. 'Did you hear what we said?' At Jamie's rapid nod, the abigail continued, 'Remember you must act the part of a boy, Miss Jamie. You're to travel on the box with the coachman, which means you won't have his lordship's eye on you. He's altogether too sharp, that one, for my liking.'

'For goodness' sake,' hissed Jamie, 'you *must* stop saying ''Miss Jamie''! Remember, I am ''Jamie'' and you are ''Annie''. What if he heard you?'

'Yes, yes, very well,' agreed Smithers, shooing her to the door. 'Now, go and load the luggage. Quickly. You don't want to draw his lordship's attention to you by being tardy.'

Jamie grabbed her pack and the abigail's bulky travelling bags and hurried out to the carriage, trying not to think about the risks of what was happening. Keep out of his way, she told herself sternly, and act simple.

But her eyes were still drawn to him, like a moth to flame. Lord Hardinge was standing by the steps, giving crisp instructions to his coachman. The grooms were stationed by the horses, ready to whip the cloths off their backs as soon as he gave the word. He exuded authority. And he was watching her!

'Jamie!' he called sharply as he mounted into the

carriage. 'Tell that sister of yours to get a move on. Quickly now!'

Jamie nodded obediently and trotted off into the taproom where Smithers was waiting, looking rather more composed than before. 'Come on, Annie! He's becoming impatient! Now, do be careful what you say to him. Don't spin any more stories, *please*. I shan't be able to keep up with them.'

'Yes, you will. Just stick to your character—backward, without many words. If you don't know what to say, say nothing. And look simple.' She turned to go.

'Annie.' The abigail turned back. 'Thank you, dear Annie. Some day—'

'Oh, stuff! Now, let's be going. He'll expect you to help me into the carriage.'

Up on the box beside the old coachman, Jamie was soon inwardly rejoicing at her escape. In just a few hours, they would reach Bath, and then she would be free. Her heart was singing. But no amount of joy could prevent her from gradually freezing. Edmund's clothes were not thick enough for winter wear and his cloak, though long, was thin, affording little protection against the bitingly sharp wind. Jamie glanced enviously at the thick greatcoat, mufflers and gloves of the coachman. Her own hands were becoming blue with cold and so numb she could barely feel them. She was sure there was a drip on the end of her nose. With grim determination, she ignored it and concentrated on mastering the chattering of her teeth. She refused to give up now. Only a few hours more...

* * *

Once Smithers was settled, Richard studiously ignored her. He relaxed in the corner of his opulent carriage, a fur rug over his knees, and closed his eyes to indicate that he did not propose to converse during the journey. He waited until the abigail fell asleep, lulled by the rhythmic rocking of the carriage. As her breathing slowed, he opened his eyes once more. And he fixed his gaze on her, thoughtfully examining every aspect of her person.

He had been surprised to find that he felt sorry for a simple lad, in spite of his suspicions of the sister's lame explanations. The boy had looked so uncomfortable in his fine clothes, obviously charity cast-offs from someone in the Calderwood family. And he would be vulnerable without his sister, if he were indeed taking a situation on his own. Richard sighed. His conscience would not allow him to draw back, when a simpleton needed his help. Besides, there might be profit in this encounter. Smithers knew more about the Calderwood household than any agent he had yet been able to employ.

Richard had noted the attempt at masculine panache as the boy slung his sister's bags into the carriage. But it was not so much the awkwardness of Jamie's movements which had attracted his attention, as the size of the abigail's baggage. Strange, if she were indeed travelling to Bath for a few days only. If she were leaving for good, on the other hand…

He smiled to himself. Things were beginning to work out rather better than he had hoped, and might yet be turned even more to his advantage. He would consider further during the journey. There was no rush, now that he had the woman under his eye.

At length, the carriage turned into a posting inn for a change of horses. The grooms were quickly about their business, unhitching the team and assessing the quality of the replacements. Nobody was paying any attention to Jamie. She sat immobile, too cold to move a muscle.

Lord Hardinge lowered the glass on his side of the carriage and poked his head out. 'Jamie! Down from there! Go and fetch me a tankard of ale. Look sharp, now!'

Jamie hurried to climb down. She made a pretty poor showing, for her fingers were so cold she could barely grip the handholds. Seeing a waiter coming towards the carriage with a tray of tankards, she rushed to grab one and immediately dropped it. The ale splashed all over the waiter's boots.

'Why, you young—' began the waiter, incensed, raising his free hand to strike Jamie.

'That will do!' commanded Lord Hardinge, flinging open the door and jumping down. 'If my servants are to be chastised, I shall do it.'

The waiter began to stammer an apology, but his lordship simply took a full tankard from the tray, threw down some coppers and turned away.

'Come here, Jamie.'

Jamie's first reaction was to run, but her frozen limbs would never have moved fast enough. Keeping her eyes lowered, she approached her intimidating benefactor. He sounded much less angry now than when he had shouted at the waiter, but still…

'Show me your hands.'

Jamie did so. They were thin and blue. The filthy fingernails stood out starkly.

'Have you no gloves?'

Jamie shook her head, still gazing at the ground.

His lordship put a hand on her frozen cheek. Suddenly it seemed as if all the blood in Jamie's body had rushed to that spot. She felt sure that the outline of his fingers was impressed in brightest scarlet on her burning skin. And that same quivering of all her body had returned.

'Why, you're frozen to the marrow, lad. No wonder you dropped that tankard. I should have known. You're much too thin—and as for these clothes… Well, you'd better come inside with your sister, before I have your death on my conscience.'

Jamie did not move. She was still trying to come to terms with the strange effects this man had on her.

'Don't just stand there, boy.' It sounded as if the Earl was beginning to regret his generosity. 'Come, jump in.' He gave Jamie a hearty push towards the carriage.

As Jamie climbed in, she registered the shock on the abigail's face. No wonder. Spending hours under the eagle eye of Lord Hardinge might well lead to discovery. Jamie dared not utter a sound. Annie busied herself with chafing Jamie's hands and clucking over her like an anxious mother hen.

'Enough, Smithers, enough!' snapped Lord Hardinge. 'I have no objection to your helping your brother to get warm but, for heaven's sake, do it without all this gabblemongering!'

Looking chastened, Smithers lapsed into silence. Eventually, she drifted off to sleep again.

Jamie soon found herself the only one awake. Cautiously, she sat up in her corner, pushing her hat back from her eyes and flexing her fingers, which tingled painfully as the sensation returned. She felt in her pocket for a handkerchief to deal with the drip on her nose. She did not have one, which reminded her that boys like simple Jamie never used them, so she experimented with wiping her nose on her sleeve instead. Ugh!

But what did that matter? She had escaped! She might never again live the life of a gentlewoman, but her future was now her own to decide. She paused to savour the luxury of the carriage, its deeply cushioned seats and the pervasive smell of rich leather. Nothing at Calderwood was half so splendid. And if Lady Calderwood had owned such an equipage, she would never have allowed her hated stepdaughter to set foot in it. Jamie sank back in her seat, longing to shout with exultant laughter.

Opposite her, Lord Hardinge moved in his sleep. He had removed his hat, presumably so that he might doze more comfortably. Jamie found herself gazing at him. It was such a handsome face in repose—thick, arched black brows, a finely chiselled nose, perhaps a little long, a generous mouth made for smiling, and a strong chin, slightly cleft. His thick dark hair became him, even in disarray. Jamie found herself wondering about the colour of his eyes. Dark, she supposed, like the rest of him, unconsciously raising her eyes to look again at his face.

Cobalt blue eyes bored into hers! Lord Hardinge had been watching her, just when she thought she was safe. And his eyes seemed to be able to see into the depths of her being! She shuddered visibly.

Glancing at the still-sleeping abigail, the Earl frowned across at Jamie, his face very stern. 'Satisfied, are you, lad?' he asked in a menacing whisper.

Jamie shuddered again.

Lord Hardinge's expression softened slightly. 'Don't worry, Jamie. I am not angry.' His voice seemed less hostile now. 'But you really must not stare at your betters in that insolent way. It could earn you a beating in some houses.'

Jamie began to stammer an incoherent apology.

'Forget it,' interrupted his lordship sharply, closing his eyes once more.

Jamie held her breath for a long time, trying to control her racing pulse and fearing another onslaught from the powerful man sitting opposite her.

The carriage remained silent. It seemed that Lord Hardinge had had enough of the boy Jamie, at least for the present.

Jamie looked enviously at the abigail, sleeping peacefully alongside her. If only she dared to close her eyes too. She was so tired—and the growing warmth inside the carriage was making her eyelids droop. But it was too great a risk. She dug her fingernails into the palm of her hand. She must not sleep where he might watch her. She must not.

At the next change, the Earl allowed them both a

bite to eat and a mug of ale. It tasted foul, and much
too strong, but Jamie could find no reason to refuse
it. Ten minutes after they had moved off, she began
to succumb to the effects of the alcohol and her sleep-
less night. Her eyes closed, but still she struggled to
stay alert.

'I am glad your brother is asleep, Smithers, for I
want to talk to you about him.'

'Yes, my lord?'

'From what you have told me, he would make a
pretty poor bootboy. Much better to place him as apprentice gardener on a large estate.'

'Yes, my lord. I intend to do so, if such a situation
can be found. But—'

'It can be. I need just such a boy on my own estate.
I shall take him.'

'I thank you for your offer, but we can't accept it.
You see…' The abigail's voice trailed off. She
seemed to be fast running out of excuses.

'Why don't you tell me the truth, Smithers?'

His slightly raised voice penetrated Jamie's half-
slumber. At the sound of the word 'truth', her eyes
snapped open.

'I don't understand…' began Smithers.

'Gammon. You know very well. No woman of
your station carries all her worldly goods with her on
a three-day trip to Bath. You have been dismissed
from your post, I collect, and are hoping to find another in Bath. Well?'

'It is true, my lord,' agreed Smithers in a whisper.
'Lady Calderwood would not keep me at the Hall

after your visit. She decided…she believed…' Her voice tailed off miserably.

'Indeed? And so both of you are turned out into the world again? I must say it makes me wonder why you will not accept my offer for Jamie.' There was an edge of irritation in his deep voice as he stared suspiciously at the abigail. The handsomeness of his face in repose had been replaced by a frown which drew his black brows together in a hard line.

Smithers began to stammer a little. 'I…I was hoping to find a situation where we could be together, so that I could look after him. You know what I mean, I think.'

'Yes, I do know. There is no need to elaborate. I assure you, he will come to no harm under my roof.' He paused to look directly at Jamie, who shrank a little under his stern gaze. 'Very well, Smithers. If I can persuade my mother to re-engage you as her abigail, will you then agree to my proposal for Jamie?'

'I don't know.' She turned to consult Jamie, who nodded quickly, taking no notice of the silent warning in the older woman's eyes. 'Since Jamie seems willing—then, yes, if we can stay together, we accept.'

'Good,' said the Earl crisply, settling back in his seat. 'I have no doubt Lady Hardinge will be delighted to have you back in her service. We should be at Harding in about an hour.' He closed his eyes once more.

Jamie looked anxiously at the abigail, who shrugged impotently. It was now clear to Jamie that his lordship never had intended to take them to Bath, but straight to Harding, his own estate. Jamie felt a prickle of alarm. What did he have in mind for them now?

Chapter Six

'What on earth possessed you to agree to his offer?' snapped Annie in exasperation, sinking on to the bed. The attic chamber was small, but better furnished than the average for servants. There were still some privileges attached to the position of lady's maid.

Before Jamie could reply, they were interrupted by the noise of heavy footsteps on the stairs. 'That will be the truckle bed for you, I suppose. Open the door and help them with it, Jamie.'

Jamie did as she was bidden, biting back the retort which had risen automatically to her lips. Annie really was beginning to treat her like a younger brother, rather than as a lady. And if she wanted to be safe, she would just have to become accustomed to it.

'Can't understand why you wants a lad like him in here, Miss Smithers,' grumbled the young footman, dragging the bed through the narrow doorway. 'He could just as easy sleep out by the stables.'

'No, thank you, Tom. Lady Hardinge has agreed that he should be with me until he's settled.' She was unbending a little more than she normally would to an inferior. 'Will you keep an eye on him, when you can, Tom? You know better than I who might be unkind to him.' The smile she gave him transformed her normally stern countenance.

Flattered by such a show of confidence from one of the highest servants in the household, Tom grudgingly agreed to look out for Jamie when he could. 'But out in the gardens he'll be on his own, for I'll not be able to go out there much. He'll be all right with old Mr Jennings. He wouldn't hurt a fly. Caleb, now, is a different kettle o' fish. Nasty piece o' work. Got a vicious temper, he has. Jamie'll need to keep out o' his way.'

'Who is Caleb?' asked Annie.

'Undergardener. Came after you left. Mr Jennings is getting too old for all the work, so his lordship wanted someone younger, ready to take over when the old man retires. Mind you,' he added with a chuckle, 'Mr Jennings ain't the kind who'll give up easily. Yon garden is his pride an' joy an' he's like to rule it 'til he drops.'

'Thank you for the warning, Tom. I'll try to make sure Jamie keeps out of Caleb's way as much as possible.'

As the door closed behind Tom, Annie set about unpacking Jamie's belongings. Jamie watched helplessly as Annie inspected her few clothes with pursed lips.

'We must sort out some more boy's clothes for you. You can't possibly work in the garden in those you have on. As for these'—she picked up a plain green gown and held it disdainfully at arm's length between finger and thumb—'I'll put them among my things. Though how anyone could think I would demean myself to wear such a monstrosity, I cannot imagine.' She dropped the offending garment on the chair.

It was that single gesture that brought home to Jamie just how impossible her situation had become. She had fully intended to revert to being a girl as soon as she reached Bath, but now she was buried on a private estate, miles from anywhere, and irrevocably cast as a gardener's boy. Could she carry it off? What if she were discovered?

Looking down at her filthy hands and travel-stained clothes, Jamie concluded that, even if she were found to be a girl, no one would ever guess she was a lady. She had needed a hiding place for a few weeks, until she came of age. What could be better?

As Annie continued to scrutinise Jamie's meagre wardrobe, muttering darkly, Jamie began to giggle. The giggle grew uncontrollably until she was laughing in great gusty whoops, gripping her aching sides. In the face of such infectious hilarity, Annie too began to laugh until they both collapsed in a helpless heap on the bed, wiping tears from their eyes.

'Oh, Annie,' gasped Jamie at last, 'however did we get into this? And how shall we ever get out of it again?'

'I don't know, I'm sure. I doubt if I shall ever find another place after this, that I do know.'

'Of course you will. If I were rich, I'd take you like a shot. Perhaps when I come of age—'

'If you were rich, Jamie, we wouldn't be in this

fix. And what self-respecting abigail would have anything to do with a lady who looks like a—'

'A dirty little scarecrow? Yes, well, perhaps with
the right sort of dresser I could be improved.' Jamie
made a face. 'What do you think?'

'I think that it's high time I found some more boy's
clothes for you, so that you can start your apprentice-
ship. Let's see how happy you are with this silly play-
acting after a week's hard work.' Annie's sharpness
failed to conceal her real concern.

'Annie, dear, don't worry. No matter what they
give me to do, I won't give myself away, I promise
you.'

Annie grunted. 'Well, see that you don't.' She
made for the door, warning Jamie not to leave the
room until she returned.

While Annie was gone, Jamie reassessed her own
position with some care. She must not be discovered,
for that would mean disaster for her—and the work-
house, or worse, for Annie Smithers.

Jamie refused to dwell on the risks they ran.
Instead, she thought hard about the handsome Earl, in
an attempt to identify what it was about him that affected her so. She could not decide. He was an
enigma. She found it impossible to reconcile his relative kindness to her with his behaviour to poor
Annie. He must have given Lady Calderwood reason
to believe that Annie was not fit for a position of trust,
considering how rapidly she had been dismissed. It
was monstrous! She said as much, yawning widely,
when Annie came back into the room with a large
pile of worn, but serviceable, working clothes.

'I don't want to talk about it,' retorted Annie flatly. 'I have no way of knowing what he might have said to Lady Calderwood and, since he has seen fit to re-engage me at Harding, I really have very little to complain about. It could have been much, much worse. As for you, young lady—' Jamie yawned again '—you need to go to bed. Did you not sleep last night?' Jamie shook her head. Annie made to turn down the covers on the bed.

'I can't sleep there, Annie. That's your bed.'

'It wouldn't be right for a lady to sleep on that little truckle there,' protested Annie, tight-lipped. 'It will do very well for me.'

'And how will you explain it to anyone who happens to come in and finds you there, while your little brother lies in luxury? Come, Annie, you know it won't do. I shall be perfectly comfortable here.' With that, she lay down on the truckle bed and closed her eyes. In less than a minute, she was asleep.

Countess Hardinge closed the book-room door quietly behind her.

Her son strode across the room to embrace her and place an affectionate kiss on her cheek. 'That was remarkably swift, my dear,' he said. 'I take it they are settled? Thank you. I'm only sorry I could not explain properly when we arrived, but with both of them listening...'

He relaxed as she nodded, lingering for a moment in his embrace.

'I understand now why you brought them, Richard—or Smithers, at least—but it seems such an unlikely route to recovering our losses. Can we really afford to spend our time on a mere abigail—situated as we are?'

He stood back slightly to look more carefully into her face, noting her worried frown and the anxiety in her eyes. 'It is nothing like as bad as you fear, my dear,' he said gently. 'We are still comfortable enough. And we shall come about.' Gently he drew her to the best chair by the fire. 'Come, sit down,' he murmured. 'Let me fetch you a glass of madeira.'

Lady Hardinge let out a long sigh as she sank into the chair. Her son could feel her eyes on him as he filled a single glass from the crystal decanter.

'I should pour one for yourself too, Richard,' she advised, before he had even turned round.

That sounded ominous. He looked questioningly at her, but her eyes had closed. Something really serious was on her mind, but surely it couldn't be money this time? They already knew exactly how much was missing. And now that he had given up his gambling and his opera dancers, they should be able to manage—just—on the income from the estate.

That left only one other possibility—another impassioned plea that he set about finding himself the wife that they had long ago agreed he must have.

As he placed her glass on the little table by her elbow, he attempted to deflect what might be coming. 'I have been thinking about what we said before, Mama, and I have concluded that you are right. I do need to marry soon. So, I have decided to offer for Emma Fitzwilliam. After all, we have known each other for nearly twenty years, so there would be few surprises. She may not be witty or clever, but she is nothing like as fickle and flighty as most of her sex. I imagine we could rub along pretty well together.'

His mother sighed again. Her features registered some inner turmoil, but she did not respond to his sweeping slight on womankind.

Richard realised he was making a poor fist of his explanations, but he was in too deep now to withdraw. And besides, his mother was the very one who constantly urged him to marry. She…no, that was not quite fair. His mother wanted him to fall in love and *then* marry. On that count, Emma Fitzwilliam most definitely did not qualify.

He swallowed hard. 'May I take it that you approve my choice, Mama? After all, the Fitzwilliam estates march with ours, and she will inherit them some day. Her dowry will be handsome. She has, besides, all the attributes a man must seek in a wife: beauty, breeding, a conformable nature—'

'She may have all the required qualities, Richard,' interrupted Lady Hardinge at last, 'but you do not!' She ignored her son's gasp of protest. 'Family tradition requires that you give the Hardinge betrothal ring to your bride as a token of your deep love for her—'

'Oh, tosh, Mama! Forgive me—but people like us do not marry for love, especially nowadays. Marriage is a matter of business. It would be a union between two families—the Hardinge title and the Fitzwilliam wealth. You're not still hoping for a love match, are you, my dear?' He softened his words by smiling warmly at her.

'The head of this family *must* marry for love,' she replied firmly. 'That rule has held true for all the Hardinges, for centuries. Your father believed in it—and so do I. You know that. And you know, too, that disaster struck on the only two occasions when the tradition was flouted.'

Richard did not reply.

'Richard?'

'Yes, Mama,' he said softly, 'I do know what happened to them, but I don't believe in the curse for a moment. It was just coincidence that both of them died, without an heir, before they reached forty. It happens in other families too. And they don't have a curse to blame it on.' He sat down and tossed off his glass of madeira in a single swallow. 'Clearly, there is only one solution—I must instantly fall head over ears in love with a lady of vast fortune. It is the obvious way to reconcile the needs of the estate with the family tradition.' He laughed bitterly. 'If only life were so simple.'

She turned slightly, looking him full in the face. 'I am sorry, Richard.'

He shook his head. 'It's not your fault, Mama. Papa was taken in by that blackguard, Calderwood, when he was too ill to know what he was doing. You could not have prevented it—even if you had known.'

He sat for some moments, grimly contemplating the dregs of wine in his glass. 'Well,' he returned at length, 'if I am to abide by your rules, I must have earned a temporary reprieve. I cannot guarantee to fall in love with an heiress, so marriage will have to wait—until the money has been recovered!' He smiled impudently. 'Every cloud has a silver lining.'

His mother could not conceal a slight twitch of her lips at his words. But there was no amusement in her voice. 'If you take that attitude, you'll make no match at all, far less a love match. I know that, after Celia, you feel—'

Richard allowed his stony expression to show her how little he appreciated any mention of that name from his past.

His mother rapidly changed tack. 'Think, Richard. You are already one-and-thirty. You have no brothers. You really must marry soon.'

She was beginning to wring her hands. Gently, he enclosed them in his own, letting her gain strength from his warmth. 'Does my marrying for love mean so much to you, my dear?'

'Not just to me. To all of us. Especially to you.'

A taut silence fell. Richard could see the strain on his mother's face, but he was not prepared to pursue this subject further, even with her. 'Come, my love. Let me take you upstairs. You will wish to rest and change before dinner.'

Lady Hardinge gave her son a smile of silent understanding as he led her out of the study and up the staircase to her bedchamber.

When Richard returned to his desk, he remained some moments toying with his pen and staring into space. So much of his ordered world turned upside-down by those few words from his mother. Words he had long tried to avoid—the Hardinge family's love matches. A fairy story, surely? And out of the question for a man like him. Yet he knew it would now be impossible for him to carry out his hastily devised plan of offering for Emma Fitzwilliam. Fate? He could not decide whether the luck was for good or ill.

Next morning Jamie rose with the lark, ravenous. She was astonished to discover that she had slept for fifteen hours.

'I am ever so hungry, Annie,' she said, as she gave herself a perfunctory wash and began to change her clothes. This was her first day of freedom, and she meant to enjoy every moment of it.

Annie eyed her balefully. 'There will be plenty to eat downstairs. But first, we must see to your appearance.' She forcibly removed the garments Jamie was holding. 'No, not those. Breeches and gaiters, a smock and an undershirt. Here.'

Jamie wrinkled her nose at the thick, rough smock. It looked thoroughly uncomfortable. Just touching it made her itch.

'It can't be helped, Jamie. You chose to be the gardener's boy. It's a good thing you're a bit thin. Boys of that age usually are. But we'll need to bind your breasts, just the same.'

Jamie blushed scarlet, but it seemed to make no impression on Annie, who was busily rummaging in the clothes press. Jamie gasped a protest as her old calico petticoat was pulled out and efficiently ripped into bandages.

'Not fit for a lady anyway,' Annie pronounced. 'If you ever become a lady again, I can provide you with better than this and with gowns more becoming than yours.'

Annie seemed to be in her element. She certainly knew how to manage a young lady, even a slightly unwilling one. In no time, she was wrapping the strips tightly round Jamie's upper body.

'Now, put on the rest of the clothes and let us see how you look.'

There was no point in protesting any more. Annie was right. Jamie had to be able to pass muster as a boy. They were both at risk if she failed.

She stood in the centre of the room while Annie inspected her minutely. 'Not bad,' the abigail conceded, 'but why did you do that to your hair? Boys don't wear it like that nowadays—it's much too long.'

'I was trying to leave myself enough so that I could be a girl again. It's just about long enough to be put up.'

'I'll tidy it up a little, at least.' Annie fetched her comb and scissors. As she freed Jamie's hair from the restraining ribbon, the dark red curls fell forward, framing Jamie's pale face. 'Why, how different you look, miss, much prettier than that severe bun you always wore at Calderwood.'

Jamie smiled shyly up at her, surprised by the half-compliment. 'Mama always insisted I wore it so, in order to tame my ''appalling red mop'', as she called it. She never permitted me to cut it.'

'She never permitted anything which would make the best of your looks, if truth were told.'

Jamie laughed. 'But I have none. I've always known I'm plain.'

'Oh? Look here.' Annie forced Jamie to sit down in front of the brown-speckled mirror and then arranged her curls becomingly around her heart-shaped face. 'Now, tell me you're plain.'

Jamie was astonished. Annie really sounded as if she meant it. But then, when Jamie did look, she suddenly saw herself through new eyes. Against the frame of titian hair, her pale complexion glowed and her deep green eyes sparkled. The plain pasty-faced dowd had disappeared. In her place, there was a pretty, red-haired—boy!

'Good grief!' Jamie hastily began to drag her hair back from her face to tie it up again. 'They'll never believe I'm a boy if I look like that,' she said, unconsciously immodest.

'True,' said Annie, with a short laugh. 'Here, I'll tidy it up for you. Then you'll do, I think.'

Annie trimmed the ends of Jamie's hair and combed it back severely from her face, tying it very tightly with a piece of twine. 'Gardener's boys don't use ribbon,' she observed sagely.

The winter sun was dipping low in the sky when Jamie finished her first day's work. She sat on her heels, stretching her aching back and looking ruefully at her grime-encrusted hands. Her body might ache, but her heart was singing. She was safe from the Calderwoods now, and surely she could remain hidden at Harding for the few weeks she needed?

She finished tidying the bed, packing all the weeds into her buckets for the compost heap and the bonfire. Mr Jennings would have no cause to complain about her ability to sort out the perennial weeds from the rest.

It was only as she passed the gardener's hut on her way to the compost heaps that she heard the raised voices. She herself was the subject of a heated discussion between Mr Jennings and another man. She allowed herself to dawdle a little.

'But this bit o' the garden's always been left ter me,' protested the unknown voice vehemently. 'B'ain't no call for nobody else, least of all a witless boy. No knowing what harm he might do.'

'The boy knows what he's about,' commented Mr Jennings calmly. 'He'll do no harm. And we can be doing with another pair of hands here, what with spring planting coming.'

'Don't need no extra hands here,' said the unknown. 'I've allus done it all m'self, ever since I been here. Why change it now? For a half-wit?'

'That's for me to decide, Caleb, not you.'

Caleb! Jamie shivered. The man was obviously angry about her arrival, even though he had never set eyes on her. It made no sense at all—for what threat was a garden boy to him? Still, she had been warned about his vicious temper. He sounded like the kind of man who would enjoy bullying a simpleton. She must keep out of his way.

The heated voices were still audible as Jamie moved slowly away. 'Let me have the minding of the boy, at least. I can't be a-running of the garden if'n I dunno what he might do next.'

'No.' Mr Jennings' voice was curt and decisive.

'I'll be responsible for the lad myself. If you want him to do work for you, you must come to me.'

'But that's—'

'That's the way it'll be, Caleb, an' no buts. That's the way his lordship wants it. You should know better by now than to cross him.'

'But—'

'Let it be, Caleb. That's the last word.'

Jamie hurried away. The men would come out of the hut in a few moments and must not find her hanging around.

From the comparative safety of the compost area, she watched the hut door. It was fully five minutes before it opened and Caleb emerged. She crouched down a little, busying herself with her work.

Caleb was a huge man, almost as tall as Lord Hardinge, but of much heavier build. He had immensely broad shoulders with massive arms and hands. He seemed to be carrying a lot of surplus weight—he had the belly of a drinker and a nose to match, its purplish colour easily distinguishable even in the fading light.

Jamie tried not to think about how she could handle a confrontation with this brute of a man. He—and his temper—must be avoided at all costs. She must make herself indispensable to Mr Jennings and perhaps allow him to see that she was afraid of Caleb. Given Lord Hardinge's explicit orders, that might serve to keep her apart from the undergardener. She prayed that it would.

Chapter Seven

The next morning, while Jamie was weeding around the parsnips, she was dumbfounded to see Lord Hardinge come into the kitchen garden with a lady on his arm. Jamie felt herself flushing bright red at the thought that he would be scrutinising her yet again. He seemed to see so much. And the more often she came under his eye, the more likely he was to penetrate her disguise.

She tried to make herself as small and inconspicuous as possible, hoping her dun-coloured smock would help her to hide among the vegetable beds.

It was not to be. Mr Jennings hurried out of his lair to meet his master and wasted no time in commenting on the skill of the new apprentice. At his summons, Jamie rose reluctantly to her feet and stood staring bashfully at the ground. She dared not look up to see what Lord Hardinge's reaction might be.

'Yer cap, Jamie,' whispered Mr Jennings out of the corner of his mouth.

Jamie looked up then, bewildered.

'Mr Jennings thinks you should remove your cap

in the presence of a lady,' said his lordship laconically, with a sidelong glance at the lady on his arm.

Jamie blushed furiously as she pulled off the offending cap, murmuring an apology.

'You will know next time, I am sure,' said a soft female voice. 'Jamie, is it not? I am glad you are doing so well in our garden.'

The kind undertones prompted Jamie to glance briefly at the speaker. She was tall for a lady, taller than Jamie, and, judging from her delicate bone structure, she had been very beautiful in her youth. Now, though still beautiful in a faded way, she was a middle-aged lady with greying hair. Her figure remained trim and her carriage erect, but there was a look of sadness about her deep blue eyes. The likeness between the lady and the Earl was very strong. Jamie could tell at a glance that the lady was his lordship's mother.

In her guise of simpleton, Jamie felt it was necessary to speak. 'Thank you, mum,' she said in a low voice, rather hesitantly.

Mr Jennings made to intervene. 'Not "mum", m'lad—'

'I am sure he is doing his best, Jennings,' interrupted the lady smoothly, in her soft voice. 'But he does not know who I am, so why should he be expected to know how to address me?'

Mr Jennings nodded.

'Now Jamie,' continued the lady, 'you must know that I am Lady Hardinge, your master's mother. You must address me as "my lady". Can you remember that, do you think?' She smiled warmly as she spoke.

'Yes, my la-dy,' said Jamie slowly, articulating every syllable as if the expression were totally new to her.

'Excellent,' said the Countess. 'And this gentleman is Lord Hardinge, as I think you know. You should address him as "my lord".' The lord in question was looking indulgently down at his mother as she spoke.

'Yes, mum—my lady,' said Jamie again, correcting herself laboriously. The Countess must be in no doubt about the boy's want of wits.

'I think that is enough learning for one day, my dear.' The Earl laid his free hand gently on his mother's gloved one where it rested on his arm. 'We should let Jamie get on with his work. Eh, Jennings?'

'Aye, m'lord. There's a tidy bit to do afore dusk, I'll grant ye.' He gestured to Jamie to return to her weeding. 'Not that I've any concerns about the lad, though. He works hard, whether I'm watching or no. Born to it, I'd say, m'lord, even though he don't have many wits.'

'Good,' agreed the Earl. 'He must earn his keep, of course. But I do not want him to be the butt of jokes and pranks here, Jennings, pray understand that. He is too much of a weakling to defend himself— even if he understood such things, which I doubt. You will see to it?'

'Aye, m'lord,' affirmed Mr Jennings with a slight bow. 'Ye can trust me.'

With a nod of acknowledgement, Lord Hardinge led his mother out of the walled garden towards the shrubbery to finish their winter constitutional.

Out of the corner of her eye, Jamie watched them

go. She continued to work diligently, apparently oblivious of everything else, but in the silence she could feel Mr Jennings' eyes on her back. He was probably thinking over what his lordship had said.

A blackbird's sudden alarm call echoed round the garden. 'Jamie,' called Mr Jennings. 'That's enough for this morning. Be off to yer dinner now.'

In the afternoon, Jamie was set to her first task outside the walled garden—weeding the beds by the side of the house. She bent to her work, nimbly picking out the young weed seedlings, while inwardly she smiled, dreaming of what it would be like when she was finally free of the threat from the Calderwoods.

The sound of a horse interrupted her search for an appropriately damning curse to call down on her stepmother's head. It was Lord Hardinge, astride the most beautiful black stallion Jamie had ever beheld.

She sat up to gaze at it. The stallion was truly magnificent—he had an arched neck and a fine aristocratic head with flaring nostrils. Strength and speed were written in every line of his glossy, glowing body. He seemed to be more than a little spirited too, for he was doing his best to unseat his rider.

The horse whinnied as she watched and then started to buck in an attempt to rid himself of his unwanted burden. Jamie gasped aloud, which drew his lordship's attention to her for just a split second.

The stallion reared. For a moment it seemed as if the rider would be unseated. Jamie's heart was in her mouth as she watched. But no. Lord Hardinge was much too good a horseman to lose to such an obvious trick. He lay along the horse's straining neck and brought him under control with knees and hands.

Jamie could hear him speaking softly to the big animal, though she could not make out his words. The effect seemed almost miraculous, for in less than a minute the horse was totally calm. Jamie watched in admiration, forgetting the role she should be playing and the chores she was neglecting.

Then Lord Hardinge turned towards her, fixing her with an enquiring stare. She noted the beginnings of a frown creasing his brow. She could not move, impaled by that stern gaze.

'Have you no work to do, boy?' His lordship's voice was not loud, but the unmistakable thread of authority carried easily across the distance between them. 'Well?' His irritation was manifest.

Still Jamie could not move. She felt a blush start at her neck and rise rapidly to her hairline. She knew she should stand up when the master addressed her, but her limbs would not obey her. She tried to speak. Her lips moved but there was no sound.

Lord Hardinge's frown eased suddenly. 'There is no harm done, Jamie. Now, get on with your work.' Without waiting to see whether she obeyed, he turned the stallion and gave it its head.

Jamie allowed herself the luxury of watching the superb beast as it galloped down the drive. Horse and rider were well matched, she decided. Only a very fine horseman could control such an animal. Or a horsewoman...

She forced herself to return to her weeding, but her thoughts kept returning to the horse and rider as she mechanically pulled the weeds and dropped them in her bucket. *She* could ride that stallion. Of course she could. There had never been a horse she could not ride. He'd be a handful, but her hands and heels itched at the very thought of him. If only…

Jamie rose from her weeding as the sun was dropping behind the top of the avenue of limes. She straightened her weary back, trying to ease her stiffness, and started towards the compost heaps with her buckets of weeds.

This part of the garden was deserted. In the gathering silence, the sound of horses carried easily from the nearby stables. She found she could not ignore them. It seemed as if the beautiful animals were calling to her, offering her friendship and comfort in her isolation.

In the space of a few moments, she had emptied her buckets and crept into the stable yard. It seemed to be empty. Jamie stood for a moment, her practised eye admiring the order and cleanliness of the place. A horse whickered nervously from one of the stables, perhaps a little disturbed by her unfamiliar scent. Without another thought, she moved towards the sound. The animal must be gentled, settled with hand and voice. She unbolted the door to slip inside, momentarily blind in the gloom.

The horse snorted uncertainly at her unexpected arrival, turning to face her. It was the black stallion! Close to, he was huge and powerful. He did not seem best pleased to see an intruder.

Jamie stood very still, allowing him to get used to her presence and her scent. Then she began to croon softly to him, encouraging him towards her out-stretched hand. After a few seconds, he took one rather hesitant pace towards her, then another. Soon she was blowing her scent into his nostrils, and he was allowing her to stroke his velvet muzzle.

Her head was laid gently against his glossy neck when she felt, rather than heard, the stable door open behind her. The big horse shifted nervously, but she stilled him quickly with a soft murmur, before glancing round to see the newcomer who had caught her where she had no business to be.

'Well, now. And what might you be doing here?'

Jamie closed her eyes in momentary panic. Lord Hardinge—again. Where had he appeared from this time? He sounded more surprised than angry, but still…

Jamie was torn between the need to calm the highly strung horse and the need to maintain her disguise. She stroked the stallion's neck reassuringly and crooned again, wordlessly. Then she blew gently into his nostrils once more. His ears twitched and relaxed, as she continued her stroking and crooning. Let his lordship make of her what he would. He was too good a horseman, she was sure, to lose his temper in front of such a nervous animal.

Richard had no intention of losing his temper. His initial shock at finding the stable door unbolted had been quickly replaced by concern. Othello was un-predictable and potentially dangerous. No one but himself had really been able to handle him. Until now, that is. For here was a skinny stripling who could barely string two words together, yet had reached a level of understanding with Othello which nobody else could match. Richard stood and—against his will—he marvelled. The boy had a most amazing gift, however backward he might be.

'Jamie?' he said softly, at last. The boy half turned. He ventured an uncertain half-smile. 'All right, lad,' Richard murmured. 'I can see you're doing no harm. Do you like horses?'

Jamie nodded vigorously. ''Osses,' he said eagerly. It sounded as if that single word was as much as the boy could manage.

At that moment, the head groom appeared round the corner of the stable block and hurried over to join his master. He looked shocked when he saw Jamie stroking the temperamental black stallion.

Richard ignored the new arrival. 'Good,' he said. Then his voice became stern. 'But you should not be neglecting your work, should you? Back to the garden with you now.' He watched thoughtfully as the boy trotted out of the stable yard.

The groom gulped guiltily. 'M'lord! I were just—'

'Easy, Weaver, easy. I'm glad you were not here to turn the boy away, for I should have missed something well worth seeing. Especially with Othello.'

Weaver gulped again, reddening noticeably as he made to speak.

'Save it, Weaver.' Richard paused. 'I wonder… Seems to me that boy is wasted in the garden. Could you use him here?'

'Aye, milord. Surely. Wi' a gift like that…'

Richard smiled pensively. 'Leave it to me, then. And, meanwhile, let the lad come to the stables whenever he wants.'

The groom was still nodding in wonder, as Richard turned and strode away.

The next few weeks were among the happiest that Jamie could remember. She worked in the garden from dawn till dusk, under the benevolent eye of old Mr Jennings, preparing the ground for spring planting. She was even permitted, under strict supervision, to help in the stovehouse where the tender plants were overwintered. Every night, she fell into her little bed to sleep the sleep of physical exhaustion and dream the dreams of contentment. Her nightmarish visions of incarceration by Ralph Graves faded into the background. For the first time in her life, she was truly well-fed. Her thin frame was beginning to fill out, so much so that Annie now teased her openly about the need for her bandages.

The idyll was marred only by the louring presence of Caleb. Jamie often felt his eyes boring into her defenceless back. The hatred was almost palpable, though she could not begin to account for it, for what threat was a simpleton to him? On the few occasions when Jamie dared to turn round to look at Caleb, he made no attempt to disguise his hostility. Once, he drew his forefinger across his throat in an unmistakably threatening gesture. Jamie began to go to enormous lengths to keep out of his way.

Her luck did not last. One blustery March day, Jamie was on her knees, using a hand trowel she had picked up, when Caleb's huge shadow fell across her. Looking up, she saw that his face was contorted into a predatory grin—and that there was nobody else within earshot. Her heart began to pound.

'So,' snarled Caleb, 'old Jennings' little pet sees fit to steal my tools, does he?' He dragged Jamie to her feet by the collar of her shirt. 'Ain't nobody learned you what happens to thieves, boy, eh?' He pulled the collar tight around Jamie's neck until she could hardly breathe. 'They gets hanged, boy, hanged by the neck 'til they be dead. An' then left on the gibbet to rot.' He tore the trowel out of Jamie's hand. 'That's what'll happen to you, lad, I'll see to that. One day soon, just you wait.' He released the collar and dealt Jamie a ringing box on the ear which felled her to the ground. By the time she had regained her wits, Caleb was gone, though his evil presence still seemed to be all around her.

She sat on the bare earth, massaging her neck as she tried to overcome the wave of panic which had engulfed her. Why was he so intent on being rid of her? What was she to do? She dared not run away from Harding, for she had nowhere else to hide. And yet, it would not take many blows from Caleb's huge hands to break her bones. She swallowed hard, refusing to dwell on such images—she was determined not to give in to her darkest fears. She would need to be much more vigilant, that was all. She must make sure she was always working within sight of one of the other gardeners. And if Caleb did catch her on her own, she must simply take to her heels.

* * *

Lord Hardinge chose that afternoon to make one of his increasingly frequent visits to the garden. Although he rarely spoke to Jamie directly, she knew he watched her and that he often asked after her progress. It seemed a strange sort of behaviour for a gentleman—in Jamie's limited experience. The more he watched her, the more she was overcome by the strangest feelings. Her body seemed to go hot and cold all over, both at the same time. And whenever he came near, her thoughts turned into a jumbled, tangled mess so that it became ever more difficult for her to maintain her role as Jamie, the simpleton.

Lord Hardinge had paused to speak to the head gardener, but Jamie was too far away to hear what was said. In any case, she had no reason to suppose they were talking about her.

After a moment or two, Mr Jennings called Jamie from her digging.

Taking a deep breath, she trotted over, wiping her hands on her smock and smiling as innocently as she could. But her heart was racing, and she was praying that she would not blush under the Earl's scrutiny as she always seemed to do.

'Jamie, Mr Jennings tells me you're doing very well here,' began Lord Hardinge with an encouraging smile. 'He would like you to stay.'

Jamie beamed at Mr Jennings.

'On the other hand,' continued his lordship, 'I have a fancy you could be better employed elsewhere.'

Jamie felt a wave of anxiety wash over her. Surely he would not dismiss her? She was so close to her goal.

'What do you say to working with my horses instead?'

Mr Jennings hurriedly began to reassure Jamie that no harm to her was intended. Jamie knew his motives were kind, but she barely heard him. She was desperately trying to work out the risks of discovery if she accepted his lordship's offer. It would get her away from Caleb; but it would put her even more in the master's way. Nothing was worth the risk that that entailed. She dared not take the chance that he might discover what she was. She shook her head.

Lord Hardinge smiled. 'You were right, Jennings.' Turning back to Jamie, he added, 'Don't worry, lad. I mean you no harm. Knowing how much you love horses, I thought you might like to help take care of mine. If you change your mind, just tell Mr Jennings here. And now, back to work with you.'

Jamie ran back to her task, leaving his lordship talking to the head gardener. He had not raised his voice but, even from the far side of the walled garden, Jamie could tell that he was now furiously angry.

Chapter Eight

'Where did Jamie get those bruises on his neck, Jennings?'

'I'm sure I don't know, m'lord. Some silly accident, probably. Something he shouldn't have been doing, I'll warrant. I'll make sure he gets into no more trouble.'

'See that you do, Jennings. See that you do.' With that, Richard strode back to the house.

He marched into his book-room, trying to keep a rein on his temper which was threatening to explode at any moment. Accident, indeed! Those bruises were surely no accident. Somebody in his household had injured a backward lad, probably deliberately. So much for his pledged word that no harm would come to Jamie under his roof! An attack on Jamie was an attack on his master's honour, too.

He would not allow his fury to get out of control, however, but paused to consider dispassionately who might be the culprit. If it were one of the gardeners— not Jennings, he was a gentle old man, if a bit of a stickler—the solution might indeed be to put the lad with the horses. But it could just as easily have been one of the grooms. Or someone in the house, even Smithers?

His anger had simmered down to more manageable proportions by the time the abigail appeared in answer to his summons. She was plainly nervous. Richard surveyed her slowly. Yes, she was a big woman, and strong, much stronger than Jamie. She could easily have done it.

'Smithers, I have just come from the kitchen garden. Have you seen your brother today?'

'Not since breakfast, my lord. Is something wrong? Oh, dear, what has he done now?' The words tumbled out in a rush.

'I think you had better see for yourself.' He pulled the bell once more and gave instructions that Jamie be sent for immediately. They had to wait fully five minutes for the boy's arrival, during which Richard sat silently behind his desk, mercilessly scrutinising the abigail. She wilted a little under his stern gaze.

Jamie entered shyly, head down. Richard noticed that the boy smiled a little when he saw that he was not alone with the master of the house. But Richard made no acknowledgement of Jamie's arrival. He continued to stare at Smithers without a word.

The woman's nerve broke first. 'Oh, Jamie,' she cried, 'what have you done this time?'

The boy's head came up, a militant glint in his eye. The bruises were livid on his bare neck.

Smithers gasped. 'Good God, who has done that to you? If I get my hands on…' She broke off. Jamie looked bewildered. 'I beg your pardon, m'lord. I should not have spoken so. But just look at those bruises.'

Richard was now satisfied. Smithers was not responsible for Jamie's injuries. 'Smithers, I should like you to take care of your brother's hurts, if you please. And then I want you to find out from him how they came about. I will have no such cruelty on the Harding estate. The culprit will be punished. I expect you to bring me a name—by tomorrow at the latest.' He looked down at the papers on his desk. 'That is all. You may go now. See what you can do for the boy.'

Annie hustled Jamie upstairs to their room to begin applying witch hazel to her bruises. She paid no attention when Jamie winced at the cold liquid on her tender skin. 'Tell me what happened,' she demanded sternly.

'Nothing,' croaked Jamie. It was the first word she had tried to utter since her encounter with Caleb. It hurt.

'Jamie, I wasn't born yesterday. Bruises like these don't appear by themselves.'

'It was an accident. It's nothing.' Jamie's brain was in a whirl. Although her throat was very sore and she could barely swallow, it had not occurred to her until now that there might be visible evidence of her encounter with Caleb. She must not name him. It would only give the bully more reason to attack her. 'I caught my collar on a low branch, and it almost choked me before I could get free. I was clumsy, that's all.'

'Do you expect me to believe that? His lordship certainly will not.'

'He will if you tell it properly. And why should he concern himself anyway?'

'You heard him. He thinks someone did it deliberately, and he will not tolerate it. He's a fair man—'

'Fair? What's fair about his treatment of you? He had you turned off from Calderwood and—'

'He's a fair man, Jamie, as I said, particularly to someone as vulnerable as my baby brother. Why don't you tell the truth?'

'I've told you what happened, Annie. There's nothing more to say.' She paused for a moment, seeing the real worry on the abigail's face. 'Even if there were someone else involved—and I have told you there was not—it would only make matters worse for me. He would just make sure there were no visible marks, next time. Now, I must get back to work, Annie.' She forced herself to smile. It wobbled a little, but she did not think Annie had noticed. 'See you at supper.' With that, she hurried out.

Barely fifteen minutes after she had left it, the abigail was again in the book-room, recounting Jamie's tale. Richard sat impassively behind his desk. He let the woman see that he did not believe a word of it. 'That's all he said?' His voice was quiet, but full of suppressed anger, as he glared fiercely at the servant.

Smithers nodded.

'And did you believe him?'

'He doesn't say much, my lord, and it's sometimes

difficult to follow his meaning, but when I suggested someone else had been involved, he denied it, vehemently. It *could* have happened as he described,' she finished lamely.

'In other words, you don't believe him. And neither do I. Little good it will do us, though, without knowing the identity of the villain.' He was talking more to himself than to the abigail for a moment, but then he turned back to her with a frown. 'As his sister, you should surely have been able to extract the truth from the boy. I do not accept his explanation for a moment. You will set about identifying the true culprit at once, if you please. I leave it to you to decide how, but the moment you find out anything more, Smithers, you are to come to me immediately. Do you understand?' At her rapid nod, he dismissed her and returned to his papers.

Richard spent the rest of the afternoon reading reports from his agents in London and elsewhere, his frown deepening as the day wore on. All the money and effort he was expending in an attempt to recover the missing loans was bringing scant return. There was plenty of information about the Calderwood household, which seemed to have been in uproar since his visit—apparently as the result of some domestic crisis or other—but there was nothing about the money. Thus far, unfortunately, Calderwood had won the day.

Richard needed a new strategy but, for the moment, ideas eluded him. At length, his patience exhausted, he stuffed the papers into his desk and mounted the stairs to his mother's sitting-room.

She welcomed him with a smile of concern. 'You look tired, Richard, and worried too. Come and sit down. May I help in any way?'

'It's frustration as much as anything else, Mama,' he admitted, dropping a kiss on her cheek. 'I need to be doing something, but until I can find some lever to use against Calderwood, I can't begin to act. None of my enquiries has come up with anything yet. And now, to make matters worse, I appear to have a child-beater on my estate.'

Lady Hardinge looked puzzled.

'That backward brother of Smithers is clearly being abused by someone at Harding, but I cannot find out who it is.'

'How unfortunate.' She paused, thoughtfully. 'You know, it's not like you to take so much interest in waifs and strays, Richard. Why are you doing so with this lad?'

'To be honest, I am not sure. Oh, at the outset, it was perfectly straightforward—I wanted to have Smithers here so that I could use her to find out more about the Calderwoods. Offering a place to the boy was a means of snaring his sister. And it worked. But now, I'm rather taken with him, I admit. He's an engaging lad, very willing and hard-working, and extremely talented when it comes to growing things, as we have both seen. He seems to have a way with horses, too.'

'You shouldn't be so surprised, my dear. Very often the simpletons who find it so hard to communicate with people seem to have a natural understanding of plants and beasts.'

Richard nodded. 'What about Smithers herself, Mama? Has she let fall any clue that might help us?'

'Absolutely none. She does her work very well, as always, even though I no longer require an abigail of her talents, as you know. But she says nothing to that. No doubt she is keen to stay where her brother is.'

'No doubt,' Richard echoed grimly, staring into the fire.

His mother watched him silently for several minutes.

Richard rose abruptly. 'I must *do* something, Mama. The waiting is beginning to drive me mad. I shall go to London to see my agents and to find out whether any of their leads is even vaguely promising. They say not, of course. But perhaps I can spot something they have overlooked. At least I shall be *doing* something.'

As the days passed, Jamie continued to work contentedly in the garden, though she had become even more careful than before. There were no more attacks from Caleb. But at night, in their room, Annie continued to pester her about what had happened.

'For goodness' sake, Annie, stop this. Every time you see me, you go on and on about those bruises. I have told you all there is to tell. The bruises have gone. Do leave it now.'

'His lordship did not believe that story. He—'

'Damn his lordship!' exploded Jamie, momentarily forgetting the manners of a lady. 'What right has he to interfere?'

'Jamie! Keep your voice down, or someone will

hear you. Lord Hardinge has every right, as you know very well. He is the master here. Would you be any less concerned if it were one of your own servants?'

'No,' Jamie agreed reluctantly, 'but this is different.'

'Oh? Why?'

Jamie was in real difficulty now. She could not find words to explain the strange effects Lord Hardinge had on her, intimidating and exciting all at once. She did not understand it herself. 'It's…it's not normal for a gentleman to pay so much attention to a gardener's boy,' she managed at last, which sounded pretty feeble even to her own ears.

Annie looked hard at her wayward charge, but merely said, 'He won't be doing so for a while. He left for London four days ago.'

'Oh, so that is why he hasn't—' Jamie shut her mouth abruptly, silently cursing herself. No one must suspect that she watched for the master's frequent walks in the garden and had been disappointed every day since his departure.

Annie seemed not to notice Jamie's gaffe. 'How much longer now till you come of age, Jamie? And what do you plan to do then?'

'March the twenty-sixth. After that, well…I should tell you, I suppose, Annie. I know I can trust you.' She rose and fetched her pelisse from among Annie's clothes. Then she slit open one of the seams to extract what was inside.

'These were my mother's pearls, Annie,' she said simply, showing her the single strand. 'They are the sum total of my inheritance from her. I believe they are very fine and very valuable.'

Annie nodded.

'Once I come of age, I shall be able to sell them and go back to being a girl again. Then I shall look for a situation as a governess or a companion, so that I can support myself. The pearls will pay for my keep until I find a position.' Jamie saw that Annie's expression was registering concern. 'I thought I might use one of the Bath agencies you spoke of, Annie,' she continued.

Annie took both the callused hands in hers and sat beside Jamie on the bed. 'Oh, Miss Jamie,' she said gently, 'it won't do. To be sure, it won't. First of all, if you were to try to sell those pearls now, as you are, you would be had up on suspicion of theft, sure as eggs is eggs.'

'I'll go as a girl, then,' protested Jamie. 'I may not be richly dressed, but I do *sound* like a lady.'

'And secondly,' continued Annie, without a pause, 'no agency will even consider you without references.'

'I should have thought of that,' admitted Jamie in a small, crushed voice. Annie put a comforting arm round her shoulders. 'But I shall find a way, never fear. Somehow I shall achieve my independence. Even if I have to write my references myself.' Her face brightened. 'Yes! That's what I shall do. Miss Jessamyne Calderwood of Calderwood Hall shall provide an impeccable reference for her erstwhile companion, Miss...er...Jemima Crane!'

Annie gasped. 'You cannot!'

Jamie cocked a saucy eyebrow. 'What choice do I have? And it will harm no one. I myself shall sign it, so it is no forgery. I shall just…embroider the truth a little. It will appear that I am an elderly spinster, somewhat ailing, who employed a young companion to brighten her life.'

'Hmph!' Annie did not sound convinced. 'And why, pray, did this paragon of virtue, Miss Jemima Crane, leave her place with so kind an employer?'

Jamie thought for a moment. 'Miss Calderwood is to go abroad, for her health. Jemima will not go, not for any price. She is afraid of the sea!'

Annie had to laugh. 'You are beyond redemption, Miss Jamie. What if—?'

Jamie refused to listen. 'I have no choice, Annie, so I had better make the best of it. Oh!' Her face fell. 'But I have no Calderwood notepaper. It will not do.'

Annie sat silent for a while, studying Jamie's face. 'I have some,' she said simply. Jamie beamed. 'Honestly come by, I promise you. I was planning to write to my old mistress in London, the day Lady Calderwood turned me off. I think I still have the sheet.'

Jamie flung her arms round Annie's neck and kissed her on the cheek. 'You are wonderful, Annie Smithers. Can we do it now? Please?'

The abigail fetched the sheet of writing paper from her case and, together, they began to compose the all-important reference for Miss Jemima Crane, spinster companion.

Chapter Nine

Mr Jennings had taken to sending Jamie every morning to cut a bunch of daffodils as a gift for Lady Hardinge. Although he never explained, Jamie knew the flowers were a token of sympathy for the widowed mistress he had served ever since her marriage to the late Earl.

It was a delightful time to be out of doors. The mornings were crisp and clear and, although there was often frost on the ground, it soon melted in the early spring sunshine. The swathes of daffodils lifted Jamie's spirits with their glorious golden colour, reminding her of the rapidly passing days. Soon it would be her birthday and she would—somehow—attain her freedom!

One morning, very much later than usual, while Jamie was picking the daffodils, she came upon a tiny plant of late snowdrops, hidden among the drifts of gold. They were quite beautiful, white overlaid with green. Jamie put the cut daffodils in the trug while she fetched her trowel and a small clay pot. The snowdrops would make a delightful gift for her ladyship. It did not matter that they would soon wilt indoors.

Jamie knelt among the daffodils to dig up the tiny flowers. It took some strength to do so, for the daffodil bed was firm and stony and her trowel had to be eased through it to get under the tiny bulbs without damaging their roots. At last they were free. She laid the little clump on the grass and began to remove some of the earth and stones from underneath, before putting the flowers into the pot.

'What the hell do you think ye're at?' cried a harsh voice.

Jamie half turned, to see the towering figure of Caleb, his face purple with fury, his arm upraised with a thin stake in his hand. Before she could move, he brought it down across her back, knocking her flat on to the earth and then pinning her there with his boot. A hail of blows followed. Jamie could not stir. Her face was driven into the flower-bed so that she could not scream aloud. At every gasp, she inhaled fine soil which threatened to choke her.

On the curious thought that she had so nearly made it to freedom, she passed out.

Caleb was raining furious blows on Jamie's inert body when he was wrenched aside by a strong arm. A sharp right to the jaw knocked him backwards to the ground, where he lay moaning and bleeding from a deeply split lip.

'I shall deal with you later,' snarled Richard, lifting Jamie's senseless body and striding back towards the house. He looked anxiously for signs of life. The boy would not die from a whipping, surely? But if he had suffocated?

No—the boy was breathing; thank God. Although still quite deeply unconscious, Jamie seemed somehow aware that the terror was over and that he was safe. Richard was reminded of a trusting child, as Jamie snuggled deeper into the safety of his encircling arms, moaning a little.

Spurred on by the sound, which seemed to suggest serious injury, Richard increased his pace. As he strode rapidly through the hallway to his book-room, he threw an order over his shoulder for Smithers to be fetched at once. A moment later, he was laying Jamie gently on the sofa and throwing off his own dust-stained coat.

The boy was breathing fairly easily now. That much was obvious from a first cursory examination. The state of his back would be another matter.

Very gently, and silently cursing the delay in Smithers' arrival, Richard turned Jamie over so that he could attend to the boy's back. Lifting the heavy smock, he pulled the undershirt out of Jamie's breeches. To his surprise, he found, instead of broken and bleeding skin, thick bandages covering most of the boy's back. A few weals were visible on his shoulders, but the skin there was not broken.

Without further thought, Richard crossed to his desk for some scissors. Then he cut through the bandages from waist to shoulder, peeling them back to see what injuries lay beneath. He was more than a little relieved to find that the bandages and the heavy smock seemed to have absorbed most of the force of the blows. A few fine red lines were the only sign of the beating Jamie had received at the hands of the appalling Caleb.

Satisfied, Richard let out the breath he had been holding. Gently he turned Jamie on to his back to make him more comfortable. The bandages fell away. To Richard's astonishment, he found that his hands were cradling, not the body of a thirteen-year-old boy, but the delectable breasts of a fully-formed girl.

Richard's mind was spinning. He was remembering everything that had happened since Jamie had come into his life and discovering new perspectives on both her reactions and his own. All the strange attractions he had felt towards a simpleton boy... As he tried to gather his tumbling thoughts, his hands continued to cup her breasts, his thumbs unconsciously massaging the reddened ridges where the bandages had cut into her tender flesh.

And at that moment, Jamie's eyes opened and she looked up into his. She seemed half-dazed. But she appeared to recognise him. And then she smiled.

For what seemed an eternity, he felt he was drowning in those slumberous green eyes, responding to the invitation they contained. But when she lapsed back into insensibility, his sanity returned. He was caressing an unconscious woman. No matter what he had read in her eyes, he was taking advantage of her by touching her so. He snatched his hands away as if he had been burnt.

'Lord Hardinge!'

Suddenly, Smithers was there beside him. He had

not heard her come in. He hastily pulled down
Jamie's smock, knowing very well it was too late.

Smithers was looking daggers at him.

'You had better see to your brother, Smithers,' he
said curtly. 'Or should I say "sister"? Never mind.
What matters at present is Jamie. You must know that
I found him being severely beaten by Caleb. The bandages seem to have saved him—or rather her—from
serious hurt. But you will wish to see for yourself.'
He turned his back in recognition of Jamie's need for
privacy, as Smithers knelt down by the inert body.

Richard pulled the bell with a grim smile. 'Doubt-
less you would welcome an opportunity to concoct
yet another of your fairy tales. You have such a vivid
imagination, as I have good reason to know. But I
fear you will be disappointed there. I have no intention of leaving you alone together now, not until I
have got to the root of this business!'

The butler appeared in answer to Richard's summons. 'Ah, Digby. Be so good as to ask Mrs Peters
to come to the study and remain here with Smithers
and Jamie until I return. And ask Tom to remain outside in the hall. Neither Smithers nor Jamie is to leave
this room until I say they may.'

The butler turned to go. By not the flicker of an
eyelid had he betrayed any surprise at Richard's unexpected manner of returning from London.

'Ah, yes,' Richard murmured. 'One moment,
Digby.' He returned to his desk to pen a short note,
which he folded and gave to the butler. 'Deliver that
to Lady Hardinge before she leaves for Bath, if you
please,' he ordered. 'And send one of the maids to

attend on her ladyship while her abigail is…otherwise occupied.'

As the butler left to carry out his various instructions, Richard turned back to Smithers. 'Now,' he began, in a marginally less harsh voice, 'take care of Jamie. Whatever you have both done, nothing can excuse what that brute was doing to her.' He came to stand over Jamie, looking down at her pale face. An ironic smile twisted one corner of his mouth, as he thought about these past weeks and the strange part Jamie had begun to play in his life. He had felt such sympathy for an innocent, backward lad—who had turned out to be no boy, and was probably neither backward nor innocent. Remembering how she had smiled up at him when he was caressing her, he was now sure of it. How completely he had been gulled!

As soon as the housekeeper arrived, he left the room without another glance, pausing only in the hallway to ensure Tom understood his instructions. Then he mounted the stairs to the top floor of the house, to begin a systematic search of the room shared by Smithers and her so-called brother.

Standing in the doorway, he surveyed the neat attic room. A bed and a truckle, a chest of drawers and a small clothes press, and nothing else. Not many hiding places here, surely? But he did not know what he was looking for. The main evidence of their wrongdoing was Jamie herself. What else might he find?

Richard chose to be very careful and methodical. He examined every item in every drawer. He pulled out the drawers to search behind and beneath them.

He moved furniture and bedding so that he could search every inch of the room.

When he found what he was looking for in the clothes press, he was tempted to return immediately to confront the women, but something stayed him. There might be more. He would remain until his painstaking search was complete.

It was some two hours before he returned to the study, dismissing Tom and Mrs Peters from their posts.

As the door closed, Richard surveyed the two women slowly. Jamie had apparently recovered from her ordeal and was sitting on the end of the sofa where he had laid her earlier. Smithers was standing behind. He noticed that Jamie had not risen from her seat as he entered the room. Indeed, she seemed remarkably composed, considering her situation. Smithers, by contrast, was twisting a handkerchief in her fingers and almost ripping it in her agitation. Good, he would start with her.

'Smithers. First, you will be good enough to explain why you perpetrated this disgraceful fraud on my household.' It was a statement, not a question.

'Jamie had to get away. She was being persecuted. It…it seemed the only way.' Her words petered out.

'Is Jamie your sister?' he demanded.

'Yes—' began Smithers.

'No,' interrupted Jamie in clear, resolute tones.

That single word was spoken in a remarkably educated voice which the woman was making no attempt to disguise. Who on earth could she be?

'No, I am not,' Jamie repeated. 'Nor am I backward, my lord. I myself am responsible for everything that has happened. Annie's only crime is that she took pity on me. Vent your anger on me, if you please.'

She might be a fraud, and she might even be a harlot, but there was no mistaking the dignity and courage with which she faced him. For a split second, and against his better judgement, he felt like applauding.

'Who are you?' he asked sharply, refusing to be ensnared by her dangerous wiles.

'I cannot tell you.' She closed her lips tightly. From her mulish expression, Richard knew she was determined to resist his questioning.

'Do you really expect me to accept that?' he asked with withering scorn. 'Come, come. Remember, I have all the power of the law at my back. And I will use it, if I have to. Now—I ask you again—what is your name?'

Jamie returned his hostile glare. 'I cannot tell you, my lord,' she replied with quiet composure. 'Since you choose not to accept that, there is nothing more to be said.' She clasped her hands lightly in her lap and stared down at them.

Richard exploded. 'By God, I shall have the truth out of you, one way or the other. Do not doubt it.'

But he did not succeed. In spite of continuing to question them for nearly an hour, he discovered nothing more. What little patience he had was totally exhausted. 'Very well,' he said, in a low menacing voice, 'since you choose to defy me, we shall adopt a different approach, an approach which you will not

enjoy, I promise you. But first, I shall give you time
to meditate upon your transgressions. Both of you.'

With that, he gave orders for Smithers and Jamie
to be locked in separate rooms for the night. He was
resolved there would be no opportunity for collusion
between them, before he had got to the bottom of the
mystery. He was not sure what kind of approach
might be successful, but he hoped that his vague
threat would prey on their minds in their isolation and
help to bring them to confess.

Richard dined alone and then returned to his book-
room, where he remained until almost all the household was abed. Thank God his mother had gone to
stay with her sister in Bath and would not return for
a few days. He did not yet feel equal to explaining
matters to her.

He leaned back in his leather chair, gazing vacantly
into the middle distance. His mind was preoccupied
with the puzzle of the items he had brought away
from his search of Smithers' room. He just did not
know what to make of them. Jamie might possibly
make sense of them, if she could be persuaded to
speak, but somehow he doubted it. Whoever, and
whatever she was, her courage was extraordinary. She
was likely to outface him, however he tried to coerce
her.

Thoughts of coercion brought the brutal figure of
Caleb back into his mind for the first time since the
encounter in the garden. The undergardener needed
to be dealt with for his mindless cruelty to Jamie. In
spite of the lateness of the hour, Richard sent for
Caleb.

But Caleb was not to be found. He had not waited to be subjected to Richard's wrath. He had not even paused to collect his belongings. It appeared that, as soon as he had recovered his breath, he had set about putting a safe distance between himself and the powerful master of Harding.

For Richard, it was the very last straw. Frustrated at every turn, his temper again got the better of him. No insolent chit was going to defy him in his own house. He would have the truth out of her. Now! Before the night was over!

Although Richard knew perfectly well that his wisest course would be to tackle Jamie and Smithers separately in the morning, when he was fresh and better able to question them effectively, his logical mind was overridden by his now ungovernable temper. His feet led him to the attics instead of to his own chamber.

He stopped outside Jamie's room. The key was in the lock, and there was no sound from inside. Transferring his candle to his left hand, he quietly unlocked the door and went in. Once inside, he locked the door again and pocketed the key.

That single candle lit only part of the room. Beyond its range he could make out the shadowy shape of a small bed and a low chest. The room contained nothing else, not even a chair.

He moved across the room, lifting his candle so that its light fell on the bed where Jamie was sleeping. Her titian hair, freed from its daytime straitjacket, surrounded her pale face in a riot of tumbled curls. Her long dark lashes—why had he never noticed them before?—rested on slightly flushed cheeks. Was she a little feverish?

Without thinking, he stretched out his hand and laid it gently on her forehead. It was cool to his touch, the skin as soft as a petal in spite of her weeks in the open air.

Her eyes fluttered open. She seemed to register the fact of his presence in the gloom and of his cool hand on her brow. As before, she smiled at him, an otherworldly smile which almost touched his heart.

'No, Jamie,' he said sharply. 'No, I am not so easily manipulated. I have come for the truth.'

The harshness in his voice jerked her into wakefulness. Her smile vanished as she realised she was alone with the master of the house in the middle of the night—and he appeared to be in no mood to humour her if she defied him.

In a flash, Jamie was out of the bed and across the room to the door. Behind her, his lordship laughed quietly. The sound seemed very menacing in the oppressive silence of the dark house.

'A waste of time, my dear. The door is locked.'

Jamie turned to face him then, her back against the door. 'What are you doing here, my lord?' she asked, trying to control the trembling of her voice.

She put him in mind of a mythical nymph, all in white, fleeing from some marauding satyr. The image inflamed his temper even further. 'What do you think I am doing, Jamie?' he responded cynically, seeking for the most effective means of putting her under pressure. 'This afternoon, in the book-room, you made me an offer with your eyes. Did you not think I would come to collect?'

She cowered away from him. What had become of the honourable man who had taken pity on a simple lad? He had even shown kindness to the boy Jamie. How could it have come to this?

His lordship set the candle carefully on the chest and came towards her, pinning her against the door with a hand on either side of her head. 'Now, my girl, are you going to tell me what I want to know? Or do I have to force you?'

Her whole body was shaking. She tried to turn her head away, but he gripped her by the chin, forcing her to look up at him. In his eyes, she saw anger, frustration—and dawning desire. And the merest touch of his hand on her face had started that same strange quivering in her limbs that she had experienced every time he touched her. She could barely stand.

It was the fear in her eyes which first penetrated the red mist of his anger. Whatever she had done, she was now helpless—and terrified of him. Then, behind her fear, he glimpsed something deeper, reaching out to him, urging him to respond.

Suddenly, both his hands were cupping her face. His mouth descended hungrily on hers, demanding that she yield to him.

Jamie was powerless to resist the pull of that first kiss. Somehow, her arms were around his neck, her fingers threading through his thick hair, her lips opening beneath the pressure of his.

Kissing her less urgently now, teasing at her lus-

cious mouth, he picked her up and carried her back
to the bed. Questions were long since forgotten as he
stretched out beside her, caressing her soft cheek. She
moaned softly when his lips moved to her neck, nuzzling gently.

'Ah, Jamie, my beauty. Soon, I promise you, soon.'

Jamie had lost all sense of who and where she was.
Everything was pure sensation—the tingling of her
skin wherever he touched her, the magic of holding
his powerful body in her arms, the longing in her
innermost being as she responded to his ardent kisses.

Chapter Ten

It was the pull of the coarse lacing of her nightgown which brought Jamie back to sordid reality. This was not the joining of two souls in pure love. She was lying in bed with Lord Hardinge *who thought she was a servant and a fraud*. Lord Hardinge was going to ravish her. This was not love, but lust. Oh, no matter that she had encouraged him, that—if she were honest with herself—she wanted him as much as he wanted her. It was wrong, despicable, base. He must not be allowed to do this. She would never forgive him—or herself—if he did.

She caught his hand and pushed it away with all her strength. 'No, please, my lord, I beg of you. Please let me go. I cannot do this.'

Richard sat up abruptly, recalled to his senses by the renewed fear in her voice. For all his reservations about womankind, he had never in his life taken any woman against her will. But this one—for this one, he was sorely tempted. She was a tease, had led him on, and now she spurned him? Surely she deserved to be taken in anger?

'Do not do this, I beg of you,' she repeated, more urgently now. 'You will never forgive yourself if you do. I have never yet known a man.' In spite of all her attempts at self-control, hot tears had begun to flow.

The last remnants of Richard's anger melted away at the sight of those tears. He passed his hand across his brow, trying to recover his composure. 'God help me! What am I doing?' he cried, anguish in his deep voice. He rose from the bed. 'Go to sleep, Jamie. I give you my word I shall not touch you again. Go to sleep now.' Then, taking up the candle, he unlocked the door and was gone, leaving her in total darkness.

Jamie could not move, not even to find out whether he had locked her in again. She lay with tears pouring down her face, trying to understand what had happened between them—and why she had denied him when she wanted him so much. The memory of his mouth on hers sent flushes of desire coursing through her veins, making her limbs at once burning and boneless. She was unable to control the longing which filled her.

Her head told her he would have taken her in anger, and as a servant, not as a lover. Who knows, he might afterwards have delivered her up to the constable and even to the gallows?

But, in spite of that knowledge, and the self-loathing which accompanied it, she knew that, if he had persisted, she would not have denied him. Only his honourable response to her pleas had spared her. If he had kissed her again, nothing else would have mattered.

* * *

On the other side of the door, Richard was standing with his hand still on the knob, trying in his turn to come to terms with what he had so nearly done. It did not matter that she was only a servant. His behaviour had been despicable. The hand which held the candle was a little unsteady, and the tiny flame cast strange flickering shadows as it moved.

'My lord? Is there something I can do for you?'

He turned to see the housekeeper emerge from the shadows behind him. He cursed inwardly. Not only had he allowed his impossible temper to lead him to the verge of doing something contemptible, he had also been caught in the act. No matter that he had not seduced the girl. The whole household would soon believe that he had. Damn, damn, damn!

'My lord?' said Mrs Peters again.

He was not about to make any sort of apology or excuse to his housekeeper. He fixed her with an aristocratic glare and said evenly, 'This young woman is locked in her room on my instructions. She is to be kept there. And she is not to be allowed to have any dealings with Smithers. Do I make myself clear?' He extracted the key from his pocket and locked the door.

Mrs Peters still looked more than a little shocked. She shook her head unhappily as he turned and made for the stairs.

Downstairs in his study once more, Richard quickly consumed four very large brandies and poured himself a fifth. He was at a loss to account for his own behaviour. Never, in all his adult life, had he lost control in such a way. That girl—Jamie—must be part witch.

But no witch had eyes like tropical pools—or a mouth like ripe fruit, waiting to be plucked. At the memory of their kisses, he shifted uncomfortably in his chair. Even the thought of her stirred his desire.

He tried to re-ignite his anger in an attempt to control his body's responses. She had pretended to be a boy to obtain a situation in his household. And she had no explanation to offer. She had yet to attempt to explain away the evidence he had uncovered during his search earlier. He would be surprised if she succeeded there, either!

But still, somehow, he was not fully persuaded of her guilt. The vision of her, as he had seen her upstairs, rose again in his mind, her eyes opening to smile up at him. When she looked at him in just that way…

He downed his brandy in a single swallow and slammed the empty goblet on to the table. Action, as ever, was the answer, so he returned to his desk and read yet again the document he had brought down from Smithers' room. With a decisive nod, he drew a fresh sheet of paper towards him and penned a crisp but careful letter. Then he sealed it with a wafer, before inscribing the address in a firm hand and franking it with his signature.

Without pausing for further reflection on the wisdom of what he had done, he rose from the table with the letter in his hand, hesitating for only a moment over the brandy decanter. No. No more tonight. In the hallway, he dropped the letter on the tray where the servants would find and despatch it first thing in the morning. Then, drowsy from the effects of the brandy, he made his way to bed.

Having gone very late—and a little foxed—to his bed, Richard slept very long into the next day. Gregg, the valet, who had naturally waited up to see his master to bed, knew better than to disturb him, so it was well after noon before he stirred.

When Richard awoke, refreshed in spite of the excesses of the night before, he recalled with satisfaction that he had had the presence of mind to despatch that letter. Then he remembered the detail of his encounter with Jamie, which gave him no satisfaction at all, only guilt. He had no wish to confront her again until absolutely necessary. If he were honest with himself, he was not sure how well he could handle such a meeting.

Instead, Smithers was summoned back to the study in mid-afternoon. She was pale and drawn.

'You look unwell, Smithers,' he commented coolly. 'Troubled sleep, perhaps?'

'Lack of sleep is not the problem, my lord,' countered the abigail quickly, bristling at the innuendo. 'Rather, lack of food.'

'What?'

'I was released from my room barely five minutes ago, my lord. No one has come near me since last night. I fancy they do not dare.' She sounded angry and bitter. Clearly, she did not care if it showed.

'And Jamie?'

'I do not know. But if you gave no express orders…'

In spite of his justifiable anger, Richard was mortified by his own stupid oversight. 'I apologise, Smithers. Go down to the kitchen now and have something to eat. I shall see you again in half an hour. And send someone up to Jamie's room with a tray.'

Smithers looked surprised at his sudden change of tone.

It did not last. 'One moment, Smithers. You realise, of course, that someone other than you must take up the tray?'

'Of course,' she repeated, with heavy emphasis, and left for the kitchen.

Half an hour later, the interview was resumed, but it proved singularly unproductive. Smithers still refused to answer any of his lordship's questions even when, in exasperation, he threatened to turn her off without a character.

'You could end up on the parish, or worse,' he thundered. 'For God's sake, woman, tell me the truth.'

Smithers would not do so. Her mouth had assumed the same mulish expression that he had noted on Jamie's face the previous day. 'It is not for me to say, my lord,' was her only answer. 'You must ask Jamie. She must decide. I cannot help you.'

Richard ran his hand through his thick hair. 'Go back to your room. I will deal with you later—once I have dealt with Jamie.'

He had finally decided that the confrontation with

Jamie could no longer be delayed, however uncomfortable it might prove to be. As he waited for her to be fetched, he repeated the resolutions he had already made. He would not touch her. He would not allow her to provoke him—until her arrival in his life, he had prided himself on his ability to control his temper in almost any situation. And he would not frighten her. The image of her cowering away from him filled him with shame. He pushed it guiltily to the back of his mind.

This time he would be calm and persistent in ferreting out the truth. No threats, no temper, no violence.

Jamie had no sooner entered the book-room than most of his resolutions were broken. 'Good God, woman, have you no shame?' His voice was almost a shout. 'How dare you persist in dressing so improperly?' His eyes raked her figure mercilessly, finally resting on her close-fitting breeches.

Bristling with anger, she looked straight at him. 'You gave me no choice, my lord,' she countered, flushing under his angry gaze. 'Everything but my nightgown is locked away with Annie. I thought you would not wish to see me in that. Would you have me go and change?'

Richard swallowed, trying yet again to master his temper and to ignore her provocative impudence. She was clever and manipulative, this one, and might well best him if he did not remain calm. He forced a thin smile. 'No, Jamie. As you well know, it would not serve my purposes to have you and Smithers back together. We will remain as we are.'

He saw that Jamie continued to stare at him without the least acknowledgement of his undoubted power over her. He could have her carted off to gaol at a word, as she must be well aware, but she showed no sign of fear. A remarkable woman indeed. Or foolhardy in the extreme.

He sat back in his chair, forcing himself to breathe slowly and deeply until his self-control had returned. 'We will start with what happened yesterday, if you please, Jamie. Tell me about it.'

'I have been thinking about that all day, my lord. Heavens knows, I have had little opportunity for any other activity since yesterday.' That little barb hit home, and his jaw clenched. He was ashamed to be reminded of his treatment of her.

Richard sat forward in his chair, watching her intently. Everything in her manner suggested honesty and openness, but he must remain on the watch for the slightest flicker of deceit.

'You must know that Caleb has been threatening simple Jamie ever since we arrived,' she began. 'I cannot see what threat a simpleton could be to the undergardener, but he clearly wanted to be rid of me. You suspected that no accident was responsible for my bruises last week.' Richard remained impassive as she looked defiantly at him. 'You were right. It was Caleb. Then, yesterday—' She swallowed hard. 'Yesterday,' she began again, in a slightly wobbly voice, 'I went to cut daffodils for her ladyship, as I have been doing for some time now. I found a tiny group of snowdrops buried among the taller daffodils. I imagine Caleb must have planted them.

'I decided to dig up the snowdrops for Lady Hardinge. But Caleb caught me just as I was tidying up the clump to put it in the pot. The rest, my lord, you know.' She clasped her hands loosely in front of her and rested her open, direct gaze on his face.

Under that calm gaze, Richard felt himself flushing. He had been a fool not to secure Caleb from the first. Now he could see that he had been obsessed with Jamie to the exclusion of all else. He did not dare pause to wonder why that should be so, saying merely, 'I shall speak to him in due course. It is clear he has much to answer for, not least his attacks on you, for which I am sorry.'

Jamie seemed to relax a little at his words. Good. Now was the time to find out the real truth about who she was.

'Let us turn to other matters now, Jamie. I want explanations for your presence here and for this blatant fraud.' He waved a hand in the direction of her rough male clothes. 'And I want an explanation for this,' he added sharply, holding out a sheet of paper.

A single glance was sufficient to show her what the paper was. 'How came you by this?' snapped Jamie, all remaining signs of deference gone.

Richard smiled with satisfaction. He had her on the defensive now, and he meant to follow up his advantage ruthlessly. 'That is of no importance. I am waiting for your explanation.'

For a moment, judging by her tight-lipped expression, he thought she would take refuge in silence.

'That is my reference, my lord, from my previous

employer, Miss Jessamyne Calderwood. You will have seen that she speaks very highly of me.'

He raised an eyebrow. 'She speaks very highly of Miss Jemima Crane,' he said, pointedly staring at her trousered figure.

'I am Jemima Crane,' said Jamie, sounding remarkably composed.

Both brows shot up. 'Are you, indeed? Then why, pray, did you not say so yesterday? Why this disreputable imposture? How comes it that such a woman'—he paused, reading from the paper—'''honest, reliable, well-educated in the ways of society''— should stoop to such impropriety?'

'I had to leave because Miss Calderwood was going abroad for the sake of her health. And for my own protection. Lady Calderwood has a distant cousin—his name is Graves—who was becoming very persistent in his attentions, which were not honourable. He gave every indication of being ready to follow me wherever I went, perhaps even to possess himself of my person by force. I admit I was very frightened.'

She shuddered—very realistically, Richard thought.

'Lady Calderwood would do nothing to help me. But Miss Jessamyne was more than kind. She procured boy's clothes for me and helped me plan my escape. We thought that, if I could lie concealed for a few months, Ralph Graves would lose interest. That is why I could not tell anyone who I was.

'I had intended to leave on my own. But, following your visit, when her ladyship dismissed Smithers, Miss Jessamyne suggested we might go together and, out of the kindness of her heart, Smithers agreed. Now, see what ill fortune it has brought her!'

'Ill fortune?' He reached into the drawer of his desk to bring out the string of pearls, which he placed carefully on the desk in front of Jamie. 'I should have said, rather, good fortune. Would not you?'

Jamie blanched. 'Those pearls, my lord, are mine, not Annie's.'

'And may I ask how you came by them?' he asked silkily.

'They were given to me,' she said unhelpfully.

His eyes bored into hers, demanding that she say more. He thought she looked guilty.

'They belonged to Miss Jessamyne. They were a parting gift to me, before I left Calderwood Hall.'

'I see. What a very generous lady she must be, as well as—shall we say—a little eccentric in her dealings with her servants?' He was anything but convinced and he wanted her to know it. Suddenly he smiled. 'No doubt Lady Calderwood will be able to substantiate your story. I expect her reply to my letter any day. We shall return to this matter then.'

He had the satisfaction of seeing her turn dead white then. So she *was* lying! About the necklace— and probably much more. His tactics were working. The waiting would give her time to dwell on her transgressions, provided she had no further opportunity to escape.

He leaned back in his chair. 'That is all for the present, Jemima. You may go.'

As she turned to leave, he added, 'And I do not wish to see you improperly dressed again. Return to your old room and see to it. You and Smithers will have the freedom of the house, for the present. But that is all. I intend to get to the bottom of all this and to ensure that the guilty are punished. So, until I am satisfied on that head, you will not be permitted to leave Harding.'

Jamie fled from the room.

Chapter Eleven

It was a great relief not to be locked into the bare attic room. Jamie mechanically folded her nightgown as her mind ranged over her options. She must get away before Lady Calderwood found her. It was that—or forced marriage to Ralph Graves. How long would she be able to resist him? And how would she live with herself if she did not? No—it must be escape. And it must be now!

Jamie knew that it would be very wrong to involve Annie this time. The abigail had already suffered quite enough as a result of her kind-hearted espousal of Jamie's cause. Lord Hardinge would expect them to try to escape together, probably after dark. Well, she would surprise him. She would go immediately. Alone.

Taking up the folded nightgown, she went back to the room that she and Annie had shared. Annie was still locked in.

'Jamie!' she gasped as the younger woman entered alone. 'What has happened?'

Jamie sat down on the bed. 'His lordship has decreed that we need no longer be separated,' she said bitterly, 'since he has discovered my imposture.'

'I don't understand.'

'He searched this room yesterday. He found the reference we wrote for Jemima Crane. And my pearls.'

'Oh, God!'

Jamie paused. It would not do to tell Annie that his lordship had written to Lady Calderwood. 'We are not to leave the house for the present, but he has *kindly* said that we need not remain locked up,' she continued, staring fixedly ahead. 'And I am not to wear boy's clothes any more.'

'That's one good thing, then,' said Annie. 'With a little work with our needles, I am sure we can make you quite presentable.'

'That will take too long. He is insistent that I change immediately,' Jamie lied, 'but I have nothing of my own to wear. I shouldn't have allowed you to send that green gown to the orphanage. If I had kept it—'

Annie shook her head. 'It was only fit for the fire.'

'I have an idea,' cried Jamie innocently. 'The second parlour maid is about the same size as I am. Perhaps we could borrow something from her. Just for today.'

'Well…'

'If *you* went to Mrs Peters and asked her, I am sure she would help. Especially if you tell her that it's on his lordship's instructions. Please, Annie!'

Annie did not stop to question why Jamie was suddenly so keen to please his lordship. 'Oh, very well. I'll go and see her now.'

The moment the door closed, Jamie flew to retrieve her store of money. Surprisingly, it was still there. No doubt his lordship would not deign to touch such a pitifully small sum. Stuffing the money in her breeches pocket, she grabbed an old woollen scarf and gloves and made for the door. There was no time to leave a note for Annie. She would be hurt, but at least she would not be implicated—and she would be sure to understand, once she found out about the letter to Calderwood.

Jamie crept down the back stairs. There seemed to be no one about. She supposed most of the kitchen servants were making ready to serve his lordship's dinner. The others would be in the servants' hall.

She paused at the bottom of the stairs to decide on her escape route. She dared not go through the kitchens, for she would certainly be seen there. The front door was impossible. And the side door was much too risky—too near his lordship's study. She would have to find a window instead. The breakfast parlour would be a good choice. Nobody used it at this time of the day. And from that side of the house, she could easily make her way through the gardens without being seen.

The breakfast parlour was deserted. She crossed to the window and lifted the sash. It squeaked in protest and stuck halfway. Jamie cursed. But there was enough room for her to squeeze through into the welcoming gloom beyond. She would just be able to see her way for a while, but it would soon be pitch dark.

She would need to get as far away as she could, before finding somewhere to bed down for the night.

Standing in the soft flower-bed, she reached up to close the window behind her. She cursed again as it refused to budge. She knew she was wasting precious seconds in trying to cover her escape route.

'Perhaps I may help with that?'

Lord Hardinge! Jamie spun round in horror, blanching at the sight of his sardonic smile.

'We shall return by a more conventional route, I think,' he said, taking her by the arm to pull her on to the path. 'Come, Jamie.' Without another word, he marched her into his study and slammed the door behind them.

'Now,' he began grimly, 'an explanation.'

Jamie glared back at him. In spite of everything, she was not afraid.

'I am waiting. Or perhaps I should summon Smithers?'

'No,' Jamie bit out. 'She knows nothing of this. I slipped out while she was with Mrs Peters.'

'Leaving her alone to face me? I see. There is indeed no honour among thieves.'

'I am not a thief!' cried Jamie hotly. 'I have taken nothing from you!'

'Indeed? Empty your pockets.' When Jamie made no move to obey, he came towards her menacingly. 'Do as I bid you, or I shall do it myself!'

With a final shrug of defiance, Jamie obeyed.

She dropped her little heap of coins on to the desk. There was also some string and a few pins. Nothing of value. Watching Lord Harding gazing at his meagre haul, Jamie wondered what he had expected. It must be obvious now that she was desperate to escape, since she had been prepared to run away with little more than the clothes on her back, in spite of the harsh March weather.

What would he do to her now?

'It seems I have no choice but to lock you in your room,' he said flatly.

'No, please,' begged Jamie instinctively.

'How else am I to be sure you will not leave Harding?' he countered sharply.

'I will give you my word—'

His sudden laughter cut her short. 'Are you really suggesting that I should accept *your* word? By God, your impudence is beyond belief!'

Jamie knew she had turned scarlet. With as much quiet dignity as she could muster, she said, 'I offer it to you, none the less, my lord. Since I have so little time left, I should rather spend it with Annie Smithers than locked in solitary confinement.'

He raised an incredulous eyebrow. Perhaps he had expected tears or tantrums.

'Very well,' he agreed at length. 'Will you give me your word not to try to run away from Harding for…shall we say, three days?'

Jamie looked sharply up at him, making no attempt to conceal her surprise at his offer. There was a very strange expression on his face, half-stern, half-indulgent. 'You have my word, my lord.' Then greatly daring, she added, 'I take it I may run away at first light on the fourth day with your good will?'

Her riposte shocked him into laughter once again,

but this time she knew it contained no malice. 'You do not want for courage, Jamie, I grant you that. Now—be off upstairs before I change my mind.'

She smiled at him then, and left the room without haste.

'If you are to be a girl, we may as well make you presentable.' Annie was obviously delighted at the chance of using her talents on Jamie. The attempted escape was behind them now. 'Mrs Peters was no help, so—'

'It's the future we should be thinking about, not appearances, Annie. He has written to Mama! They will know where to find me. And I have given him my word to stay here for three days. My only hope is that the time will be up before he hears from her. Then I can still escape.'

'But his lordship is determined you shall not do so, Miss Jamie. Besides, time is on your side. Just consider—today is March the twenty-fourth. Her ladyship probably will not have his letter until tomorrow at the earliest, so she cannot be expected to arrive before the twenty-sixth. You will be of age by the time she comes. She will have no power to coerce you.'

Jamie brightened. She had become so obsessed by the encounters with Lord Hardinge that she had lost count of the days. 'Oh, Annie, thank you. Of course, you are right. Only two more days.'

'And then you will be able to tell Lord Hardinge the truth. Once he knows you are a lady, he will surely lose his suspicions of you, even if he don't approve of your conduct.

'Now let us see whether any of my fine gowns can be made over for you.' Annie began to pull out the silk and muslin gowns she had been given over the years by past employers. It would be a difficult task to adapt any of them to fit Jamie's shorter, fuller-bosomed figure. Two gowns were immediately discarded. One was much too matronly for a lady of Jamie's age. The other could not be altered to fit.

'That leaves the green silk,' said Annie. 'It always was my favourite—'

'Then you must not dream—'

'—my favourite,' repeated Annie, 'but this particular shade of green does not suit me. For you, however'—she held it against Jamie—'it will be perfect.'

'Oh, Annie!' breathed Jamie, touched.

'Enough of that, Miss Jamie. We'd better get to work on this gown. And when we have done that, I shall dress your hair for you. I've been itching to do that for months, so don't try to stop me. I promise you will be pleased with what I can do. Even Lady Calderwood appreciated the styles I created, and *she* was never one to give praise lightly. If you'll just allow me to—'

'I give in, Annie, truly I do. After all the trouble I have brought you, that is the least I can do. I have nothing else to offer.' Her voice cracked a little as she spoke.

Annie began to busy herself with unpicking a seam. 'We had best get started, don't you think?' she said briskly. 'The light will soon be gone.'

By the time their work was completed, next day, Jamie had been transformed from a grubby boy into an elegant young lady. She twirled round in the green silk gown, revelling in its luxurious softness and flowing lines. 'His lordship will not doubt that I am a proper lady's companion now, Annie.'

'No, he will not. Though I am sure he was convinced as soon as he heard you speak. As long as he does not think you are the lady herself. Then there would be the devil to pay.'

Jamie's agitated response was interrupted by a knock at the door. 'Miss is to come down to the drawing-room at once, his lordship says,' reported the little maid. 'A lady and gentleman have arrived,' she added helpfully.

'Oh, God! It is Papa and Mama! What am I to do?'

Annie looked steadily at her young charge, her eyes full of pity. 'Miss Jamie—'

'There is nothing I can do, for he is bound to learn the truth now,' continued Jamie, more resolutely now. 'I shall go down and face him.' She straightened her shoulders, threw a nervous smile at Annie and followed the maid downstairs.

'Ah, come in, Jamie.' Richard had forgotten, in his shock at the sight of her transformation, that she claimed to be Miss Jemima Crane. For she *was* transformed. Gone was the awkward boy whose apparent gawkiness was emphasised by overlarge smock and breeches. In his place, Richard saw a svelte, elegantly clad young woman with titian curls and an elfin face, dominated by huge—and terrified—green eyes.

'Pray be seated, Lady Calderwood. And you, Mr

Graves,' Richard began politely. He was determined that he would not betray his inner feelings by so much as a look or a gesture.

For a moment, Jamie seemed to be transfixed by the menacing glare from Lady Calderwood who was standing in the centre of the room, looking as if she were about to take charge. Then Jamie put her hand on the arm of the nearest chair and sank into it—strangely forward behaviour from a paid servant, Richard thought. But the girl's skin was ashen—and she seemed to be about to faint.

Richard was not a man to allow Lady Calderwood to take the initiative from him. He continued to look after his guests as though nothing untoward were happening, forcing an exchange of empty pleasantries on to Lady Calderwood while the butler served refreshments. Meanwhile, he watched Jamie out of the corner of his eye. Only when he saw that her colour was returning a little did he turn his full attention back to his guests. He was determined to maintain complete control over this unexpected encounter.

The woman was a harridan—that was crystal clear. God help her poor benighted husband! Even Calderwood deserved better. The man Graves? A singularly appropriate name, he felt, for someone who looked as if he belonged among the stench of death and decay. No wonder Jamie had fled from him. In spite of what she was, the thought of her in the power of such a disgusting creature made his blood run cold.

As soon as the door closed behind the butler, Lady Calderwood began her attack. 'You wrote that you had in your household a young woman bearing a reference from Miss Jessamyne Calderwood, my lord. You understood that Miss Calderwood was an elderly relative who had gone abroad for her health.'

Richard did not move a muscle.

'I must tell you, sir, that you have been grievously misled. No Jemima Crane has ever worked in my household.' Lady Calderwood seemed to be enjoying the play of anxiety and dismay on Jamie's face. 'Nor has there ever been any elderly spinster at Calderwood. Besides my husband, my children and myself, there is only one other member of the family—my stepdaughter, Jessamyne Calderwood.'

She turned in her chair to level an accusing finger at Jamie. 'And there she sits, the wicked undutiful daughter who ran away from her home, rather than fulfil her obligations to her family.'

Lady Calderwood's eyes were fixed on Jamie, who was now clutching desperately to the arm of her chair.

Richard quickly masked his shock with an expression of polite concern. 'May I ask, ma'am, what obligation it was from which your stepdaughter fled?'

Lady Calderwood turned back to her host. She ploughed on, obviously secure in the power of her position.

'Marriage,' she spat venomously. 'Her father had gone to considerable lengths to arrange an advantageous match for her—she has no dowry, you must understand, and is singularly lacking in accomplishments—as I said, a most advantageous match. But Jessamyne refused, positively refused to comply with Sir John's wishes. I have come to take her back and to ensure that she does her duty.'

She glared at Richard, daring him to defy her.

Richard was well aware that all the might of the law and all the rules of polite society were on her side. No one could refuse to yield up a girl to her rightful guardians. 'Let us be perfectly clear about this, Lady Calderwood.' His voice was measured and reasonable, if a little clipped. 'Your stepdaughter ran away from you in order to avoid a marriage which was—shall we say?—distasteful to her? May I ask the name of the bridegroom?'

Before Lady Calderwood could reply, the whining voice of Ralph Graves intervened. 'She is betrothed to me, sir! I am here to reclaim what is owed to me!'

'Indeed?' Richard's tone was suddenly icy. 'I had not noticed any betrothal announcement.'

'The engagement is understood between the families,' said her ladyship soothingly, 'but no public announcement will be possible until my stepdaughter is safely back at Calderwood. Engagement visits and the like, you understand.'

'Oh, yes, I do understand. Believe me, I do.' He favoured his guests with a tight smile, as he reviewed the situation. He had no choice, in honour. None at all. He knew now exactly what he must do.

Lady Calderwood was also smiling, in expectation of imminent triumph, it seemed. 'We are most grateful to you, sir. We shall all, I hope, endeavour to forget that she was ever here. No one at Calderwood will ever speak of it. And the wedding will take place without delay.'

'One moment, ma'am, if you please. You were speaking of duty, of your stepdaughter's obligations to her family. Far be it from me to disagree with you. I shudder to think that any member of my family might ever be guilty of such unnatural conduct as you have described.' He glanced briefly towards where Jamie sat, apparently on the point of collapse. 'But do you not agree that there is a yet higher duty, owed by a woman to her husband?'

'Well, yes, of course,' replied Lady Calderwood, sounding perplexed at this new turn of the conversation. 'Jessamyne will certainly owe her first duty to Mr Graves, once she is married. But—'

'I am glad we are agreed on that point, Lady Calderwood. I do *so* want to avoid any unpleasantness here. As you say, a wife's first duty is to her husband. And so you will agree that your stepdaughter's first duty must be to me, her husband?'

'What?' shrieked Lady Calderwood, springing up from her chair.

'Impossible!' screamed Ralph Graves. 'Such a marriage could not be legal. She is under age.'

Richard rose slowly from his seat to confront his visitors, drawing all their attention on to himself and away from Jamie, who was sitting in stunned silence. His eyes narrowed menacingly and his voice made clear that he would brook no opposition. 'As my wife, she has the protection of my name and of my position in society. I suggest to you, sir, that it would be most unwise in you to meddle further in this matter.'

Mr Graves did not reply, but his jaw worked unconsciously. The grinding of his teeth could be heard in the sudden silence.

Lady Calderwood's shock had temporarily deprived her of the power of speech. She stood gasping for breath, turning redder and redder, like a broiling lobster.

'Do, pray, resume your seat, ma'am,' invited Richard smoothly. 'You will wish to rest, I am sure, before you start back to Calderwood. I shall arrange for a nuncheon to be sent in.'

He smiled tightly. 'Now, if you will excuse us, my wife and I must attend to some urgent business which will, I fear, prevent us from returning to bid you farewell. So we shall take our leave of you now.'

He bowed politely to Lady Calderwood and, with barest civility, to Mr Graves. Then he crossed the room to take Jamie's trembling hand and raise her from her chair.

'Come, my dear,' he said, smiling gently down at her as he led her swiftly from the room.

As the doors closed behind them, Jamie tried to find her voice.

'Say nothing now,' Richard warned in a low voice, squeezing her hand meaningfully. 'Come.' He led her downstairs, pausing only to ensure the butler understood his instructions about the prompt despatch of the visitors and the need for absolute discretion. 'We shall be in the book-room,' he added. 'We are on no account to be disturbed.'

With studied politeness, Richard then ensured Jamie was comfortably installed in the privacy of his library. He pressed a glass of brandy into her hand.

'Oh, no, my lord, please!' she protested.

'Drink it,' he instructed. 'I promise it will do you good. You have been through an dreadful ordeal these last few days, mostly at my hands. Come, humour me, Jamie.' He smiled again, trying for a semblance of the irresistible smile which had melted so many hearts, and was rewarded when she sipped gingerly at the fiery liquid.

She spluttered a little, as the brandy burned its way down to her stomach.

'Good,' he said. 'Now, a little more, Jamie.' He watched approvingly as she sipped again.

He took his seat beside her on the leather sofa, but not close enough to make her feel in any way threatened. He knew he must handle this interview with kid gloves. 'First, you must tell me what I should call you. "Jamie" reminds me too much of grubby gardener's boys.'

Jamie was beginning to feel the warming effects of the brandy. Coupled with Lord Hardinge's apparently light-hearted approach, it was exactly what was needed to enable her to respond lucidly to him. 'My name, as you will have collected, sir, is Jessamyne. It was my father's choice, I'm afraid. I have never liked it. Neither did my mother. Indeed, it was she who took to calling me "Jamie". It really is my name, you see.'

'Your mother?'

'She died when I was six.'

'I am sorry. It must have been very hard for you, especially when your father remarried.' He did not add 'to that woman' but it was easily inferred from his tone. He laughed suddenly. 'Well—"Jamie" it shall be, if that is your wish. I shall soon become accustomed to "Jamie the elegant lady" instead of

"Jamie the backward garden boy". Now, tomorrow—'

Jamie was almost ecstatic and, in her relief, burst out, 'Tomorrow, I come of age, at last. My lord, I shall never be able to thank you enough for what you have done in saving me today. I only pray the damage to your reputation will not be irreparable. It was the most chivalrous action I have ever known and oh!— I thank you!'

His lordship seemed to be avoiding her gaze. He continued briskly, 'Chivalry had nothing to do with it, Jamie. It was the only possible solution for both of us. I admit I had not reckoned on your being under age but, thankfully, that difficulty will be resolved by tomorrow. I shall be able to get a special licence and then—'

'But you cannot!' cried Jamie.

'Have a little more faith, my dear,' he drawled laconically. 'Of course I can. An Earl, even newly made, does have some influence, you know.'

'But, I meant… You cannot intend to go on with this?'

'Why not?' he asked baldly. 'It is the obvious solution.'

'But you cannot want to marry me. Why, I am a nobody, penniless, and my reputation must be in shreds. I am no fit bride for you, my lord.'

He took both her trembling hands in his. 'Jamie, you are the daughter of a baronet and a perfectly suitable wife for an earl. I have not the slightest need of a dowry. And as to your reputation'—he laughed bitterly—'*I* brought you to Harding. *I* forcibly parted you from Smithers. And if your reputation now lies in ruins, it is because *I* tried to take advantage of you, when I had promised you would be safe here.'

Jamie could not tear her eyes away from his and from the anguish and guilt she saw there.

'Jamie,' he continued earnestly, 'there is no other way to protect you, to restore you in the eyes of the world. You *must* agree to accept my name. You must! You have nothing to fear from me. I shall not force my attentions on you again, you have my word on that.'

Jamie gulped back a sob at this evidence of his unselfish regard for her honour above his own desires. 'My lord, I cannot allow you to do this. It is not necessary, believe me,' she pleaded, trying unsuccessfully to free her hands from his grasp. 'From tomorrow, I shall be a free agent. I shall find a situation and make my own way in life. That is, if you will return my pearls to me, so that I may sell them,' she added, with the merest hint of a smile.

He smiled a little sadly in response. 'Your pearls shall be returned. Were they your mother's?'

'Yes,' she admitted shyly, 'they are all I have from her—my dowry, you might say.'

'Then you must keep them, Jamie. It would be a crime to part with them.'

Jamie felt an overpowering need to make him laugh, to lighten the intense atmosphere a little. He was thinking too much about his own guilt. And overlooking hers. 'You thought that I had already committed a crime to get them, did you not, my lord?' she ventured.

His smile widened a little. Clearly, he had not expected wit. 'I did. And I humbly beg your pardon, ma'am. May I hope for forgiveness?'

'After what you have done today, I believe I could forgive you anything, my lord.'

'Richard.'

'No, my lord. It would not be right for a mere servant—'

'But perfectly right for my wife. Jamie, listen to me! You really do not understand what risks you run. Consider, for a moment, what could happen if you find paid employment as you intend—which, I have to tell you, will be difficult, if not impossible. However elevated you may be, you will still be a servant, with no protection against your stepmother's machinations or against the odious Graves. No one would lift a finger to take the part of a paid companion against a gentleman. You could be abducted, forced into marriage—or worse.

'Jamie! Do you understand what I am saying? Marriage is the only way of protecting you. You have no other choice.'

Jamie sat very still and silent for a long time. She had ceased trying to free her hands from his. She gazed at them now, her reddened, callused hands lying within Richard's elegant white ones. Then she raised her eyes to his. 'I cannot answer you, my lord, not now. So much has happened in these last few days that I must have time to think. Will you allow me a little time?'

'I will. On one condition.'

'And that is?'

'Jamie, I have not forgotten that tomorrow you will be twenty-one, and free, and that you believe you do not need my protection. I know otherwise. At first light tomorrow, I shall leave to procure a special licence, which will then be perfectly legal since you will be of age. I should be back the following day. *Then* you can tell me what you have decided. I shall not try to force you. I ask only that you remain until I return.'

'But how will you explain the licence? Surely it is not done for an earl—'

'It is perfectly normal, when a family is in mourning, for marriages to be small, private affairs. No one will raise an eyebrow. The announcement will be made later, once the wedding is safely over. Now, Jamie, what do you say?'

Jamie could not read the expression in his eyes, but his voice betrayed his growing tension. She answered as calmly as she could. 'I shall be here when you return, my lord. You still have my word.'

Richard's answering smile was a mixture of triumph and pleasure. It lit up his face. He lifted Jamie's hand to his lips and kissed it gently.

'Now, my dear,' he said briskly, rising from his seat, 'do you remain here until we are sure those vultures are safely on their way. No one shall disturb you. And, in the meantime, I shall make arrangements for your new accommodation.'

Jamie began to protest.

'It will not do, you know, for a lady to be sleeping in a bare attic,' he said teasingly. 'But, if it will put your mind at rest, Smithers shall be given a bed in your dressing-room, at least for the present. Will that content you?'

Jamie nodded. Her heart was too full to speak.

'Good. I shall send Smithers to you directly. I leave it to you to decide how much you tell her.'

Chapter Twelve

Richard paused for a moment outside his mother's sitting-room, trying to collect his thoughts. How was he going to tell her what he had done? And how would she react? He had had no opportunity to speak to her since her return from Bath. She knew nothing about the revelation of Jamie's real identity. And his terse note, before his mother left, had simply warned her that he was detaining Smithers while he investigated her suspicious behaviour.

He reached for the handle, still hesitant. He would look in quietly, he decided, and if Lady Hardinge were resting after her journey back from her sister's, he could return later. Without knocking, he silently opened the door.

Lady Hardinge was seated in a chair in the window bay, staring vacantly at the park. His brain registered that, in profile, she was still a beautiful woman, in spite of her years. A single sheet of paper lay in her lap.

'Forgive me for disturbing you, Mama,' he said

quietly, closing the door and crossing to where she sat.

She turned to smile up at him, with a little frown of puzzlement on her brow. Lifting his scrawled note, she said simply, 'I hope you have come to explain this, Richard. I admit to being intrigued and, I am afraid, a little saddened. I had not thought it of Smithers.'

'Nor were you wrong, my dear,' he confirmed quickly, pulling up a chair to sit at her side. 'I have a great deal more to tell you now.' He explained in very matter-of-fact terms about Caleb's assault on Jamie and the discovery that she was a girl.

Lady Hardinge was aghast. 'I cannot understand what on earth Smithers was about, to embroil herself in such a disgraceful imposture. I had thought her so honest—so trustworthy.'

'There is more to it than that, Mama. I must tell you—Jamie is a lady.'

The Countess was shocked into silence for fully half a minute. When she found her voice again, she fastened on the key word in what her son had just said. 'A *lady*? Surely not?'

'She is Miss Jessamyne Calderwood, Mama, only child of Sir John Calderwood and his first wife.' When his mother made no response to that staggering revelation, he continued, 'She ran away from home because she was being forced into marriage with an old man who is, it appears, both a miser and a lecher. Forgive my plain speaking, Mama, but I must have you understand the way of this. You see, I...' he

cleared his throat '…I have compromised her, Mama.
In all honour, I must marry her.'

'Dear God,' breathed Lady Hardinge. 'Oh, my
dear, surely not? You cannot marry a girl who has
behaved in such a shockingly improper way. It was
she who compromised herself, by coming here
dressed as a boy. Why should you rescue her from
her own folly? Oh, Richard, no!'

Her son took a deep breath and looked into his
mother's sad eyes. 'It is worse than you know, Mama.
Until two days ago, she had taken great care never to
be in a compromising position in spite of her mas-
querade. But after I found them out, I locked Jamie
and Smithers into separate rooms. I wanted to prevent
any further collusion between them. That was my
only motive, I promise you.'

He put his hand to his brow and ran his fingers
through his hair.

'Two nights ago…' He stopped and tried again.
'Two nights ago, I went to Jamie's room. I…' Guilt
overcame him then. He found he could not continue.

'You seduced her?' whispered his mother in horror.

'No,' he replied flatly. 'No. I admit I tried to, but
she repulsed me.' He could not hide the self-loathing
in his voice as he acknowledged his despicable behaviour in the starkest terms.

A long, painful silence ensued.

Then Lady Hardinge began to explore possible avenues of escape for her son. Richard half-expected her
to raise the question of the family curse once more,
but his mother was much too practical for that. 'If
you did not seduce her, then I do not see that you

must marry her. I am sure something can be arranged. If I—'

'No, Mama, the die is cast. I have ruined her. And there is yet more to this sorry tale.' He had recovered some of his normal composure now. 'This morning I received a visit from the present Lady Calderwood and Ralph Graves, the man to whom Jamie was to have been forcibly betrothed. He is quite the most repulsive man I have ever met. He made even my flesh crawl. I could not see her sacrificed to him, Mama. When Lady Calderwood insisted on taking Jamie away, I told her she could not, because Jamie was already married to me.'

'Good God!' cried Lady Hardinge. 'Whatever possessed you to do such a thing?'

'The expression on Jamie's face when she first recognised the visitors,' he admitted, with the tiniest hint of a smile. 'Horror, and innocence, mixed together. And then a look of such hopeless resignation that I could not do otherwise than save her. Truly, I could not.'

'I see,' said his mother meditatively.

Richard was quite sure that she did not see.

'What is her dowry, do you know?' asked Lady Hardinge, after a pause.

'She has none, Mama,' he replied in a flat voice. Before she could speak, he continued, 'It is of no moment, in any case. This marriage is a matter of honour—and honour only.'

'I see,' said his mother again. 'And when is the wedding to be?'

'As soon as I can procure a special licence.
Tomorrow, Jamie comes of age and so—'

'A minor!' gasped Lady Hardinge. 'Richard, for
heaven's sake—'

'She will be twenty-one tomorrow. All will be well
once I have married her. If she will have me, that is.'

This last information clearly put a new complexion
on the matter for Lady Hardinge. 'You mean she has
refused you?' she asked incredulously.

'She has certainly tried to do so. I wish you will
see her, Mama, and convince her that she has no
choice.' As his mother stared at him in disbelief, he
added, 'She thinks she can earn her own living once
she is of age. As a governess, or some such. It is
madness. No one would employ her without references. And I fear Graves would seek to revenge the
insults she has heaped upon him. Will you not see
her, Mama, and persuade her?'

'I will see her, certainly. As to the rest—we shall
see.'

When Richard rose to leave, his mother smiled
anxiously up at him. 'It is a dreadful coil, Richard, I
admit, but there may yet be another way. Send her to
me, and I shall see what may be done.'

Jamie's approach to the Countess's sitting-room
was very hesitant indeed. She had known the
Countess for a kind, rather sad lady who had taken a
real interest in the progress of a backward garden boy.
But Lady Hardinge was most certainly a great lady.
Having discovered how Jamie had imposed upon her
by perpetrating such a shocking fraud, the Countess

must be expected to be haughty and unforgiving. She probably intended to read Jamie a stern lecture on the proper conduct for a lady. Perhaps even to insist that she return to Calderwood and Ralph Graves?

At that point, if she had dared, Jamie might have fled, but it was already too late. Digby had thrown open the door. 'Miss Calderwood, my lady,' he intoned.

Jamie stood transfixed on the threshold as the butler closed the door behind her. Her head was bowed. She could not find any words to say.

Lady Hardinge turned in her chair and surveyed her visitor with careful calculation for a long time. 'Miss Calderwood,' she said at last.

Jamie raised her eyes to the Countess's face, but could not speak. She felt she was just a tangle of emotions—misgivings, principally, mixed with contrition. But she must meet this trial with courage, for that was all she had to fall back on.

'Miss Calderwood. Will you not be seated?' said Lady Hardinge formally.

From her position by the door, Jamie curtsied, but did not move to sit down. 'Lady Hardinge, I do not deserve your kindness. I have imposed upon you and your son in the most shocking way imaginable. There is no possible apology which I can make for the wrongs I have done you both, although I would make amends if I could.' She was twisting her hands together as she spoke. 'It is my intention to leave Harding, ma'am, so that you may be free of me. There can be no question of pardon, I know, but oh!— I am sorry!'

The Countess seemed to be much affected by this emotional little speech. 'Do come and sit down, Miss Calderwood,' she said again, more gently now. 'My son has told me something of your history, but I should prefer to hear it all from your own lips, if you are prepared to tell me. You need hold nothing back, I assure you. I am not easily shocked. And my son has told me what happened when he came to your room.'

Jamie blushed fierily to the roots of her hair. 'Oh, ma'am, he did not—'

'I think it best if you start from the beginning,' intervened Lady Hardinge calmly. 'Don't be afraid. Just tell me the truth.'

Jamie looked wonderingly at her, trying to decide what to do. The Countess did not seem particularly stern, though not particularly friendly either. She still had that same sad look in her eyes, perhaps even more intense than usual. Jamie hesitated a little before deciding that a simple recital of the facts would do no harm. Not now.

She sat stiffly on the edge of the chair opposite the Countess, clasping her hands tightly in her lap to hide her nervousness. 'My name is Jessamyne Calderwood, ma'am. My father is Sir John Calderwood, of Calderwood Hall in Hampshire. I am twenty years old.' Her voice was strained and her delivery stilted, but she forced herself to continue. 'The present Lady Calderwood, whom I think you know, is my father's second wife. My own mother died when I was six.'

Lady Hardinge nodded slightly.

'I have a half-brother and three half-sisters at Calderwood which is…not a rich holding. There was no
possibility of a London season for me, on account of
the expense, and unfortunately I have no dowry. So
my parents sought elsewhere for a husband for me.
They chose a Mr Ralph Graves, who is a distant
cousin of Lady Calderwood.' Her staccato delivery
faltered at that point. She could not go on, because
she did not know how to describe Graves without
straying into improper criticism of her parents in the
process.

'Is he so dreadful, this Mr Graves, that you could
not face him squarely and simply refuse him?' asked
Lady Hardinge softly.

Jamie's chin came up. 'It would have changed
nothing, ma'am. The betrothal announcement was
about to be made, whether I refused him or no. If I
had then cried off at the altar, I should have been
branded a jilt before all the world, and any marriage
for me have become impossible. My only hope
was to prevent the announcement from being made.
There was no one to help me. So I fled.'

'Why did you choose Harding? And as a boy?'

'Oh, ma'am, please don't blame Smithers for my
deception. She simply took pity on me when I could
not buy a seat on the stage.' Jamie gulped. 'You see,
it had been my intention to seek work as a governess
or companion through the agencies in Bath, but…it
became clear that it would not serve. I had been
dressed as a boy for the journey only, but when Lord
Hardinge offered to take me as a gardener's boy, it
seemed such a heaven-sent opportunity that I… The

truth, ma'am, is that I was so desperate that I seized upon his offer without thought for the harm I might do. Especially to Annie Smithers. Afterwards, it was too late to retreat.'

'And may I ask when you proposed to confess your deception to us, if it had not been discovered?' asked the Countess sharply.

Jamie stared at her clenched hands. 'To be honest, ma'am, I hoped to avoid doing so altogether. I intended to leave Harding in such a way that there would be no concerns about the boy Jamie or trouble for Smithers either.' The Countess's frankly disbelieving look prompted her to explain rather more than she had intended about her plans to make her own way in life. 'I should have taken care to contrive that simple Jamie was seen to have left Harding for a better position elsewhere,' she concluded, biting her lip.

'You did not think to trust us with the truth, my dear?' asked Lady Hardinge in a suddenly softer tone.

That voice, coupled with the unexpected endearment, was Jamie's undoing. Her carefully erected defences crumbled. Tears stood in her eyes. 'Since my mama died,' she said simply, 'there has been no one I could trust. Except—these last weeks—Annie Smithers.' She dropped her head into her hand to hide the tears that were threatening to overpower her.

'Miss Calderwood, my son tells me he has offered you marriage, but that you have refused him.'

Jamie nodded but did not speak.

Lady Hardinge hesitated. 'Will you tell me why?' she asked at last.

Jamie swallowed hard and raised her head, blinking

back her tears. 'Lord Hardinge saved me from being forcibly married, by telling Lady Calderwood that I was already married to him. That lie was successful. There is no need to make it a reality.'

'Do you not wish for marriage? For children of your own?'

'Oh, yes,' breathed Jamie, without stopping to think, 'but that is not what Lord Hardinge has offered.'

'I do not understand. Pray explain, Miss Calderwood.'

'Oh, dear,' said Jamie, biting her lip once more and cursing her too ready tongue. 'Your son, ma'am, feels he is honour bound to save my reputation by making me his wife. In that, he is…mistaken. I myself am responsible for everything that has taken place since I left Calderwood, and I alone must bear the consequences. Lord Hardinge must marry some day, no doubt, but it cannot be a marriage in name only to a woman like me, whom he does not love and cannot respect. He deserves better than that,' she added hotly.

Lady Hardinge looked shocked. Eventually, she said, 'You have much courage, Miss Calderwood. Few women would choose as you have done. I honour you for it.' Then she added, 'But I should not be too hasty in making my decision, if I were you. Perhaps you should sleep on it.'

Jamie looked at her in consternation. It sounded as if Lady Hardinge were urging her to reconsider Richard's offer. Surely that was impossible? Surely she must have imagined it? But no, Lady Hardinge was gazing steadily at her, with a half-smile on her lips and a not-unfriendly gleam in her eye.

Giving herself a mental shake, Jamie begged leave to retire to reflect on the Countess's advice. 'Thank you, ma'am, for receiving me with such kindness,' she said, as she curtsied herself out. 'It is much more than I have deserved.'

The Countess sat long after Jamie's departure, pondering the inwardnesses of what she had learned. The girl was unquestionably a lady, and a lady of spirit and courage. She was Richard's equal by birth, without a doubt. And, since she was certainly not indifferent to him, there seemed to be no rational explanation for her refusal. Nor, to be honest, was there any sound reason for Richard's having proposed in the first place. In the past, he had gloried in his affairs, and in his ability to abandon them without a backward glance. But now... The man Jamie had described sounded less and less like the son she knew—except for his determination to challenge the Hardinge curse head on. That, she felt, was very much her son.

Lady Hardinge decided to let matters take their course for a little longer yet, before she chose which side of the scales should receive her two penn'orth. She smiled to herself. It would all be really rather entertaining, if it were not quite so serious.

'She seems determined not to have you, Richard,' said Lady Hardinge later, sitting alone with her son in the drawing-room. Jamie had been persuaded, with difficulty, to join them for dinner, but she had retired to her room immediately afterwards.

'Hardly surprising,' he answered bitterly, 'considering my behaviour towards her. But she has no choice, Mama. I shall convince her, never fear.'

Lady Hardinge let that pass. 'But a marriage in name only, Richard? Is that wise, do you think? Forgive me'—she blushed slightly—'but could you abide by it, if she did agree?'

'Of course,' he replied tersely. 'I have given her my word.'

Lady Hardinge tried another approach. 'I believe Miss Calderwood may have a romantic soul, Richard,' she said slowly.

He threw her a sharply questioning glance, which she ignored.

'She will look for love in marriage. I had hoped that you would do the same. I have not forgotten the Hardinge tradition, even if you have.'

'If love is what it takes to persuade her,' he replied, after a moment's thought, 'then love there must be. God knows I have been told often enough about my ability to attract the female of the species. Obviously I must set about wooing this one, and quickly.'

His mother was aghast. 'Richard! Surely you could not be so wicked?'

His set expression gave the lie to that.

'Oh, Richard, do not, I beg you. Love is a *mutual* passion. Love which is not shared turns to hate, and despair. You know that. You must remember what Celia made you suffer when she jilted you. You may make Jamie love you now, to win her consent, but later, when she finds you do not care for her...I predict you would both be very unhappy. Better to let her go, Richard, as she wishes.'

He turned a bleak face to her. 'No, Mama, it cannot be. This marriage touches my honour. I have pledged my word that Jamie will be my wife. But I promise you that I shall try to avoid causing her the unhappiness you fear. After all, she need not know her love is not returned. Surely that is not so hard to do?'

His mother was of the opinion that such a deception was not merely hard, it was impossible. But her son would not listen. He was adamant that it was his duty to marry Jamie. He would not be moved. He would make just one concession—in deference to his mother's misgivings, he would not give Jamie the Hardinge betrothal ring, since family tradition required it to be given as a token of love.

When the door closed behind her beloved but impossible son, Lady Hardinge sighed. Richard would go to any lengths, perhaps even coercion, to enforce his will. As a result of her careless words, he had seen that he could have his way by making Jamie fall in love with him. And now, quite cynically and deliberately, he would set about winning her love. No doubt he would succeed, too. He was famous for his address. Poor, poor girl.

And yet, she thought suddenly, perhaps he may not have his way in this in quite the manner he supposes. He would never have offered marriage to any of the simpering, empty-headed females he so despises, no matter what the circumstances. There must be something more behind his willingness to do so now. Jamie Calderwood is not like any other woman he has known. And it may be that he feels more for her than he yet knows. He will woo her, certainly, but I fancy she may have more than a little say in the outcome of this strange courtship. Yes. I think it may do very well. In more ways than one.

Chapter Thirteen

Jamie lay on her back, staring up at the rose pink canopy of the great bed. She could not sleep. Her brain was churning with the extraordinary events of an extraordinary day.

Richard, Earl Hardinge, had proposed marriage to her! And he seemed intent on going through with it, even though he could not possibly love her. He desired her, that was certain. She had had ample proof of that. But was desire any basis for wedlock?

Lady Hardinge's attitude, too, was a riddle. She had received Jamie more than graciously, once Richard had explained how matters stood. She might even be favourably disposed to Jamie, to judge by the way she had treated an ex-servant. But there was something hidden beneath Lady Hardinge's outward calm, something which Jamie could not quite identify.

As for Jamie's own feelings, she was afraid to probe them too deeply. She did not love him. Of course not. How could she? She barely knew him— and only as a servant knows a master.

A picture of him rose in her mind. She felt her body

tremble at the mere thought of him. What was it about him that affected her so? His image so easily dominated her to the exclusion of all else. It was not fear, she was certain. Fear was what she felt at the prospect of being married to Ralph Graves. If she married Richard instead, she would be just as completely in his power, yet…it was not the same.

She forced herself to begin to think rationally, to banish his beguiling presence. She valued him for all his finer qualities—his kindness, his honesty, his charity. Above all, for the honourable way he had treated her. Even when he was trying to force explanations out of her, he had never been other than fair. The only exception was the episode in her bedroom, when his passions had momentarily overcome his reason—and for that she must be as culpable as he. It shamed her to admit it, even to herself, but she knew she desired Richard Hardinge quite as much as he desired her.

None of this seemed to be helping her to reach a decision on his proposal. She knew in her heart of hearts that he was right about marriage—it *was* the only solution which could guarantee her safety—but the idea of a loveless marriage appalled her. She had spent too many years as a spectator of her father's. She could not inflict that on a man like Richard.

Besides, Richard had said that it would be a marriage in name only. That would be grossly unfair on him, not least because it was his duty to beget an heir. And as for her—she was not sure whether marriage and motherhood would ever be offered to her now, but she did not think she was ready, at the tender age of twenty-one, to sacrifice all hopes of having her own children at her knee.

She shook her head helplessly as she tossed around on the pillows. Nowhere was there a spot of cool relief for her fevered cheek. Her thoughts continued to wander round and round the arguments. One single idea kept recurring—it would be absolutely wrong to accept Richard and to force him into a loveless, childless sham of a marriage. She could find no way to counter that thought. Beside it, her own situation paled into insignificance.

So—the decision had made itself. Even at some personal risk, she would not accept him. However much she might be tempted, she would go her own road, and do her best to escape from Harding and all its works for ever. It was the only honourable solution open to her. She would just have to be resolute in withstanding him.

What would Annie say? Oh, dear! Annie's reaction to the day's events—for Jamie had told her everything—had been ecstatic. She had a simple vision of a comfortable married life for the future Lord and Lady Hardinge—with the new Countess ably served by her faithful abigail, naturally! She had roundly castigated Miss Jamie for even considering refusal of his lordship's offer.

Jamie sighed. To Annie, it all seemed straightforward. She had seen many *ton* marriages based on far less mutual regard than existed between Jamie and the Earl. Annie had no time for missish notions about loveless marriages. She had a vested interest too for, as Countess Hardinge, Jamie would be sure to employ her. Whereas if Jamie left, Annie might well have to leave too.

Jamie tried not to think about that. She must not allow sympathy for Annie to sway her decision. It would be difficult to cling to it in any event, she knew, especially when faced with Richard's overpowering presence.

She burrowed deeper into her soft pillows, trying to compose her mind for sleep and watching the play of the moonlight on the wall opposite the window. At long last, she was just beginning to drift off when the shaft of moonlight disappeared. Pity, she thought drowsily, that it had clouded over. It was so beautiful.

The shadow moved across the wall. That could not be the effect of clouds, surely? Jamie tensed, listening, all thought of sleep now banished from her mind. There must be someone in the room! Without pausing to wonder whether it might be Richard, Jamie screamed at the top of her voice.

'Gawd!' muttered a man's voice from somewhere near the window. 'It's all up now! I'm off!'

Then there came a separate sound—a movement somewhere nearer the bed. At the same moment, the door to the dressing-room was thrown open to reveal Annie Smithers, clad only in her nightgown, but armed with a heavy candlestick in one hand and a pair of curling tongs in the other.

The obstruction at the window disappeared, allowing the moonlight to flood the room once more. It showed a man rushing towards the window in an attempt to escape. Annie did not hesitate for a moment. She ran across the room, arm raised, and brought the brass candlestick down on the head of the intruder. He crumpled to the floor, where he lay motionless, with Annie standing over him like a hunting dog over its prey.

Jamie reached the window just in time to see a dark figure sprint across the garden and disappear into the shrubbery. All that remained was the wooden ladder, propped up against the window sill.

'Jamie!' Richard stood at the open door to the dressing-room from where he could take in the situation at a glance. 'Fetch something to bind him, Smithers!'

Annie hesitated, looking first at the motionless body on the floor and then at Jamie in her thin nightgown.

'Quickly now! I'll look after things here.' Annie dared not disobey that sharp instruction. Richard knelt to feel for a pulse on the fallen figure.

'There was another man too,' whispered Jamie a little shakily, turning back from the window. 'He was on the ladder outside the window. But he has escaped across the grounds. You will never catch him.'

Richard swiftly bound the man's hands with the scarf which Annie had brought from the dressing-room and rose to face Jamie. 'Go back to bed, my dear,' he said in reassuring tones. 'I shall take this visitor downstairs for a while and *enquire* as to his business here. I doubt it will take long to unravel this mysterious little episode. Don't worry. You are safe now.' He hefted the inert body over his shoulder and made for the door.

'Richard.'

In spite of his burden, he turned quickly, looking both surprised and pleased.

Jamie was intent on telling him of her suspicions. 'I heard the second man's voice, the one who escaped. He was outside the window on the ladder. I think it was Caleb.'

At the mention of Caleb's name, a shadow of fury crossed Richard's face and his lips tightened in disgust. He did not attempt to argue with Jamie. But then the anger disappeared, and he smiled at her reassuringly.

'Go to bed, my dear,' he said again. 'I shall be back soon, I promise. And, in the meantime, Smithers shall remain here with you. With her candlestick!' He smiled warmly at the abigail. 'Thank you. I shall not forget this.'

With Richard gone, Jamie could not be persuaded to return to bed. How could she ever sleep now? She paced the room in her agitation. Why had Caleb and his accomplice broken into her chamber?

Richard tried to collect his thoughts as he carried the intruder down to the cellars. For that single second when Jamie had used his given name, he had thought she was warming to him. But one look at her face had confirmed that she was using it quite unwittingly. A twinge of something like disappointment had intruded on him. Now, why was that? Of course, he was on the look-out for signs that he was succeeding in his campaign to make her love him—he had to be—but he should be noting those changes coldly and rationally. The surge of emotion he had felt when she spoke his name was not in the least bit rational.

Richard pushed this riddle to the back of his mind. He needed to concentrate on his prisoner—and the identity of the second man. Could it have been Caleb? It was, after all, quite plausible, especially as Caleb had been allowed to give him the slip. Richard cursed himself yet again for that mistake but dared not dwell on it. He forced himself to focus on the task before him.

Richard's interrogation of the second man produced results surprisingly quickly. By the time he returned to Jamie's bedroom, he was very grave.

'Jamie!' he cried. 'You should be in bed!' He signalled to Smithers to withdraw, but she stubbornly ignored him. Her expressive face registered her strong disapproval—a man should not be here in the middle of the night, especially when her mistress was dressed in only a fine lawn nightgown!

Richard's eyes narrowed angrily. He was about to utter a very sharp rebuke when Jamie forestalled him.

'Thank you, Annie,' she said firmly, nodding towards the door. The abigail withdrew unwillingly into the dressing-room.

'She will still be listening, I expect,' smiled Richard, opening his arms encouragingly to Jamie.

Without further thought, she went to him, breathing in the scent of his warm body and allowing his strength to enfold her. She felt so safe now, leaning her head against his chest and closing her eyes thankfully. Only then did she realise that, under his thin silk dressing gown, he was practically naked!

'My lord!' she cried, all the years of her proper upbringing automatically asserting themselves as she tried to pull away from his dangerous embrace.

Richard held her tightly so that she could not break free until he chose to let her go. She must be made to begin to trust him. 'Don't be afraid, Jamie. I shall not attack you again. I have given you my word. Come.'

He sat her on the bed and looked down at her. How lovely she was! The cold fire of moonlight glowed with a pearly lustre on her pale complexion in its frame of titian curls. Most of all, her eyes—huge and shining, dominating her beautiful face—seemed to gaze hauntingly into his. For a brief moment, thoughts of Caleb were forgotten as he drank in the vision before him.

Then cold sanity returned. His face assumed a stern cast.

Jamie shivered a little under his scrutiny.

'I have not learned very much from the man in the cellars,' he began. 'You *were* right about Caleb, I think. He may have been trying to steal from us as some kind of revenge. But that was certainly not the prime motive.' He sat down beside her, taking her cold hand in his.

She did not attempt to pull away. She knew this was a gesture of reassurance, not of desire.

'Jamie—I am sorry—their object was *you*. They were paid, by someone who seemed to be a gentleman's servant, to carry you off.'

'Who?' whispered Jamie through a constricted

throat. She could not begin to understand this impossible nightmare.

'I have no name, nor any proof. But can there be any doubt about it? Who but someone from Calderwood could have any reason to try such a thing?'

It was all too much—fantastic, horrible, unbelievable. Jamie bit back a sob.

Richard enfolded her in his arms once more. He kept his touch gentle, though his taut voice betrayed the anxiety he too was feeling. 'Jamie, you really do *not* have a choice. Lady Calderwood—or Graves—is determined to seize you. If they would dare to break into Harding itself, then there is nowhere you could be safe. Don't you see?' His voice had risen a little, as he attempted to convince his unwilling charge. He sensed that his moment had come.

Jamie nodded slightly, thoroughly bewildered. She no longer had the strength of mind to think straight, particularly when Richard's arms were round her. What was happening to her? None of it made any sense, least of all Richard's steadfast determination to sacrifice himself to save her.

'Then you do agree? You *will* marry me? Answer me, Jamie!'

There was a long pause. Jamie felt the strength and comfort which flowed from him, as he held her cradled gently against him. She knew she wanted to hold on forever to this glorious feeling of warmth and belonging. Maybe, just maybe, theirs could become a real marriage, a union of love, instead of a marriage of convenience? After all, he had shown her that he

was a passionate man. And he seemed to care, at least
a little…

She must stop this wishful thinking. She had resolved to refuse him. Why couldn't she just tell him
so? But he was still waiting expectantly for her response, smiling warmly at her, in a way that touched
her heart.

It was no contest. 'Yes.' Her whispered response
was barely audible.

His arms tightened round her for a moment, his
eyes closed, and he placed a tender kiss on her titian
curls. 'Thank you,' he breathed into her hair. After a
moment, he straightened and said briskly, 'I promise
you will not regret it. We shall be married before
Graves learns his plot has failed. The ceremony can
be performed as soon as I return.

'And in the meantime, my dear, I beg you will take
no risks. Stay indoors. Go nowhere without escort.
And make yourself beautiful for your wedding day!'

A strangled sound escaped Jamie, half-laugh, half-
sob. No chance for second thoughts now. She knew
he would not allow her to retreat.

Richard kissed her softly on the lips, laid her back
on the bed and pulled the bedclothes over her. 'Sleep
now, little one,' he said, stroking her hair. 'I shall
send Smithers back to you. You will be safe now.'

As he started to open the dressing-room door, he
turned back for a second to smile generously at his
betrothed. 'Happy birthday. Sleep well.'

Jamie glanced down at her wedding band as
Richard led her back from the chapel to the house. It

was done! They were married!

It seemed strange to be entering the house by the main door. The butler stood rigidly to attention, holding open the door for the Earl and his new Countess. Jamie wondered what was going on behind that expressionless face. What could he possibly think of her?

'Thank you, Digby,' said the Earl affably. 'We shall be in the blue drawing-room. Bring some refreshments.'

'Certainly, milord.'

To Jamie's horror, he brought not tea, but champagne! 'Excellent, Digby,' commended his lordship. 'Will you take a glass with us, Mama?' He seemed to take it for granted that Jamie would not refuse to join the celebration.

'I shall propose a toast,' announced Lady Hardinge, taking her glass. 'To Jamie and Richard—long life, love, and happiness.' She sipped her wine, watching the faces of the newly-weds over the rim of her champagne flute.

Jamie was embarrassed by her words, especially the mention of love.

Richard seemed to conceal his feelings rather better. He merely smiled inscrutably.

'The second toast is mine, I think,' Richard responded. 'To the new Countess Hardinge, my beautiful wife.' Jamie averted her gaze. 'I couple that with another toast,' he added mischievously, 'to the other Lady Hardinge, my beautiful mother, the Dowager Countess.'

His mother spluttered a little over her wine. 'Oh, dear,' she murmured. 'Yes, I suppose I am now. I imagine I shall become accustomed to it after a while.' Her expression of chagrin caused the others to smile. Soon all three were laughing gaily.

'We had better change for dinner soon, I think,' warned the Dowager. 'No doubt something rather special has been prepared below stairs. I hope it has not spoiled as a result of the delay.'

'Oh dear.' Jamie could not hide her concern. 'I have no evening gown, I am afraid—'

'You look delightful just as you are, Jamie,' interrupted the Dowager, smiling with approval at the cream silk gown which she had pressed on her prospective daughter-in-law for the ceremony. 'In any case, a bride should sit down to her wedding breakfast in her wedding gown, however late it may be. Let Richard change. You and I shall sit here comfortably until he returns.'

Their waiting was not comfortable, however, for Jamie was very awkward in her new position. She felt more of an impostor now than she had ever done as Jamie the simpleton. A lady she might be—by birth— but she felt she had long ago forfeited that status. How could she ever attempt to regain it?

The two ladies were sitting in silence when his lordship returned. He took in the scene at a glance. Then, in an attempt to break the ice, he ordered a fresh bottle of champagne.

'Richard! What are you about?' cried his mother, the moment the door closed behind Digby.

'Celebrating,' he replied simply, refilling his empty glass.

Dinner might have been a difficult occasion without Richard's careful planning. He knew that his mother must be expected to yield up her place to Jamie. He was sure, too, that Jamie would not wish to oust his mother from the foot of the table. In other circumstances, he would have watched in amusement as two women jockeyed for position. But these were not any two women—these were his mother and his wife. So he solved the problem by putting Jamie on his right at the head of the table and his mother on his left. Both were too surprised to make any kind of fuss.

The meal was indeed sumptuous. They marvelled at how so much had been done in so little time. Where had the lobsters appeared from, for instance, and the ducklings? Someone had worked miracles for Jamie's wedding day.

Richard rose from the table with the ladies, refusing to remain drinking port in solitary state. He preferred, he said, the company of the two ladies in his life.

'Do you play, Jamie?' asked Lady Hardinge, nodding towards the piano, when they were back in the drawing-room once more.

'I was used to, ma'am, but of course I have not done so since I came to Harding. I was going to ask you if I might—'

'Of course you may practise here, if that is what you wish. Remember, you are mistress of Harding now, not I. You may do just as you like.'

'Within reason, Mama,' added Richard, with a grin,

'for a wife must still defer to her husband, must she not?'

The Dowager threw him an eloquent look. Intercepting it, Jamie giggled uneasily, wishing Richard had not pressed quite so much champagne on her. She was feeling really rather strange.

'If you will excuse me,' said the Dowager, rising from her seat, 'it has been a very long day, and I should prefer to retire now. Jamie will deal with the tea tray, Richard, I am sure. Goodnight, my dears.' She kissed each in turn. 'Bless you both.'

As he closed the door behind his mother, Richard smiled across at his bride. 'A model of diplomacy, do you not agree, Jamie?'

'Yes, indeed,' agreed Jamie, too eagerly, then lapsed into silence. Heavens, where were her wits? She was behaving like a green girl just out of the schoolroom. Surely she could think of something to say?

No words came. The only thoughts swirling in her mind were of Richard Hardinge—who was now her husband!

Richard came slowly across to where she sat and took her hand. Raising it to his lips for a whisper of a kiss, he took his place at her side. 'You are bemused by all that has happened, I fancy, my dear. Do not let it worry you. You have all the time in the world to learn your new role. And you are safe here, I promise you that.'

Jamie nodded, her gratitude visibly written in her beautiful eyes.

'Come, my dear,' he said then, raising her to her

feet. 'You too are tired. Let us retire.' He led his blushing bride into the hall.

Too late for regrets now, thought Jamie, as they made their way up the main staircase to the suite of rooms which had always been occupied by the Earl and Countess Hardinge. She glanced at the powerful man at her side, immaculate in his evening dress. She shivered, unaccountably, for she did not fear him, of that she was certain, even while she hesitated to delve too deeply into what her feelings really were.

When at last they stood alone together in the splendid sitting-room which lay between the two bedchambers, she raised her eyes shyly to his and found that he was gazing at her in a most disconcerting way.

'My lord,' Jamie began uncertainly, 'I—'

'Ah, yes,' interrupted Richard, recalled to the present by her words and trying to bring his own ragged thoughts into some sort of order, 'that reminds me—did you, or did you not, just promise to obey me, wife?'

What was she to make of an ominous statement like that? She nodded apprehensively, unable to tear her eyes away from his strange expression.

'I do not expect to be much in the habit of issuing orders, but when I do, I shall expect them to be obeyed. Always,' he added sternly, glaring down at her. 'And my first—and only—order for this, your wedding day, is that you cease to address me as "my lord". Or else!' All of a sudden, he was openly grinning at her.

'Why, you...!' She burst out laughing. All the earlier tension between them was dispelled. 'Or else what, *my lord*?' she demanded impudently, echoing his mood.

'Or else I may be forced to tan your delectable backside, you witch. I mean it, you know.'

'Really?'

'Really. Now—say it, Jamie.' His tone was suddenly very serious indeed.

She looked up into his eyes which seemed more black than blue in the shadowy room. She could not read his expression. The pressure of his hands on her shoulders was strong. 'If it is truly your wish, I shall call you by name. Richard,' she said caressingly, making the single word sound almost like an endearment.

He held her to him for a few seconds. Her defences seemed to be crumbling, but it would not do to go too fast. 'Thank you,' he whispered into her hair. 'And now, I suggest we go to bed. You need your rest, my dear.'

The new Lady Hardinge blushed to the roots of her hair.

'No. I have not forgotten my promise.' He moved to open one of the doors off the sitting-room. 'Your chamber is here, and you will not be disturbed. Mine is on the other side.' He indicated a door in the opposite wall. 'Goodnight, Jamie.' Richard pushed his hesitant wife gently into her bedchamber and closed the door on her before retreating to his own room and the decanter of brandy which awaited him.

Then, for the very first time, he began to review his position dispassionately.

Jamie Calderwood was his wife—in name at least.

He had given her his word that he would not force himself on her, so he could not bed her, not unless *she* released him from his bond. But if he did not bed her, she could *still* be at the mercy of the Calderwood clan—for if they regained control of Jamie, the marriage could be forcibly annulled. Dear God, this solution of his might be no solution at all!

Why had it mattered so much to him? Why had he risked so much for a red-haired waif who had it in her power, now, to deny him both comfort and children? He shook his head in bewilderment, sipping abstractedly at his brandy. Truly, he did not know. He had done it, but he did not really know why, except that he had felt an overpowering need to atone for his earlier dishonourable treatment of her and to protect her from her appalling family. Jamie affected him strangely, as no other woman had ever done. Was it her indomitable spirit that made him want to stand between her and all the world? She had rare courage—and beauty besides. She was fit to be a queen, not just a countess.

But she was his Countess now. And if he wanted a true marriage—which he was at last prepared to admit that he did—he would have to gain Jamie's trust, and overcome the disgust he had surely engendered on that fateful night, so that *she* would agree to release him from his vow. He was not sure whether she would ever do so. She had repulsed him when they were alone in her room two nights ago, even though his only desire had been to reassure her. And today she had seemed to be afraid of him, shivering at the merest touch.

For a man who was famous for his ability to charm women, he had been singularly unsuccessful so far with the one who was now his wife. Had it not been for the attempted abduction, she would probably have continued to refuse him. He knew he had taken advantage of her when she was at her most vulnerable. And he had given her no chance to withdraw. Now honour was satisfied—but in a loveless union. His mother's concern about a one-sided passion seemed laughable in the circumstances. Jamie certainly did not love him.

It would not be an easy task to win her, nor quickly achieved. But now that they were married, they could spend a lot of time together. He would be able to keep her safe from her terrible family. And she would come to know him better without feeling threatened. Perhaps eventually she would be charmed into trusting, even loving him?

Chapter Fourteen

Jamie lay awake a long time, her thoughts full of the enigmatic man who was now her husband. Eventually she slept, but she could not escape him even there. Her wedding night was disturbed by erotic dreams she did not fully understand.

When Annie eventually drew the curtains, the sun was already well up. 'You must make haste, my lady,' she chided, proudly reminding her charge of her new status. 'His lordship went down to breakfast some time ago. Will you not want to join him?'

Jamie allowed herself to be persuaded and made haste to dress. As Lady Hardinge, she should now be in mourning like the rest of the family, but she possessed no blacks. Indeed, she had only two presentable gowns to her name—the cream silk in which she had been married and the green gown which Annie had made over earlier. She would have to create an opportunity to ask her husband's permission to order mourning gowns, or she would disgrace him in public. She swallowed hard. Richard could be very intimidating, and she did not relish the thought of applying to him for money on the very first day of their marriage. But what choice did she have?

The butler greeted her warmly at the bottom of the staircase, pointedly ignoring her inappropriate green gown. 'Good morning, my lady. You will find his lordship in the breakfast parlour.'

'Thank you, Digby,' answered Jamie with a winning smile. 'And Lady Hardinge too?'

'No, my lady. The Dowager Countess is taking a tray in her room this morning.'

Jamie paused a moment to reflect on that interesting snippet of information. Richard's mama had always made a point of breakfasting downstairs, having made clear to all that she did not believe in assuming die-away airs. This careful absence was yet further evidence of her tact and consideration where her new daughter-in-law was concerned. Jamie felt herself warming even more to the older woman, and hoping very much that they could become friends for, in all her twenty-one years, Jamie had never been permitted a real friend from her own station in life. She felt the beginnings of a glow of happiness.

Digby showed her into the breakfast parlour and discreetly withdrew. Richard, sitting at the head of the table, looked up, smiled and sprang to his feet. 'Jamie! I had not expected you to come down.' He came round to help her into her seat, placing a gentle kiss on her cheek as he did so. 'You look a little pale, my dear. Are you quite well?'

How considerate he was. 'I am very well. Truly, I am.' She smiled reassuringly at him and was rewarded when his anxious frown disappeared. 'Idle-

ness is my problem, more like. You must remember
that I am not used to such luxury. I had to earn my
keep at Calderwood. And when I was employed by
the fearsome Lord Hardinge,' she added impudently,
'I had to work like a slave from morn 'til night. Just
look at my hands!'

Richard laughed, resuming his seat. 'You are a
minx, madam. With the hands of a scullery maid!' He
sipped his coffee meditatively. 'We shall have to do
something about them, you know. They really are not
fit to be seen, and you cannot always be wearing
gloves. Still, there are bound to be remedies. I imagine Mama will be able to give you some cream to
make them presentable.'

'About that… It's not just the state of my hands. I
am afraid I am not in the least presentable. I have no
mourning clothes. Do you think—?'

'You have no clothes at all, as far as I can see,' he
responded quickly, coming immediately to the nub of
her problem. 'But don't worry about that. I have already arranged for Mama's dressmaker from Bath to
wait on you, later today. You should order whatever
you need from her.'

'Oh, but—'

'And not only blacks,' he continued. 'You will
need half-mourning soon too, and eventually society
wear. I should like you, if you will, to order something in green now, to match your eyes.' He smiled
conspiratorially. 'You can wear it here at Harding, so
that I can admire you in secret. No one else need
know.'

Richard's smile was captivating. But on this occasion, it did not exercise its usual charm on Jamie's vulnerable heart. She was merely surprised into a chuckle at his swift resolution of her problem. And now she had to face another. 'I have very little experience of modistes, I'm afraid. Mama—Lady Calderwood, I mean—never allowed me new gowns.'

Jamie was glad to find that Richard could stick to practicalities when it mattered. And that he had a ready solution to offer. 'If you would like it, Mama would be very willing to assist you. You may trust her judgement too, for she has exquisite taste.'

Jamie agreed gratefully. She could not do better than the combination of Lady Hardinge and Annie. Apart from welcoming Lady Hardinge's advice, she would be glad of an opportunity to know her mother-in-law better.

'You should know that I have sent the announcement to the *Gazette* and to the *Morning Post*. It should appear tomorrow, so, in a day or two, our marriage will be common knowledge and there need be no more worries about the odious Graves.' He sipped his coffee slowly, watching Jamie as she toyed with a slice of bread and butter. 'And, just in case that does not suffice, I have also written to your father.'

Jamie began to relax a little, soothed by his deep voice and his apparent mastery of all eventualities. She felt so secure with Richard around. Surely no one could harm her now?

Before she had a chance to speak again, he put his cup down and moved to take the chair next to hers. 'One more thing, my dear. I omitted to give you a gift for your coming of age. Happy birthday, Jamie.'

'Oh,' breathed Jamie, as he laid a flat leather case by her plate.

'Open it.'

Jamie did so, to reveal a beautiful square-cut emerald pendant on a gold collar set with tiny diamonds. Matching emerald ear studs, on a slightly smaller scale, completed the set.

'These are not Hardinge family jewels—though you will have those too, of course, as soon as we are out of mourning. Mama will tell you all about them, and the history of the family too, if you let her. But these emeralds are just for you. For your green eyes.'

'But how…? There has not been time.'

Richard grinned impishly, almost like a schoolboy. 'There are ways of beating time, if one puts one's mind to it. I happened on them in London yesterday, and I knew I had to buy them for you. A messenger brought them this morning.'

Jamie could not take her eyes from his fabulous gift. Or her mind from his thoughtfulness. 'Thank you, Richard,' she whispered in awe. 'They are quite beautiful.'

He rose and made for the door. 'Forgive me, Jamie,' he explained in a serious voice. 'I must leave now. I have to deliver our unexpected visitor to Bristol so that he may face his trial. I am hoping that, once he is confronted with the full panoply of the law, he will tell us more than he did three nights ago. It is *just* possible, I suppose, though I am not very confident.

'He came from Bristol, too, so there are one or two

leads I may be able to follow up. Who knows, I may even find the elusive Caleb.'

'Please take care, Richard,' Jamie whispered.

'Have no fears, my dear. I shall not be alone with our friend. And besides, I go armed.' He patted the pocket of his coat reassuringly. 'I am counted an adequate shot, you know,' he added modestly.

'I shall try to be back before dinner,' he promised, 'but do not wait if I am late. And make sure you enjoy yourselves with the dressmaker. I expect you to be quite ravishingly gowned by the time I return.'

'Oh, but—' began Jamie, in protest. Too late. Her husband had already gone.

The Dowager and the new Lady Hardinge prepared to spend a very pleasant and expensive day with Madame Françoise, the modiste from Bath. She was, according to the Dowager, more than competent to provide a wardrobe for Jamie while the family was in mourning.

'But, when you go to London, I advise you to have your gowns from Célestine,' said Lady Hardinge. 'There really is no one to equal her. Do you not agree, Smithers?' Annie did.

Jamie was more than happy to learn from their experience. For what did she, a penniless country mouse, know of such things?

Madame Françoise brought with her a number of part-finished gowns and two of her seamstresses to work on them. By the time the consultation was over, Jamie would have both a day dress and an evening dress fit for a countess.

Encouraged by the Dowager, Jamie ordered a bewildering array of gowns and accessories. She had never thought to own so many clothes in all her life. She was even persuaded to a grey velvet riding habit, so that she might begin to ride again as soon as the family was out of full mourning. Just the thought of being on horseback again made her want to shout for joy.

Madame Françoise was beginning to pack away her samples by the time Jamie mustered the courage to broach the subject of that other dress. 'Have you any green among your samples, *madame*?'

Lady Hardinge looked up sharply but said nothing.

'Why, yes, *madame*. I shall fetch zem on ze instant.' She bustled out.

Jamie looked guiltily at her mother-in-law. 'Forgive me, ma'am. I do not mean to shock you. You see, Richard wants—'

Lady Hardinge smiled indulgently. 'No need to explain. I understand very well. Let us order exactly the kind of creation Richard has asked you to wear. Green—to match your eyes, of course. He always did have good taste. I am sure we can create something to please him.'

How well she understands her son, Jamie thought. If only I could read him half as well.

Madame Françoise returned with her samples. Both ladies lit immediately on the same glowing silk and on the same style from the many drawings. 'Simplicity is the key,' said Lady Hardinge knowledgeably. 'Let the gown enhance your youth and beauty without drawing attention to itself.'

Jamie blushed but agreed. Her new wardrobe was complete. But would Richard approve?

When Jamie was finally gowned in her new black-silk day dress—which was finer than anything she had ever before possessed—she felt more than a little self-conscious. But Lady Hardinge welcomed her warmly when she returned to the sitting-room. 'Ah, my dear, that is splendid, especially now that Smithers has re-done your hair in just that way. Those loose curls do become you. She is a treasure, is she not?'

'I owe her a great deal, ma'am.'

'So I believe, though I have only the sketchiest notion of how you came to be together in the first place. I hope you will do me the honour of confiding in me some day. I am not really an ogre, you know!'

'Oh, Lady Hardinge, I never for one moment thought that you were!'

Lady Hardinge's eyes twinkled mischievously. 'My dear, you really must try to call me "Mama". What would Richard say if he heard you?'

Like mother, like son, thought Jamie, recalling how Richard had teased her into dropping all formality with him. She felt as if she were being surrounded by a warm protecting cocoon. How could she deserve all this?

'I shall try to remember, Mama,' responded Jamie with a shy smile.

'Excellent, my dear. That sounded almost natural!' She beamed at her daughter-in-law. 'Now, about Smithers. It is clear that your need of her talents is much greater than mine, and so I shall not even suggest taking her to the dower house with me. Besides, she would not come, not if it meant leaving you, of that I am sure.'

'But surely, ma'am—Mama—you do not mean to leave Harding?'

'Of course I do—though not immediately. The dower house is not yet ready, even though the work was begun months ago. It was so very neglected. Richard—bless him!—had the work put in hand not long after his father died, for he knew how much needed to be done, and we had agreed it would be best if I were to remove there as soon as his marriage had taken place.' Lady Hardinge stopped suddenly, a slight flush rising up her neck. 'You see, Jamie...' she began uncertainly.

Jamie felt all her hopes tumbling around her. 'Marriage? But—'

Lady Hardinge bit her lip. She hesitated uncharacteristically. 'Er—he is an only son, you see. He accepted, some time before his father died, that he needed to marry to...to secure the succession.'

Now Jamie was absolutely mortified. She had considered many aspects of her marriage to Richard, but never this. Still, it had to be faced. She continued as bravely as she could. 'Did he...did he have anyone particular in mind?'

Lady Hardinge hesitated even more, as if desperately searching for words. 'It was a matter of duty rather than of inclination, I am sure,' she said.

If Lady Hardinge expected that platitude to satisfy Jamie, she would be disappointed. Jamie gazed directly at her, waiting patiently for a name.

'I believe he had settled on Emma Fitzwilliam,'

said Lady Hardinge at last. She looked very flushed. 'Her father's estate marches with ours.'

Jamie felt as if all the breath had been knocked from her body. Dear God, what had she done?

Richard had already chosen a bride and had sacrificed her—and his own inclinations, no doubt—for Jamie's honour. How could she ever hope to make a true marriage based on such infamy? She had been wicked to accept him, when all her better instincts had prompted her to refuse. Now what was she to do?

She dimly perceived that Lady Hardinge was still speaking, but she did not understand a word of it, as she fought to regain control of her whirling thoughts.

'…as soon as it is finished. Will that be convenient, my dear?'

Jamie forced a smile. 'Whatever you wish, ma'am,' she said evenly. Heavens! What had she just agreed to? She needed some time by herself to sort out what to do now.

But the Dowager would not allow Jamie to escape. 'Splendid,' she said, sounding totally confident again. 'Now, will you pull the bell, my dear, and order us some tea?'

Over tea, Jamie gradually recovered a little from her shock, as she was skilfully drawn out by her mother-in-law's gentle questioning. By the end of an hour, Jamie had given Lady Hardinge all the important details of her life at Calderwood and of her subsequent flight.

Lady Hardinge was looking at Jamie with a mixture of envy and admiration. 'You have great courage, my dear. Have you told all this to Richard?'

'No, not all,' admitted Jamie. In truth, she had told her husband very little. For when could she have done so?

'You should. Or, if you prefer, I could do it for you?'

Jamie shook her head. 'I shall tell him myself—when the moment is right.' Seeing her mother-in-law's knowing smile, she changed the subject abruptly. 'Will you tell me more about the family history, Mama? Richard said I should ask you.'

'You do surprise me. Do you tell me he did not warn you against my superstitious nonsense?' As Jamie looked at her blankly, she said, 'I see that he did not, which is something of a surprise. In any case, you shall judge for yourself.'

She sipped her tea delicately. 'The Hardinges have served the kings of England for centuries—ever since the Conqueror, we believe.' She laughed gently. 'And they have almost always managed to be on the winning side too, which must have required a remarkable amount of luck, especially during the Wars of the Roses.'

Jamie nodded, fascinated. At Calderwood, she had read all the histories she could lay her hands on. Almost every noble family had found itself in disgrace at some time or other during that period.

'I like to think that the family has prospered because of the tradition that the head of the house must marry for love. It has been upheld for centuries. In fact, it goes back so far that we do not really know how it came about. All we know is that, when the rule is flouted, a curse descends on us.'

Jamie listened in increasing wonder. She did not dare to think what such a curse might mean for her—and for Richard. She held her breath, waiting for her mother-in-law to continue.

'At least, that is how it appears,' added Lady Hardinge. 'There have been only two occasions when the head of the house did not marry for love. Twice they flouted the tradition—and twice they died without an heir.'

Jamie felt the blood draining from her face. She swallowed hard. This could not be real.

'And then there was the Hardinge diamond,' continued Lady Hardinge with a mischievous smile. 'It was given to Major Richard Harding for his services to an Indian prince. You must understand that the major belonged to a cadet branch of the Hardinge family—he did not even have the ''e''!'

'I beg your pardon, ma'am? I am afraid I do not quite understand.'

'Goodness. Richard has been remiss!' chuckled Lady Hardinge. 'When the first Earl Hardinge was created, for services to Charles II, there was a mistake in the letters patent—an ''e'' was added to the end of the name. Of course, it had to remain. One does not cavil at the gift of an earldom. Only the main branch of the family took to using that spelling, though. The rest remained plain ''Harding'' without an ''e''. That is why this estate, which predates the earldom, is also ''Harding'' without an ''e''.

'But, to return to Major Harding—there were probably well-nigh twenty people between him and the earldom, yet in the five years following the gift of the stone, every single one of them died. The title fell into his lap.

'And there have been similar happenings since. The diamond brings luck—but it cannot undo the curse. It did not help the Earl who married a woman he detested, purely for her money. He was crippled shortly after, by a fall from his horse, and died in agony. He had no son. The title went to his cousin.'

Jamie nodded, fascinated—and more than a little unnerved. Was the curse the reason for Lady Hardinge's underlying sadness about Richard's marriage to her? What would happen to Richard, she wondered, to punish him for marrying where he did not love? And to her, for accepting him?

Chapter Fifteen

Jamie determined to wait up for her husband, however late he might be. She needed to know whether his enquiries had produced any result. But she dare not allow herself to be idle, for then her thoughts would stray towards Emma Fitzwilliam or the Hardinge family curse. Instead, she explored the glories of the Harding library, finding that it included just the sort of novels and frivolous books which had never been permitted to cross the threshold of Calderwood Hall.

To her surprise, she soon found herself absorbed in *Sense and Sensibility* in spite of the questions nagging in the back of her mind, and the evening passed swiftly until a soft tap sounded on the door of their sitting room. That would be the butler, summoning her to meet her husband. She rose and smoothed her gown, trying to look totally composed.

The door opened to reveal, not the butler, but Richard, looking a little damp from his travels.

'Digby said you were waiting up for me, Jamie. But you should be in bed, my dear. It is very late.'

He smiled wearily down at his wife, and found himself thinking how well black became her. He felt a sudden desire to take her in his arms, just to hold her against his travel-worn body, but he managed to resist the impulse. He was not sure he would be able to control what might happen afterwards.

'Digby was supposed to fetch me down to you,' Jamie began anxiously. She had hoped for a little longer to prepare herself.

'He did try, I promise you.'

Although he was tired, there was mischief in his eyes, but his wife did not respond to it. 'I see,' she returned seriously.

They sat down side by side on the sofa, not touching. He thought she seemed a little wary of him. It hurt to think that she could not be at ease with him, though he was not sure why it mattered so much to him.

He raised one of her hands to his lips and dropped a feather-light kiss on her palm. Then he repeated the gesture with the other, gazing deep into her glorious eyes and recognising how truly troubled she was. 'You have no need for concern, Jamie,' he said in a soft, but serious voice. 'You are my wife, remember?'

She looked away, unable to hold his gaze. His words shamed her, for she knew she was no true wife. Unconsciously, she withdrew her hands and clasped them in her lap.

Richard's jaw tightened at the thought that Jamie was repelled by his simple reminder that she was his wife. The fact that he had intended it as a reassurance made it worse. Clearly he had been wrong to believe

he was making progress with her. Even a kiss on the
hand was too much, too soon, apparently.

Swallowing his defeat, he smiled at her. 'I have to
admit that I have achieved little today, in spite of all
my efforts. Our intruder has been delivered to the
Bridewell but, even there, I could get nothing more
out of him. To be honest, I think he has told all he
knows. My search for Caleb has been equally fruit-
less.' The smile was a little rueful now. 'That is my
account of myself. A thoroughgoing failure, I'd say.
So, if you have any more thoughts on what we might
do, let me have them, I beg you, for I am at a stand.'

How weary he is, Jamie thought, trying to resist
the urge to touch his furrowed brow and smooth away
his cares. 'I do have one thought,' she ventured, ruthlessly subduing her softer feelings. 'My father has an
agent in London. I think Ralph Graves may use him
too.'

Richard slapped his open hand down on his thigh
with a loud crack. 'Good God, where are my wits? I
should have guessed as much. I shall start for London
in the morning.' He smiled broadly at his wife. 'Well
done, my dear. In fact, if you—' He broke off in mid-
sentence, apparently embarrassed.

Jamie could not imagine what might be in his mind,
but, encouraged by that generous smile, she allowed
herself to voice her own thoughts. 'Might I come with
you, Richard?' At the look of astonishment which
crossed his face, her precarious composure shattered.
She found herself beginning to stammer apologetically. 'I'm sorry. I did not mean... Please, do
not—'

'I should be delighted if you would accompany me, my dear. In fact, I was just about to ask if you would agree to come. I cannot imagine a better partner in this adventure than my quick-witted wife.' This unexpected compliment provoked a rosy blush from his now thoroughly confused wife. 'Good. That's settled then,' he said quickly, keeping his tone light and practical. 'Can you be ready early tomorrow?'

'You forget, my lord,' she returned archly, trying to regain some vestige of her earlier self-control, 'that, until recently, I was wont to rise with the dawn.'

'Witch!' he laughed, getting up from his seat and dropping a kiss on her titian curls. 'Now, get thee to thy rest, wife, for we have much to do tomorrow.'

Jamie listened as he descended the stairs, probably to return to his study. She sighed wistfully, wondering why she made such a mull of every encounter they had.

Back in his book-room, Richard forced his mind on to practicalities. Summoning Digby, he gave instructions for their early departure for London in the morning. In view of the chilly weather, and the presence of his wife, they would travel in his carriage, rather than by curricle. A messenger must be sent ahead immediately to warn the staff at Hardinge House to prepare for their master's arrival. And his valet and her ladyship's abigail must follow with all speed, together with the baggage.

'Does your lordship expect to make a long stay?' The butler was responsible for calculating quantities of baggage and allocating packing duties.

'A week, perhaps two, I should think. We shall not

be going into society, of course, so there will be little
need for baggage. We can always send back for anything more we need, if we decide to extend our visit.'
The butler bowed himself out to set about rousing the
household to meet this sudden change of plan.

Richard had turned meanwhile to penning a long
explanatory note to his mother, in case she was not
awake before they left on the morrow. He paused to
wonder about the wisdom of taking Jamie with him.
In London, they would be thrown together much more
than at Harding. Could he resist the temptation she
presented?

Her lovely face, framed by her glorious hair,
seemed to appear before him, tantalisingly. Dear God,
how he wanted her! What was it about her that stirred
him so? He could not tell. Nor when and how his
feelings had begun to change towards her. But he
knew now that he felt something for his wife which
he had never experienced before in all his dealings
with womankind. And that he did not dare to put a
name to it. Not yet.

Very early next morning, Lady Hardinge entered
the cheery breakfast room where her daughter-in-law
was calmly pouring coffee for her husband. Richard
was dressed for travelling. Jamie had put on her black
silk again, since it was the only appropriate day gown
she now possessed.

Richard rose in surprise to greet his mother. 'What
are you doing down at this hour, Mama? I had left a
note for you explaining everything.'

'I am quite well aware that you think I am in my

dotage, Richard, but you are mistaken if you think me incapable of rising early. I have come to ensure that Jamie is properly taken care of, before this mad escapade gets under way. Your note of explanation'— she waved a sheet of paper in his direction—'says much, but it does not say that.'

Richard grinned, a little sheepishly, and politely helped his mother to her seat. He threw Jamie a look suggestive of the persecuted fugitive.

'If you have your way,' continued Lady Hardinge, without allowing either of them to say a word, 'this poor child will freeze to death. Have you no conscience?'

Jamie tried to suppress a giggle. 'Oh, Mama, you really are most kind to worry so about me, but truly there is no need. Only think—on my last journey in Richard's carriage, I was left to freeze to death on the box! I am sure this trip will be most comfortable by comparison.'

Lady Hardinge interrupted her son as he made to defend himself. 'That is nothing at all to the point, Jamie. Your husband has a duty to look to your well-being and, in my opinion, he is failing in it. What, for example, did you plan to wear over that thin silk gown you have on?' There was no response, except for a muffled choking noise from Richard's end of the table. 'Quite. However, there is a solution. After breakfast, you shall come upstairs to my dressing-room and we shall make a selection from what I have there. I have, for example, a black sable cloak and muff which will be just right for you.' She glared at her son. 'I take it you do not object, Richard?'

'Not in the least, Mama,' he admitted, grinning cheerfully at her. 'Against such a formidable combination as my mother and my wife, how should I dare to say a word?'

Jamie gasped with laughter.

'Stuff!' exclaimed Lady Hardinge inelegantly. 'You, my son, are bound for a bad end—unless a good woman can save you.'

'I recognise it might be a tall order,' quipped her son, glancing towards his wife for a split second.

Lady Hardinge sipped at her coffee and turned to Jamie. 'Do go to Célestine's while you are in London, my dear, and order your half-mourning. You will need it quite soon.'

'But, Mama, I have already spent a fortune on my wardrobe here. I cannot...' She broke off, looking guiltily towards her husband.

'Why not?' demanded Lady Hardinge. 'It is surely up to you how you spend your allowance. Why, what on earth is the matter, my dear? I did not mean to embarrass you—'

Richard's deep voice intervened. 'Jamie is embarrassed for me, I collect, Mama. She has no allowance—not yet. With all the other events happening around us, I am afraid I overlooked it. But no matter.' He turned to Jamie. 'How much do you think you will need, my dear?'

'I—'

'Richard! How is Jamie supposed to know the answer to that? Really, men are quite witless sometimes, I do believe!'

Jamie was again trying not to laugh. She dared not look at Richard's face.

'Why don't you start with the same allowance I had from your father and see whether it is enough? But you will need to be prepared to increase it, I warn you. A young bride's needs are bound to be much more than those of an old woman in her dotage.' Lady Hardinge finished her coffee and rose to leave. 'I shall expect you upstairs in five minutes, Jamie.'

As the door closed behind her, Jamie dared at last to look directly at Richard, whose eyes were brimming with laughter. In a matter of seconds, both of them were convulsed, trying vainly to muffle the sounds of their mirth.

'What on earth came over Mama?' chuckled Richard, as soon as he could speak. 'I have never seen the like.'

'I think she feels I need a champion. And she was splendid, quite splendid. If you had seen your face when she said men were witless…' Jamie succumbed to another peal of laughter which she stifled as best she could with her now damp and crumpled handkerchief.

'What could I say?' pleaded Richard. 'A man may not contradict his mama, after all.'

'Oh!' If there had been a loose cushion on her chair, Jamie would have thrown it at him. 'How outrageous you are, my lord!'

'And how beautiful you are when you laugh, my lady,' countered Richard, with a hint of deeper meaning in his voice. Too much, he realised immediately. She looked like a frightened doe again. His recover was very swift this time. 'However,' he continued smoothly, 'your first duty now, ma'am, is to attend on my mother, before she demands my head on a charger for dereliction of duty! If you would save me, I beg you, go!'

Good humour restored, Jamie did as she was bid.

His laughing voice followed her as she made for the stairs. 'But delay at your peril, my lady. After fifteen minutes, I depart, with you or without you.'

Jamie picked up her skirts to run nimbly up the stairs to Lady Hardinge's dressing-room, and was still smiling broadly as she entered.

'I am delighted to see you in such spirits, Jamie, my dear. And Richard too. He has not laughed like that in a long time.'

'I do believe you provoked him deliberately,' said Jamie suspiciously, spying the twinkle in Lady Hardinge's eye. 'If I may say so without giving offence, Mama, I think I know from whom he has his wicked sense of humour.'

Her mother-in-law seemed pleased at this. 'I take it from that, my dear, that my son has been showing you at least a little of his lighter side. Good. In my opinion, that is what you both need.'

Before Jamie could reply, the Dowager turned to the cupboard and began pulling out clothes, all of which she tossed to the protesting Jamie. 'Come, Jamie, you need them, at least until your own wardrobe is delivered, whereas I have no need of them now. Humour me, if you will.'

In the end, all was agreed. Jamie would wear the sables, and the matching hat. The other clothes would be packed up immediately and loaded into the second carriage with Smithers and Gregg. Honour was satisfied.

Precisely fourteen minutes later, Jamie arrived back in the hall, swathed in sables, just as Richard came out of the study with some papers in his hand. 'Well!' he said, admiring the picture she made. 'You lost, I see!' He grinned. 'But you had the good sense to take your fall quickly. Most commendable! What a wonder you are, my dear.' With an exaggerated bow, he offered her his arm. 'May I see you to your carriage, my lady?'

In less than five minutes, they were under way. Jamie sank back into her corner, relishing the comfort of her sables, the fur rug across her lap and the hot brick under her feet. Even as Miss Calderwood, she had never dreamt of treatment like this. It seemed… unreal.

Richard, too, sat back in his corner, idly watching the play of expression on his wife's face. She was sometimes very easy to read. And at the moment, her childlike pleasure in her surroundings was evident. Good. So far. He would try to keep the journey lighthearted. And he would not touch her. He knew well enough the mistakes he had to avoid.

'How are we going to set about finding my father's agent, Richard?' Her practical question broke into his careful calculations, dispelling his increasingly dark mood.

'Ah, now, there I do have some ideas. I daren't let my wife do all the thinking, lest she, too, conclude I am witless.'

Jamie chuckled, as he had known she would. He found himself thinking again how beautiful she had grown since her unmasking, like a flower blooming under a dedicated gardener's careful nurturing. But he pushed such delicious thoughts to the back of his mind. He was nowhere near ready for such temptations, especially now, with the prospect of many hours alone in her company.

'I shall go, first of all, to my own agents. They should be able to furnish some names, which will give us a start.'

As he spoke, the carriage lurched, throwing Jamie towards him. Their hands touched. Even through their gloves, Jamie felt as if a bolt of lightning had shot up her arm. She felt herself flushing with embarrassment and pulled her hand away sharply. Why could she not control her reactions to him? What on earth would he think of her behaviour? She clasped her hands in her lap, trying to concentrate on counting the tiny stitches in her kid gloves.

Richard looked steadily at her and cursed silently. So lovely, so desirable—and so afraid of him! How was he ever going to win her trust?

Chapter Sixteen

A slightly uncomfortable silence prevailed for several miles. Jamie had suddenly become conscious that she was truly alone with her husband for the first time since their wedding ceremony. On other occasions, there had always been the likelihood of imminent interruption—or it had been clear that Richard had no intention of prolonging their tête-à-tête. But now…his presence seemed to fill the carriage. The scent of him was all around her, preventing her more rational self from functioning. And after that single touch, she could think of nothing but Richard, of how close he was, of how much she wanted to be in his arms.

Jamie transferred her gaze to the sable muff. She sensed that her husband was watching her, but she felt unable to raise her eyes to look at him. She focused instead on the lustrous black hairs of the beautiful fur. How thick and soft it was.

Richard shifted deliberately in his seat, but his tactic did not succeed—Jamie still would not look at him. He frowned, racking his brains for some way of putting her at her ease again. Why did she recoil from him so? Was she still suffering as a result of his attempt to seduce her? Then why had she agreed to marry him? Had he really coerced her?

He shook his head a little, trying to clear his thoughts. It really would not do to continue along this 'if only' road. Nothing could be undone. They had to go forward from where they were.

He smiled across at her tense figure. 'I hope you are more comfortable today than on the last occasion when we shared this carriage,' he said lightly.

She looked up briefly, a slight flush rising on her neck. 'Thank you, it is most comfortable,' she said in a rather strangled voice, before lapsing into silence once more.

He groaned inwardly. This was not going to be easy. But still—their first encounter was as good a topic as any. He continued in a bantering tone, 'I wonder you did not think to take some gloves when you fled from Calderwood. But then—perhaps better not, for I should not have known you were freezing. I could not tell how thin your clothes were.' She must say something now, surely?

'It was kind in you to notice. Many a master would have left me to freeze on the box.'

That was true. Richard had surprised himself when he had taken the boy inside. 'I wonder I did not. It must have been the effect of your soulful eyes, my dear. You looked so helpless, so lost.'

Jamie thought back to that incident. She remembered every second of it, especially the burning touch of his hand on her cheek. She could feel it still. And now he was waiting for her to continue the conversation, but no words would come. In desperation, she turned to the window, rubbing the mist from the pane with her black kid glove. 'Where are we now? We seem to be making very good speed. Shall we reach London tonight?'

Richard sighed. Still, it was better than silence. He began to describe the route they would take. With luck and good horses at every change, they should make London in the day. The important thing was to make progress while the light lasted, for once darkness fell, their speed would be very limited.

'I hope you will not mind, Jamie, but I do not propose to stop to eat. Mrs Peters has provided a basket of provisions which—if it is up to her usual standard—would feed an army for a week. We can eat as we go. We should be able to get some coffee or a glass of wine while the horses are being changed.' He looked towards her for some sign of acquiescence.

'That will suit me very well,' she nodded. 'Thank you. I...I must say I am rather too excited to eat in any case. I have never been to London before.'

'Truly?' queried Richard. This was too good an opportunity to miss! 'Then I hope you will allow me to show you some of the capital, my dear.'

Jamie looked uncertain.

'It would be my pleasure to do so,' he added with his most charming smile.

'Oh, I should like that above all things, Richard, only... Would it be proper to do so while we are in mourning?'

Richard cursed silently. She was quite right. He did not try to hide his chagrin as he admitted his fault.

'But some few amusements may be possible, none the less,' he added. 'Even in mourning, we may visit Westminster Abbey and St Paul's. If you would like to go, that is.'

'Oh yes, very much,' she began eagerly. She was about to launch into a description of all the things she wished to see in the Abbey—like Queen Elizabeth's tomb and the Coronation chair—when she remembered that her father had called her a 'bluestocking' for just such a display of erudition. She lapsed into sudden silence.

Richard threw her a wondering look. 'It sounds as if you know about them already, Jamie,' he began, with a smile. 'Are there particular places you wish to visit? The City?' His smile broadened. 'Or the London gardens, perhaps?'

'Well—yes.' Jamie tentatively began to describe things she longed to see. Hesitant at first, she soon became animated, as she warmed to her subject and forgot all her father's strictures. She spoke knowledgeably of historic buildings and described London's gardens in the spring as if she already knew and loved them.

Richard was entranced. Not only was his wife courageous and beautiful, she was also well read and displayed a fine intellect for one so young. With nods and smiles, he encouraged her to talk, so successfully that the miles flew by. He was on the point of suggesting that she might like to redesign some of the gardens at Harding when the slowing of the horses brought Jamie up short.

'Goodness,' she exclaimed, flushing, 'how I have been rattling on!'

'Nothing of the sort. It was most interesting. I am delighted to discover we have so many tastes in common, my dear. Clearly you must be given free rein in all my gardens. And given your obvious love of history and of books, we shall never want for a topic of conversation.'

Jamie felt her blush deepen. Was he roasting her?

'Now, this is Marlborough, Jamie. May I order you some refreshment? You must be thirsty.'

Jamie could not deny it. 'A cup of coffee would be very welcome,' she admitted. 'If it will not delay us.'

'It shall be done forthwith, madam, if you will excuse me a moment. And I shall get you another hot brick too. The drive through the Savernake Forest can be cold and gloomy.'

So it proved to be, but they made good speed, none the less. It began to look as if they would certainly reach London in the day. And then, in the afternoon, in the Maidenhead thicket, the mist came down. The carriage slowed to a bare walking pace, as the coachman eased his team through the murk.

Richard's face bore a set expression. There was nothing to be done. If they came through the other side of the mist, they might still make London. Otherwise...

It was Jamie who first voiced a doubt. 'If we cannot go faster than this, we shall never make London tonight, surely? Do you know where we are, Richard?'

'Aye. Just outside Maidenhead. If the mist does not lift soon, we shall have to rack up somewhere for the night. Don't worry. There are some quite tolerable inns hereabouts.'

'Oh, I have no worries,' exclaimed Jamie blithely. But she had. She was still alone with Richard—and anything might happen at a strange inn.

When the coachman dared drive his team no farther, they stopped at the Castle Inn, a small but high-class hostelry, hard by Maidenhead. Unfortunately for the Hardinges, they were neither the first nor the only travellers to seek shelter there.

The landlady was wringing her hands as she apologised to her high-ranking new guests. 'I have but the one chamber left, milord, milady. We've so many guests arrived unforeseen this evening, and I couldn't be turning them out, milord, not in this weather. You see—'

'I see exactly your dilemma, my good woman. Do not fret over it. We shall be quite comfortable in the chamber you have, I am sure. Now, if you would take my wife upstairs…'

The landlady bustled up the staircase, apologising volubly all the time. She flung open the door at the end of the passage. 'Please to go in, milady. The fire is lit, as you see, but I'll send up hot water in two shakes.'

'Is there a private parlour?'

'Well, no, milady, I'm afraid not. I only have the one and some earlier guests have taken that. I could ask them—'

'No, indeed,' said Jamie quickly. 'We shall be quite comfortable here, if you could send up some supper.'

The landlady agreed at once. 'Your ladyship's abigail…' She let the question hang in the air.

'I have no idea where she may be. Or my husband's valet either. The second carriage was some time behind us. We must suppose that they have stopped somewhere. Would you…?'

'Have no worries on that score, your ladyship,' responded the landlady promptly. 'If they do arrive, I can find them a bed somewhere. And my daughter can wait on your ladyship, if you wish.'

'That is most kind,' said Jamie gratefully. 'What is her name?'

'Annie, your ladyship.'

Jamie grinned. 'How appropriate. I am sure we shall do very well. Pray send her up to me.'

As the door closed behind the landlady, Jamie surveyed the room. Although the chamber was large, it was dominated by a huge, curtained bed. There were two easy chairs by the fireplace and a small table at which they would no doubt sup. There was a washstand in the corner. And there was plenty of hanging space for clothing. But there was no dressing-room. And there was nowhere else to sleep but that one great bed.

Jamie swallowed nervously when the door opened, but it was not Richard. It was Annie, the landlady's daughter, much flustered at being asked to serve such a great lady. 'Will you change your gown, milady?' she asked shyly, moving to unpack Jamie's travelling portmanteau.

Jamie knew a moment of panic. Where was Richard? Surely he might walk in on her at any moment? Trying to control her voice, she gave the maid to understand that she thought it unnecessary to change. She washed and tidied herself, rather more hurriedly than was her wont. She tried to hide her relief as Annie refastened the last hook of her gown and began to redress her hair.

'Shall I tell his lordship he may come up now, mi-lady?' asked Annie, when she had finished.

Jamie lifted her chin at such impertinence. 'His lordship will come up when he is ready,' she said icily.

'Oh, no, milady. Beggin' your pardon, but his lordship asked me to tell him when you had finished your toilet. He is waiting in the coffee-room.'

How thoughtful he was! And all her haste for no reason!

'Thank you, Annie,' she said, with an apologetic smile. 'Pray tell him so. And bring up some more hot water too.'

Moments later, a soft knock announced Richard's arrival. Jamie rose uncertainly from her chair. His powerful presence seemed to fill the chamber. Richard—and the huge double bed.

Richard was not slow to read the situation. He crossed to where his wife stood by the fire. 'You look much refreshed, Jamie. Is that hot water over there? I should like to be rid of my dirt.'

'I have ordered some more for you. It will be here directly.'

He smiled at her. 'How thoughtful. Thank you.' He began to strip off his coat and waistcoat, then paused.

'Forgive me, Jamie, but as there is no dressing-room…'

She shook her head, trying to smile confidently at him. 'No matter,' she said quietly, resuming her seat so that her back was towards the washstand.

As soon as the hot water arrived, Richard stripped to the waist and began to wash. In the little mirror on the wall, he could see his wife sitting rigidly in her chair. But as he began to shave, she moved. It was a barely perceptible shift of position but just enough, he fancied, for her to watch him out of the corner of her eye. Even curiosity was better than nothing, he decided. He chuckled to himself, but continued to ply his razor as if nothing untoward were happening.

Jamie had failed to resist the temptation to take just one look. She consoled herself with the knowledge that he could not see what she was doing and, since they were bound to share that bed, she might as well know something of what lay in store. But one single look was not enough, she found, for his broad shoulders and smooth skin drew her eyes like a magnet. She had seen him in a dressing gown, but somehow his naked skin was different, making her long to stretch out to touch him.

He put his razor aside and began to wash the traces of shaving soap from his face, reaching for a towel. Jamie edged back into her earlier position, her face flaming. What would he think if he caught her? Luckily, he did not turn. By the time he had put on a fresh shirt and neckcloth, she knew her flush had subsided.

In deference to Jamie, who unaccountably had not

changed her dress, Richard resumed the same coat and waistcoat, even if they would not have been acceptable to Gregg's critical eye. Then he relaxed into the chair opposite his wife with a long sigh. 'You must be tired, Jamie, after all those hours cooped up in the carriage. I am sorry I insisted we should try to make London in the day. It was foolhardy. I should have arranged for us to break our journey at somewhere more comfortable than this. Forgive me.'

She looked up at him then, surprised by his apparent seriousness. His eyes smiled warmly at her, though there was a little hint of annoyance there too. 'You should have organised the mist better,' she ventured and was rewarded by his rich chuckle.

'Indeed I should, madam. But next time, I beg that you will remind me of it *before* we set out.'

That was too much. In a moment, both were laughing merrily. The gay mood, carefully nurtured by Richard, lasted throughout the wholesome supper which the landlady served for them, even though Jamie declined to share Richard's wine.

Jamie pushed her plate away. 'I could not eat another bite. The landlady must believe her guests are starved, I fancy.'

Richard smiled at her across the top of his wineglass. 'Probably. And she has a reputation to maintain. The Castle is small, but well known for the quality it offers its guests. I must say that the claret is excellent.' He sipped it approvingly.

'Shall you ring for some brandy?' asked Jamie a little hesitantly. It was so difficult to know what to do in a shared room doubling as both bedchamber and supper room.

He cocked an impudent eyebrow. '*And* cigars, do you think?'

'Oh!' She gasped with laughter. 'Pray smoke, my lord, if you wish. I should not for the world spoil your enjoyment of your meal.' She made to rise to ring the bell.

'Jamie, don't you dare!' he warned dramatically.

She turned back and gave him an arched look.

He slowly finished his wine and replaced the glass on the supper table. 'I shall take a glass of brandy downstairs, madam wife, as a gentleman should. Shall I send the maid up to you, once the covers are cleared? You are tired, I know, and will wish to make ready for bed.'

Suddenly all the good humour left her face, and he kicked himself for his lack of tact. How thoughtless to remind her now...

'Thank you,' she said in that familiar strained voice. 'You are very good. I am a little tired, I admit.'

He made his way to the door. 'Go you to bed then, my dear. I shall try not to disturb you when I come up.'

Jamie did not know what to make of that last remark, but she decided there was no point in fussing over it. She would go to bed, as he had suggested, and wait to see what happened. Perhaps she would be able to sleep, in spite of not knowing... Perhaps he really would not wake her...

Two hours later she still lay awake, alone in the great bed, wondering how much longer he would wait

before coming up. He would have consumed a considerable amount of brandy by now, surely? She did
not know whether that would make matters worse, or
better.

The flickering shadows on the wall betrayed the
draught from the opening door. She closed her eyes
and lay still. She heard the tiny fizz as he snuffed his
candle and then the soft sound of his steps as he approached the bed to look at her in the glow of the
firelight. She knew he was gazing down at her. And
she knew she could no longer pretend. She opened
her eyes.

'You should be asleep, wife,' he smiled softly at
her.

'I c-could not,' she stammered in a whisper.

'No, I can see that.' He moved round to the other
side of the great bed and began to pull back the
covers.

Jamie stiffened.

'Since there is no sofa, it will have to be "bundling", I am afraid.' He smoothed the top sheet up
and under the pillows on his side of the bed. Then he
looked across at his wife. 'If you do not let out that
breath you are holding, Jamie, you will surely expire,
you know.'

Jamie gasped and turned the colour of the glowing
embers in the hearth. 'I don't understand,' she managed at last.

'About "bundling"? It's an old country custom,
my dear, for courting couples who have nowhere to
go in winter but the...er...family bed. They are put

into bed together but with the sheet between them so that they cannot…er…' He coughed. 'I believe that, in medieval days, the knights used a sword for the same purpose—but as I do not happen to have a sword by me this evening, I thought the sheet might serve instead.' He smiled mischievously at her and sat down on the bed, waiting for her embarrassment to subside.

It was some moments before she was able to look at him.

'That's better. You have nothing to fear, Jamie. We shall share the bed to sleep, that is all. Now, close your eyes, my dear.'

Obediently, she did so. She could hear him moving about as he removed his clothing to make ready for bed. She dared not look. Even when he came round to close the bedcurtains, she dared not look.

Presently, the bed dipped as his weight descended on it. He pulled the remaining bedcovers over himself and closed the curtains. Inside the great bed, it was quite dark. She began to feel the warmth from his body stealing through the thin sheet which separated them. She lay totally motionless, hardly daring to breathe.

'Goodnight, my dear,' he said gently. 'Sleep well.' Then he turned on his side and said no more. In less that five minutes, his breathing had become deep and regular. He was asleep!

What a fool she was! She should have known he would find a way. He always did. He had told her he would keep his word. She should have trusted him.

She continued to reproach herself for quite some

time, lying in the dark with her sleeping husband by
her side. But at last, exhausted, she too fell asleep.

When she eventually awoke, it was broad day, and
Richard was gone from the bed. Annie, the little maid,
was drawing aside the bedcurtains and offering her a
cup of chocolate.

'His lordship is out in the stables, milady,' supplied
the girl helpfully. 'Not that it'll do much good, I'm
afraid, seeing as how the mist is worse than ever this
mornin'.'

It was mid-afternoon before it lifted. Richard hesitated before deciding to drive on to London. The mist
might easily descend again. On the other hand, it
would be better to take the risk. Jamie needed to be
properly installed in Hardinge House as soon as possible. 'Bundling' was a temptation best not repeated!

Chapter Seventeen

It was very late indeed by the time they reached Hardinge House in Hanover Square. Although the remaining distance had not been great, there had been further patches of mist to delay them. But, by dint of perseverance and some good luck, they had eventually reached their goal.

For Richard, this final part of the journey had been very instructive. Although Jamie had been quite reluctant to speak, he had eventually acquired a tolerably good understanding of what her past life had been like.

Her father had treated her abominably. Her stepmother was quite unspeakable. No wonder Jamie had been so shocked to find Lady Calderwood at Harding.

And yet, in spite of everything, Jamie had emerged without bitterness from their shadow. His wife was— he now knew—quite as strong and courageous as he had believed. But she was also much more vulnerable. In all her one-and-twenty years, no one had really cared for her, except perhaps her long-dead mama. She needed to be loved and cherished, of that he was sure, but she was afraid to lower her guard in order to let it happen.

Hardly surprising, considering what had been done to her. He wondered whether he could succeed against such odds—and what it would mean to him if he did. To be sure, he had never before been daunted by a female's defences—the stronger they were, the greater the satisfaction in breaching them. He had never failed. But now... He could not be sure. Jamie was so different from his society women. All he could do was to work on her defences, slowly and carefully, in hopes that, eventually, they would crumble.

As the carriage pulled up, Richard looked down at his wife, who was sleeping peacefully with her head on his shoulder. He felt again a great yearning for her, but he managed to master his desire to touch her. 'Jamie,' he said softly. 'Wake up, my dear, we have arrived.'

'Oh!' Jamie came suddenly awake, blushing to find how she had slept. 'Oh, dear! I beg your pardon, Richard. How very uncomfortable for you.' She drew away from him, busying herself with her hat.

'My pleasure, ma'am. After all, we witless men have to have some uses, do we not?'

She smiled uncertainly, but at least her flush had subsided. A moment later, he was helping her down from the carriage.

Jamie was surprised, next morning, to find Annie opening her curtains and offering her a cup of chocolate. The abigail did not even look especially tired.

'Oh, it was nothing, my lady,' she responded airily to Jamie's question. 'We just plodded on until we got here, about five o'clock this morning. What will you wear today, m'lady?'

'The black silk again, I suppose. I have no choice. Lady Hardinge's gowns will need to be altered for me.'

'Beg pardon, my lady, but you do have a choice. Three gowns from Madame Françoise were delivered just before we left. I have taken the liberty of pressing one of them for you this morning.'

As Annie moved aside, Jamie saw that a new gown was hanging on the dressing-room door. Like the first, it was black and demure in style, with a high neckline and long sleeves, but this one was lightened by a little ruff of lace around the collar and some rather fine beaded embroidery. Jamie was delighted with it, and with Annie's ability to work such miracles.

Jamie was not in time to join her husband in the breakfast parlour. Instead, she had to content herself with exploring the house and interviewing the house-keeper.

It was well after mid-day when Richard returned.

'I have seen my people this morning,' he said, 'and set them to finding your father's agent in London. I have also arranged to offer a reward—discreetly—for information on Caleb. If he has gone to ground in the rookeries—'

'Rookeries?'

'I beg your pardon, Jamie, for my language. It means those parts of the city where the poor are crowded together in the most abject squalor, where no gentleman would dare to go alone. Many of the people there are totally honest, I'm sure, but a great many of them are villains—thieves, burglars, coiners—and worse. If Caleb is in hiding in London, that is probably where he will be. We shall have to trust to the greed of his neighbours to discover him.'

Jamie looked unconvinced. 'He may not be in London.'

'That is true, though London is certainly the best place to hide. I suppose he might have gone to your father's estate…'

'Or to Ralph Graves' estate at Bathinghurst,' Jamie put in, her voice almost a whisper.

'True, but in either place he would be much more difficult to conceal. Country people always know what is going on, I find.'

Jamie nodded. Calderwood had been just the same.

'If we have no news of Caleb in a few days, I will go to Calderwood myself,' said Richard decisively. He saw that all the colour had drained from Jamie's face. 'Don't worry, Jamie. I am quite capable of dealing with your father myself—and with Lady Calderwood, too, if it should come to that. If Caleb is there, I shall find him. And it is time I paid another visit to Calderwood. I have some unfinished business to discuss with your father.'

Jamie looked truly puzzled, but she said nothing.

Richard smiled down at her, admiring her tact. 'Now that you are my wife, Jamie, I should not conceal this from you, but it is not an edifying story. You see…my father… Towards the end of his life, my

father was severely ill—not physically, you understand, but in his mind. His memory was…uncertain.
Sometimes he did not recognise his own family. And
he had unpredictable changes of mood. At times, he
would be in a violent temper—even towards Mama.
It was very…distressing.'

Jamie nodded, her eyes full of concern.

'At some time during those last months, my father
made a very large loan to yours.'

Jamie gasped.

'There must have been some kind of document, of
course, but I have not been able to find it. I think your
father may have it.' He was looking increasingly
grim. 'Without the evidence of that contract, I have
been unable to recover the money.'

Jamie closed her eyes in mortification. Her father…yes, it was all very much in character. He
would have borrowed the money to finance his gambling. And he would have had no qualms about im-
posing on a sick, old man to do it.

'I am so sorry, Richard,' she said, after a moment.
'If only I could…' A sudden, horrifying thought
struck her. 'And yet you married me, his daughter—
without a penny of a dowry.' She felt like crawling
away to hide.

Richard could read his wife's emotions from her
expressive face. Gently, he took both her hands in his.
'Jamie, you are in no way responsible for what your
father may have done. And I told you once before—
I have no need of a dowry. Oh, I admit that I will be
glad when I have recovered the loan money—I have
plans for extensive changes to the estate, which I

cannot fund easily without that capital—but I am not yet running from my creditors, I promise you.' He smiled mischievously. 'Believe me, the estate is still wealthy—your mantua maker's bill will be paid.'

Jamie smiled back at him, but her guilt remained. What about the bill for those emeralds?

'Now, this afternoon,' continued Richard briskly, 'I plan to enquire in the clubs about your father's contacts in London. And Graves', too, for that matter. I'm afraid I shall have to do that by myself, Jamie.' He grinned. 'Unless you would like to dress as a boy again?'

Jamie burst out laughing. 'My lord,' she said, trying to look severe, 'you are quite incorrigible.'

'How true! How true!' He was still grinning, delighted that he had diverted her mind from her appalling family. 'Oh, by the bye, I forgot to mention… I met an old friend in the City this morning—Sir Edward Fitzwilliam.'

Jamie looked down, trying desperately to conceal her dismay.

'He is a very old friend of the Hardinges. I hope to introduce him to you, one day soon. And his daughter, Emma.' He laughed at some fleeting memory. 'She and I lived in each other's pockets when we were younger. She was a little urchin then, though, seeing her now, no one would believe that. She was the toast of London, last season. Blondes were all the crack.'

Jamie managed to mutter an appropriate, but noncommittal reply. She had long ago determined to avoid Miss Fitzwilliam's company if she possibly could.

'It was a happy coincidence that we should meet,' Richard continued. 'I have been wishing to find you some congenial female company, and I can think of no one more suitable than Emma. She is a delightful girl, and most accomplished. And she has exquisite dress sense too. You could perhaps take her with you, when you go to visit Célestine, do you not think?'

Jamie did *not* think—but she could hardly admit to the fact, especially to him.

'Are you all right, Jamie?' asked Richard, seeing her strained expression, but unable to guess its cause.

'I have the headache a little,' admitted Jamie, not untruthfully, for a pain had begun to nag behind her eyes.

Richard was all polite concern. 'It's the after-effects of our dreadful journey, I expect.' He immediately summoned Smithers and insisted that Jamie rest in her chamber.

Soon Jamie lay on her bed, frustrated in her desires and in her curiosity, wondering what to do next.

She began to review her situation, overcoming her earlier emotional reactions and forcing herself to think logically. Emma Fitzwilliam could indeed have been the ideal bride for Richard. But, although he must have had many opportunities to offer for her, he had never taken any of them. For whatever reason, he had not married Emma. Had he really wished to? If so, why had he waited so long? It made no sense, except in the light of his mother's words that he had chosen Emma out of duty, not inclination.

In the end, he had married Jamie, not Emma. A little voice murmured that he had offered for her, too, out of duty not inclination, but she resisted its siren call towards dark despair. She would have none of it. Richard was married to her and, somehow, she was going to make their marriage a success.

When Jamie woke again it was evening. The headache was gone. She felt refreshed and renewed. The emotional turmoil over Emma Fitzwilliam was a distant memory, as if it belonged to another world.

'What time is it, Annie?' she asked brightly.

'It wants about an hour until dinner, my lady.'

'Excellent. I should like to take a bath first. Have you pressed my black evening gown?'

'Yes, my lady, and also the green one, in case you felt like wearing it this evening.' She bustled to the door. 'I'll go and see to the hot water now.'

Annie's words had conjured up the memory of Richard's tantalising smile as he had asked Jamie to order it. A shiver ran down her spine. Intrigued, and a little fearful, Jamie made for Annie's sanctum. The black silk evening dress, much adorned with beading and ruffles, hung just inside the door. On the far side, the green gown caught her eye, and she let out a little gasp of surprise.

She had chosen the sea-green silk and the pattern under Lady Hardinge's expert guidance, but she had not thought it could be quite so lovely. The style was simple enough—a ruched bodice, cut very low and edged with matching satin ribbon, a slim draped skirt, totally plain, to show the rippling silk to advantage, and short tucked sleeves, again edged with ribbon. Jamie reached out to touch it, relishing the luxurious feel of the delicate fabric in her fingers. As the skirt moved, the colour seemed to shimmer in the half-light.

'You are pleased, my lady?' Annie was a little out of breath from having run upstairs from the kitchen. 'Your bath water will be here directly.' She hurried into the bedchamber to make ready for its arrival.

Jamie stood transfixed, gazing at the glorious green gown. Richard had asked her to order it, and it was he who had suggested she wear it when they were alone, instead of black. Did she dare? Now? Tonight?

Her wandering thoughts were recalled to reality by the clank of copper water cans being carried in for her bath. She could decide while she bathed, she concluded, wavering uncharacteristically. After all, she did not know whether the dress would become her. It might be better to settle for the safe, black gown. Still, she might just try the green, to see how it looked, before resuming her mourning. Yes, that would be best. For, if she wore the green, what would Richard think—and do?

She settled back into the scented water, allowing the warmth to relax her muscles and the perfume of jasmine to invade her senses. She had never known such luxury. It seemed like a delicious dream. And she definitely did not want to wake up.

In no time at all, it seemed, Jamie was dressed, all but her gown, and her hair was arranged in a riotous tumble of loose curls. 'Better than that horrid bun, my lady?' asked Annie impudently, regarding her handiwork with satisfaction.

Jamie had to concede. While she still found her complexion overly pale and her hair colour unbecoming, she was forced to admit that, under Annie's skilful fingers, she had become just about presentable.

The abigail fetched the sea-green gown and slipped it carefully over her mistress's head before fastening the back. 'That does look well, m'lady, very well indeed,' she beamed. 'Now, if I was to add a green ribbon to your curls, it would be quite perfect.'

'Oh, but I am not going to wear this gown, Annie. I just wanted to try it on, to see whether it fitted properly, that's all. I shall, of course, wear the black.'

Annie snorted. 'Why?' she asked sharply, reverting for a second to her previous role of elder sister. 'You look beautiful in it, and his lordship specifically asked you to wear it. You told me so! Do you not wish to please your husband?'

'Annie! How dare you?' If Annie had forgotten their present relationship, Jamie had not. Annie blushed and looked away, mumbling an apology. 'It is for me to decide when I am ready to leave off my blacks, Annie, not you, nor even his lordship. What I told you about my conversation with his lordship was in confidence. I did not expect you, of all people, to abuse my trust. Oh, don't take on so,' she added more gently, patting the older woman's hand. 'I didn't intend to fly up into the boughs. It's just that…I am not ready yet.' On that unfathomable statement, she proceeded to remove the green dress.

Standing before the glass once more, Jamie admitted to herself that the sea-green gown had been much more flattering than the safe, black silk. For a second, she even toyed with the idea of changing again, but quickly overcame the impulse. She had no idea how Richard would react if she wore it, or what he might read into her choice. She did not yet know her husband well enough to be able to deal confidently with him. Until she was better prepared, she did not dare to make herself even more vulnerable than she already was. Squaring her shoulders, she left the room.

Richard was waiting in the saloon when she appeared. 'How splendid you look, my dear,' he smiled appreciatively. 'With your colouring, you make black seem the colour of choice, rather than of convention. Many women would envy you.'

Jamie blushed rosily, wondering traitorously whether his compliments were sincere. Black could look just as good on blue-eyed blondes, she would have thought.

He drew her to a seat and brought her a glass of sherry. As he took his place beside her, the faint fragrance of jasmine filled his senses for a second, temporarily halting his practised flow of words. She is like an exotic flower, he thought idly, so fragile, so easily crushed.

Just then, dinner was announced. He rose and offered her his arm.

Apprehensively, Jamie rested her fingertips lightly on his immaculate black sleeve, waiting for the jolt of electricity which happened every time she touched him. But, this time, it was different. As he smiled down into her eyes, a great feeling of warmth spread through her body, making all her nerves tingle expectantly, and heightening all her senses. It was not frightening, nor unpleasant. It was a feeling difficult to describe in words. All she knew was that she was waiting for something to happen, something beyond her wildest imaginings, something somehow magical.

Her husband stood quite still, looking down into her eyes and trying to unravel the emotions he saw there. He could have sworn that there was no hint of fear, even if there was not yet trust. But there was something else, hidden behind a misty veil which he could not penetrate.

Richard was recalled to himself by the butler's discreet cough from the doorway. 'Are you ready, my lady?' Richard said softly, covering her hand with his.

Jamie jumped. *Now* she had the bolt of lightning again. Her body quivered slightly. 'Oh, forgive me, my lord,' she said quickly, trying to make a recover. 'I was miles away for a moment.' She forced a warm smile for her husband, who had not removed his hand from hers. 'Shall we go in?'

Dinner was a light-hearted affair. Richard had taken the unusual step of having both places laid at one end of the long dining table, 'so that we do not have to be forever shouting to each other'. He set out deliberately to exercise all his considerable charm on her, regaling her with amusing tales of his childhood at Harding and of his less reprehensible adventures at Oxford.

Jamie allowed the warmth of his presence to envelop her like a cloak and smiled indulgently at his more madcap escapades. She hardly noticed that he refilled her champagne glass more than once, or that she drank it. It was all part of the dreamlike quality of the evening, which she attributed to their closeness and harmony, as her husband wove his potent spell around her.

'And now you must tell me more about you, my dear,' he said, topping up her glass once more and signalling to the servants to withdraw. 'Tell me about your escape from Calderwood. I've never understood quite how you managed to get away without being caught.'

Jamie was now beginning to feel more than a little light-headed, but she set about explaining, as best she could, trying to overcome her natural embarrassment about 'borrowing' her brother's clothes and stealing out at dead of night.

'How did you manage the horse? It's a wonder you weren't heard in the stable.'

'I was not in the stable long, just a moment to put a halter on Cara and lead her out. She's very good.'

'Just a halter?' repeated Richard, amazed.

'I… Yes, well, it was too dangerous to spend time saddling her. And besides, they would have known then that I was dressed as a boy. So I rode bareback and let Cara find her own way home. I hoped they would think she had got loose by accident.'

Richard was gazing at his wife with new respect. 'You can ride bareback?'

With a slightly giggly laugh, Jamie admitted that she could. 'Astride too, I'm afraid,' she added guiltily, 'but only on Cara. At least, I have never tried on any other horse.'

'Cara. Is she your horse?'

'Not exactly. She belonged to my mother, and I sort of adopted her. Strictly speaking, she belongs to my father, I suppose, though no one else would want to ride such an old horse.'

Richard rose to escort his wife to the saloon, happy to forgo the solitary splendour of port or brandy for her increasingly fascinating company. Life with Jamie would never be dull. As he offered her his arm, he said softly, 'As soon as we are out of mourning, I must see you properly mounted. There is a mare at Harding that might suit... Or should you like me to try to buy Cara for you?'

'Richard!' gasped Jamie, her eyes shining. 'Oh, Richard, would you? Oh, thank you so much!' She was so overjoyed at his generous offer that she forgot all remaining constraint and, throwing her arms round her husband's neck, hugged him impulsively. No one had ever been so kind to her before.

For a second, Richard's hands hovered over her back, but then he forced them to his sides again. Like an endearing child, he thought, as she pulled away from him, looking a little sheepish. But the lady in her soon returned. Her hands went automatically to her hair.

'No, it's perfect, believe me,' he said with a warm smile. 'Not a curl out of place.' As he spoke, he reached out to touch the single ringlet which hung down on to her bare shoulder and moved it an infinitesimal distance to the right. 'Absolutely perfect,' he repeated, not quite succeeding in his attempts to keep his voice light and playful.

Jamie had managed not to shiver this time, perhaps because his fingers had not actually touched her skin, but she felt again that weird tingling of every nerve. She could not read his expression either. He seemed to be admiring *her*, of all people, when he could have had any number of beautiful women, like Emma Fitzwilliam. And he was going out of his way to be gentle and amusing. Oh, she did not understand it, even as she basked in it.

'How are your hands coming along?' he asked, when they sat once more in the saloon. He reached out to lift her right hand for examination in a very practical way. 'Those calluses will take a while, I suppose, but at least the skin is losing its redness.' He placed her hand back on her lap, noticing that she seemed to be reacting a little strangely. 'Jamie—are you all right, my dear?'

'Oh…yes. Yes, perfectly. It's just…' She giggled a little. 'I feel a little strange, that's all, as if everything were becoming hazy. I can't explain.'

'I can, I'm afraid,' he said flatly, remembering the champagne, which had been meant to relax her, not to make her sleepy. Obviously he had given her too much. 'May I suggest you retire now? You will feel better in the morning.' His voice betrayed the harshness of his self-criticism.

'Oh!' Jamie was conscious of the sudden withdrawal of all that enveloping warmth. 'Certainly, if that is what you wish, my lord.'

With surprising swiftness, considering her slight inebriation, she rose, bobbed a tiny curtsy and was gone, leaving him standing alone by the fire, cursing his own stupidity but quite unable to account for his wife's devastatingly sudden change of mood.

Tears were streaming down Jamie's cheeks as she ran up the stairs to her room and threw herself on to the bed. How could he change so much, so quickly, from gay and laughing to hard and withering? To send her to bed like an errant child! It was no better than Calderwood, to be sure! She continued to sob bitterly into her pillows, perversely grateful that she could indulge in her woes in private for once.

Jamie's sense of justice returned eventually. Hardinge House was nothing like Calderwood. Here she was cosseted, her every whim immediately gratified...except one. She wanted a true marriage, while her husband, however friendly he might be, seemed determined to keep her at arm's length. But he had wanted her before their wedding. Why not now?

Her inner devil whispered that he probably preferred the embraces of serving-girls to those of his lawful wife, maybe even unwilling serving-girls. No. No, that could not be, for he had not taken advantage of her when he had had the opportunity. She refused to believe him base.

And yet she could not account for his behaviour now. It was almost as if he were afraid of her. He never came into her chamber of his own free will— and he never stayed there a moment longer than necessary, even when he was forced to come. What if she were to go into his chamber instead?

She half-rose, wondering whether she had the courage to do such a thing. Why not? She was his wife! She tidied her hair before the glass, noting that the signs of her self-indulgent weeping had almost gone. Then she slipped her feet back into her evening shoes and crossed into their sitting-room.

There was no sound from Richard's chamber. He could be asleep. He might even be angry at being disturbed. She hesitated a moment. Then, squaring her shoulders and swallowing hard, she knocked softly and opened the door into Richard's room.

The fire blazed in the grate, the huge canopied bed was turned down and the brandy decanter stood ready on the table. But apart from those, the room was empty.

In the silence, the clock on the mantelshelf chimed twice. Two in the morning! How long had she lain in despair on her bed? And where was her husband?

Assailed by thoughts of where he might be—and with whom—Jamie ran from the room.

Chapter Eighteen

Next morning, Jamie forced herself out of bed at the usual hour, in spite of overwhelmingly low spirits and an aching head. How much champagne had she drunk last evening? She supposed that must be the chief cause of the terrible state she was in, although it could equally well be the shock of finding Richard absent in the middle of the night.

Annie took one look at her mistress's face and disappeared, returning five minutes later with a glass of murky liquid. 'Drink this, my lady,' she advised sternly. 'It will settle your stomach—and your head.'

Jamie bridled. 'What is it?'

'Sovereign remedy for the after-effects of overindulgence, m'lady,' said Annie smoothly, making little attempt to hide her disapproval. 'The valet's secret potion. If you swallow it quickly, you won't hardly taste it.'

Jamie flushed deeply at the thought that the whole household knew of her predicament. 'You asked Gregg for this for me?' She was outraged.

'No one else knows, m'lady. Gregg was making it

for his lordship in any case, so he just made a little
more than usual. Do drink it.' Her disapproval had
been replaced by concern now.

Jamie sniffed at the cloudy liquid. 'Ugh!' Then,
gritting her teeth, she tossed it off. 'Good God!' she
spluttered, after a moment of gasping for breath.
'What on earth is in it?'

Annie shrugged. 'Gregg will not say. He won't let
anyone watch when he mixes it either, so your secret
really is safe.'

After a few minutes of distinctly odd churnings in
her stomach, Jamie found she was indeed beginning
to feel better. Time to satisfy her curiosity. 'I am surprised my husband needs such a remedy this morning,
Annie. I had not noticed that he drank much at dinner
last night.'

The abigail commented airily, 'Oh, his lordship
never overindulges at home, my lady. At his clubs,
it's different of course, especially when they're playing deep. Last night, he…' She stopped, flushed, and
began to brush Jamie's hair.

Gaming! No wonder his chamber had been empty.
Dear God! If Richard were addicted to the tables, who
knew how it might end? Jamie knew well enough that
most of the Calderwood financial problems had re-
sulted from her father's insatiable appetite for gaming. Richard certainly lived well, but surely no estate,
however large, could withstand continued losses?
Especially after that iniquitous loan to her father.
What if…?

She forced herself to halt this totally unwarranted
descent into pessimism. One night at the tables—and

she knew of only this one—did not mark her husband out for a gamester, even if she dearly wished that he did not gamble at all. And at least it was better than what she had suspected last night.

She found herself wondering again if he kept a mistress, like so many men of his rank. A man who was past thirty could not be expected to live like a monk, even if he were now married. A cold lump settled in the pit of her stomach, like a lead weight, at the thought of Richard in the arms of another woman, any other woman.

Annie's bustling activity recalled her to the real world. She must join Richard at breakfast as if nothing had happened. She must try to use their time together to re-establish their rapport.

But there was no need, for her husband had already reached precisely the same conclusion and was a much more skilled practitioner of the art than she. He smiled a little apologetically as she took her seat at the breakfast table. 'Morning, m'dear.' Richard's greeting was quite breezy, considering the night he had had. 'Are you well this morning? I fancied I should make you an apology for plying you with a little too much champagne last night but, to be frank, you look to be blooming on it! Should I repeat the offence, do you think?'

'If I am blooming, it is thanks to Gregg's magic potion.'

'Works miracles, don't it? I was wondering why I seemed to have had short measure this morning. I shall have to speak to Gregg.'

'Oh, no, please,' gasped Jamie, blushing scarlet at the thought. 'If you—'

Richard grinned wickedly at her. 'I shall have to tell him that he must on no account provide his remedy to my wife when she is foxed. She should be left to endure the consequences of her own excesses. An appropriate penance, don't you agree?'

'Oh, by all means, my lord—on condition that you impose the same penance on yourself, of course,' Jamie retorted. 'For sin does not distinguish between the sexes, does it?' she added, with a sweet smile and a decidedly warlike glint in her eyes.

Richard raised both hands in token of surrender. 'I yield to your superior force, madam. Believe me, without Gregg's ministrations this morning, I should not be sitting here.'

'Indeed?'

He had the grace to look a little guilty and to admit that he had been rather too self-indulgent on the previous evening, both in terms of his gambling and his wine. 'But, thanks to the invaluable Gregg, we are both able to face the world again. And we shall have the whole day to ourselves. My agent will not send his report until this evening, and there's nothing more I can do until it arrives.' He smiled generously. 'So— I suggest we make that trip to Westminster Abbey. Can you be ready in half an hour?'

Jamie was just about to don the sables once more, when a maid brought up a message that some visitors were with his lordship in the blue saloon and her presence was requested. Intrigued, Jamie allowed Annie to hang up the sables again. It was very strange that Richard should be prepared to receive callers while the family was in deep mourning. 'I wonder who it may be?' she said almost to herself as she checked her appearance in the glass.

Richard came to take her hand as she entered the saloon. 'I have a delightful surprise for you, my dear. I want you to meet Sir Edward Fitzwilliam and his daughter Emma, two of my dearest friends.' He led her across to the visitors, continuing cheerfully, 'We have never stood on ceremony with one another, you must know. Why, Emma and I were thick as inkle-weavers when we were children.'

Jamie forced her leaden feet to move across the room to meet the visitors. If Richard noticed that she was pale, she hoped he would put it down to shyness.

The introductions were rapidly completed. Sir Edward was a large hearty gentleman, rather red-faced, which Jamie attributed to a love of good living. He took Jamie's hand in his own much larger one and expressed himself delighted to make her acquaintance. He had been intrigued to hear of Richard's sudden marriage, he admitted, but now that he had met the new Lady Hardinge, he could understand it perfectly.

Jamie was a little embarrassed by such fulsome compliments, especially from the father of the girl who had been Richard's intended bride, but she could detect no hint that Sir Edward's words were at all insincere. She smiled prettily, if a little shakily, and said all that was proper.

Miss Fitzwilliam seemed to be as open and friendly

as her father, both in her congratulations to the newly-weds and in her hopes that she and the new Countess might come to know each other better. Although Jamie agreed readily to the proposal, for to refuse would have been churlish, she shrank inwardly at the thought of friendship with the lovely Miss Fitzwilliam. On closer inspection, she proved to be everything that Jamie was not—tiny, blonde, blue-eyed, apparently possessed of every perfection of form and manner, and with the easy confidence which comes from long experience of the society world.

By contrast, Jamie felt large and clumsy, and ill-prepared for her new elevated station in life. No wonder Richard had planned to marry such a pattern card of feminine virtue! Jamie's small stock of confidence seemed to be ebbing away as she watched the easy intercourse between her husband and this lovely girl. It had been more comfortable to be a gardener's boy.

'I am so glad you have both come up to London, Richard, for otherwise we should not have seen you until the Season is over.' Miss Fitzwilliam had adroitly avoided asking directly why they had come, though the question was clearly uppermost in her mind.

'I had to come on business, Emma, so naturally my wife accompanied me. I am sorry I shall not have the pleasure of waltzing with you this Season, but no doubt there will be so many other gentlemen vying for your hand that you will not notice my absence.'

'Rogue!' exclaimed Miss Fitzwilliam. 'That is non-sense, and you know it! Not one of them waltzes half as well as you do.'

'Well, my dear,' interrupted her father, 'you will have to make the best of it, for Richard cannot possibly dance while he is in mourning. Perhaps that will encourage you to pay a little more attention to the eligible bachelors among your cavaliers instead of giving your hand to all comers. This will be your fourth Season, my girl. Beware! You are almost on the shelf!' It was clear from the indulgent smile which accompanied this warning that Sir Edward did not believe a word of it.

'I have paid attention to them, Papa,' protested the young lady, throwing him a look of reproach. 'You know that most of them covet my fortune rather than my person. I do so wish to marry a man I can both love and esteem, rather than one I must suspect of base motives,' she said a little wistfully. 'I suppose that means I shall have to marry someone with a fortune of his own, like Richard.'

'Well, we'll see, we'll see,' said Sir Edward placidly, smiling at his daughter. 'I have no wish to see you leave my roof, I'll readily admit.'

'Nor I,' echoed Richard. 'You must find a husband within ready striking distance of Harding, Emma, so that we may continue just as before.'

Suddenly, Miss Fitzwilliam laughed wickedly. 'I can tell you now, Richard, that Papa once had ambitions in your direction.'

'Emma!' Her father started to cough and turn very red.

She continued regardless. 'I had to tell him that we should not suit. A woman cannot marry a man who has been like a brother to her. We should have strangled each other before a month was up. Do you not agree, Richard?' Her eyes were dancing with suppressed mirth.

Richard laughed too, and nodded, moving to refill Sir Edward's glass. He threw a conspiratorial glance at Jamie and said, 'I doubt we should have lasted a week.'

Jamie was astonished. Richard did not look in the least embarrassed. Perhaps he was relieved to learn that Miss Fitzwilliam would have refused him?

Sir Edward had recovered his composure as he downed his sherry. 'Heaven preserve me from my wilful daughter,' he said, shaking his head. 'My only consolation is that she behaves with the utmost propriety when she is in company.'

'I am delighted to hear it, sir,' said Richard with an indulgent smile. 'And I know it to be true. I am only sorry that she and Jamie will not be able to go into society together—at least, not this Season. But perhaps they may become better acquainted in private. I am sure Jamie would welcome a chance to have a friend of her own age and station.' He looked enquiringly at his wife.

'"Jamie"?' repeated Miss Fitzwilliam, turning to Jamie with a friendly smile. 'Forgive my impertinence, ma'am, but may I ask about your unusual name? I have never heard of "Jamie" as a lady's name before.'

'My given name is Jessamyne,' admitted Jamie with a genuine, if rueful smile. Emma Fitzwilliam was no rival, that much was now clear. And she might even become a friend. '"Jamie" was a name given me by my mama. I much prefer it to Jessamyne.'

'No wonder,' added Richard with a grin. 'And I hope you will allow Emma to use it, my dear. I should hate to see you both standing on ceremony, such old friends as we are.' He raised his eyebrows expectantly.

'Of course,' conceded Jamie immediately.

'And you must call me "Emma", of course,' beamed that young lady. 'I do so hope we shall become friends.'

Jamie returned her smile with interest. 'I am sure we shall,' she said, with decision.

It was late afternoon by the time they returned from their delayed expedition to Westminster Abbey. Richard had insisted on taking Jamie all over the building, exploring every corner. And in the face of his determined good-humour, she had found herself enjoying every moment in his company and forgetting her lingering doubts.

When Jamie came upstairs to change for dinner, she saw that Annie had left the green gown in view, as a silent reminder. No such hint was necessary now. Jamie had already decided that she must take the initiative with her husband—somehow—and that it could no longer be delayed, if the distance between them were ever to be bridged. Waiting could only make matters worse for their marriage.

Not for the first time, she wished she had more experience of dealing with men, as she embarked on what would, she fervently hoped, be a seduction.

Heavens, she did not even know how to flirt, far less seduce! Still, if she let her love lead her… Love?

As she stood gazing fixedly at the green silk gown, she at last admitted to herself how she felt about her husband. She loved him! And now, she could see that it had been so for weeks, perhaps months. No wonder she had accepted his proposal, though all her finer instincts had prompted her to refuse him. He might have been better off with someone more like Emma Fitzwilliam, but he had chosen Jamie instead, and she could never give him up. She was able to recognise, finally, that her heart would be broken if she lost him now.

These moments of soul-searching served to strengthen her nerve for the encounter ahead. She would have to behave in a way she had never done before, never in all her life. And she must be prepared for her husband to reject her advances, as he had seemed ready to do every time the possibility of intimacy arose.

She had supposed that he still desired her, but what if he did not? Perhaps he was even thinking about someone else? She swallowed hard, trying to slow the thumping of her heart. She had to know the truth, she decided, whatever the cost to her self-esteem. If he did not want her as a true wife, she would be ready to settle for whatever lesser status might be on offer. Galling though it was to her pride, she knew there was no other choice for her. She could never leave him now.

Annie was allowed free rein over her mistress's appearance that evening and surpassed even her own high standards. The sea-green gown fitted Jamie to perfection, gliding over her slender figure, yet emphasising her feminine curves. With the matching ribbon threaded through her loose titian curls and Richard's emerald pendant clasped round her neck, she looked the complete antithesis of the pasty-faced dowd of Calderwood Hall.

Annie sighed as Jamie started to descend the stairs. 'Good luck,' she whispered softly.

Richard turned at the sound of the door opening and then stood transfixed as Jamie entered the room. He had not expected this. If she had been blooming before, she was now quite breathtaking. His heart lurched and began to beat very fast. Pushing aside all the questions which rose in his mind, he strode across the room to take both her hands and raise them, one by one, to his lips, drinking in the faint breath of her jasmine scent. This time she did not pull away. He felt a slight pressure of her fingers as she smiled up into his eyes.

'My dear, you look quite lovely tonight,' he began, a little uncertainly, searching for the proper words, 'and that green is exactly right, even more becoming than the black.'

She wondered for a moment if he were teasing her, but no, his eyes were warm and serious, perhaps too serious. 'I am glad you approve, my lord,' she answered rather primly, but smiling still.

'Madam, you tempt me with your words,' he said, with a mischievous twitch of the lips, trying to assume a stern tone of voice.

Jamie frowned a little, unsure of his mood, but did not pull away.

'Have you forgotten so soon, my dear, what I promised your punishment would be, if you continued to address me so formally?' He had forced his black brows together into a frown which was totally at variance with the sparkle in his eye.

'Oh,' gasped Jamie, 'but you would not!' She tried unsuccessfully to retreat. He was clasping her hands too tightly. 'Richard, you—'

'Better,' he pronounced solemnly, kissing her hands again and looking warmly into her eyes, 'but if I were you, I should not hazard too much on my husband's capacity for mercy. I pride myself on never making idle threats.'

'I had not thought that applied to your wife.' She allowed him to lead her to a seat and turned to look him full in the face. 'Does it?'

'Now, what am I supposed to say to that?' he teased. 'If I tell you that I shall never lay a finger on you, I shall be inviting you to become a disobedient, unmanageable wife. But if I promise to force your obedience with threats and violence, I risk losing your trust altogether.' He sought and held her gaze. 'Advise me, wife. What should I say?'

Jamie knew instinctively how she must reply. She did not hesitate. 'You should remind me of my marriage vows, husband, to love, honour and obey. You should ask me if I have so quickly forgotten all that I then promised.'

'And have you?' His voice had become suddenly husky.

She looked deep into his blue eyes, searching for some sign which would reveal what he wanted her to say. She could not be totally sure of what she saw there, but she quickly decided that she had no choice any more. The offer must be made—now—while her courage was high. In a low voice, which surprised her with its firmness, she said, 'I married you most willingly, my lord husband, and I shall keep my wedding vows—every single one—if I am permitted to do so.'

His sharp intake of breath proved that he had not misunderstood the import of her words. His cobalt eyes glowed with a new fierceness as he looked down into hers.

Richard could not tear his eyes from the green ones gazing unflinchingly into his. She was offering herself to him in the only way she could and waiting, totally vulnerable, like a cornered doe, to learn her fate— whether her husband would accept or reject her.

Richard's hand was gripping Jamie's so tightly that her fingers were starting to go numb, but she did not move a muscle to pull away.

Richard was quite oblivious of what he was doing. He was lost in those limpid eyes.

A discreet knock on the door broke the spell. 'Dinner is served, my lady,' intoned the butler and then quickly withdrew.

'Damn,' muttered Richard, releasing her hand. He rose from the sofa and turned to find that Jamie was still seated, apparently lost in thought. Had she even heard the butler's words?

'Jamie,' he said softly.

She looked up into his face and rose, a little unsteadily. Her eyes seemed to be brimming with tears.

Richard felt an answering tenderness welling up within him. Did she believe he was rejecting her? For a moment, he was at a loss for words as he gently cupped her face in his hands and gazed at her tempting lips. When he eventually spoke, his voice was very serious. 'Jamie, my dear, are you sure? Do you know what you are doing? I gave you my word, and you have it still. You do not need to do this.'

A single tear overflowed, running unheeded down her cheek and on to his hand. 'But I do, Richard,' she said simply. 'You gave me your word. Now I give it back to you, if you are willing to receive it.'

Richard found he had no words any more. Trying desperately to master the tide of passion which was threatening to drown him, he kissed her lips, gently at first, tasting her sweetness, but then, as she began to respond to him, with increasing fervour, pulling her tightly against his hardened body. For what seemed an eternity, both were lost in the whirling waters of that deepening kiss, until the realisation that Jamie's legs were no longer able to support her brought Richard back to a sense of where they were.

He tore his mouth away from hers, gasping for breath. Her eyes were huge and brilliant in her pale face. Her body was trembling. Without his arm around her, she would have fallen.

'I think we should go in to dinner, wife,' he began prosaically, trying to regain control of his treacherous body.

Jamie responded, not to his words, but to the tender

inflection in his voice and the warmth and desire in his eyes. He did want her—and he would make her his true wife, she was sure of it now. For the moment, it was enough. 'As you command, husband,' she said, bowing her head in mock obedience. 'Will you give me your arm?'

For Jamie, the meal passed in a dreamlike haze. She picked at the food served to her and drank a little—a very little—of the champagne which accompanied it. Although she was once again seated on her husband's immediate right, they did not touch once throughout the meal, for both were fully aware of the dangers which lay along that path. None the less, Jamie felt as if the warmth and tension in his body were radiating out to hers, making her nerves tingle and setting a whole flock of doves fluttering in her belly.

She could not know how much the play of these emotions enhanced her looks. Not daring to touch, Richard feasted his gaze on her instead—the brilliant eyes, the petal-soft complexion framed by silky curls, the wide mouth, ever so slightly bruised from his kisses, the elegant column of her neck tempting him down towards the beautiful breasts rising above her low-cut gown. The vision fired his flesh. He wanted nothing more than to slam his chair back from the table and carry her upstairs on the instant.

He tried instead to concentrate on the food on his plate and the wine in his glass. Presently, the second course was served. He watched as Jamie toyed with a little vanilla cream. Her wineglass, never more than half-full at the outset, was barely touched. 'Will you take a little more champagne, my dear?' he asked politely, ready to summon the butler from his post.

Jamie shook her head, murmuring something incoherent. The meal was clearly becoming something of an ordeal for her.

Richard threw down his damask napkin. 'I am afraid we are neither of us very hungry tonight, my dear,' he said, in his best conversational voice, starting to rise from the table. As he escorted Jamie into the hallway he said, in a voice loud enough to be heard by the servants, 'I fear the excesses of the last few days are taking their toll. Will you allow me to suggest we retire early? We shall have another long day tomorrow, I fancy.'

Jamie was just able to nod slightly but, luckily, not conscious enough to be embarrassed by the blatant invitation in his eyes. She allowed herself to be led up the stairs to their suite where, magically, neither abigail nor valet was to be seen.

Richard kicked the door shut and pulled her roughly into his arms, covering first her face and then her neck with urgent kisses. She arched into him, helpless, her hands gripping his strong body for support.

He made to pick her up and then stopped, placing his hands on her shoulders so that she was forced to face him. 'Jamie. Oh, Jamie, if you want to change your mind, you must do it now, else it will be too late.'

She shook her head, lifting her mouth for his kiss. There would be no going back now.

He lifted her in his arms then and carried her

through the connecting door to his chamber, to lay her on the huge canopied bed. She watched, in something of a daze, as he methodically snuffed all the candles in the room, leaving only the flickering firelight to cast ghostly shadows across his handsome face.

He came to her then, stretching out beside her on the bed as he had done once before, and drawing her into the encircling strength of his arms. He held her close, resting his lips on the top of her head to drink in the jasmine fragrance of her hair.

'Oh, Jamie,' he whispered, pulling the pins out of her hair one by one so that her curls fell free on to the pillow, 'how beautiful you are, my little wife.'

Then he began to kiss her, more gently than before, for he knew he must not allow his own desire to dictate the pace, lest he frighten her.

But he had reckoned without Jamie's own responses. She had loved and desired him for so long that, innocent though she was, the first touch of his hand on her breast set her whole body aflame. Her every sense was alive to his presence, eagerly responding to his lead as her clothes disappeared, one by one. She was no longer in the real world, but in a sensuous paradise where she felt as if she were floating towards oblivion.

Richard had stopped kissing her. Her eyes flew open to find he was simply gazing at her, with loving tenderness. Apart from the emeralds at her throat and in her ears, she was now naked, her body glowing rosily in the warm light. The glint of desire in his eyes was unmistakable. Jamie found she was blushing all over. Without thinking, she tried to cover herself.

He laughed throatily, pushing her hands gently back to the bed. 'Your blushes make you even more beautiful, love. Do not try to hide yourself from me, please. Just let me look at you.'

In spite of herself, she felt her blushes deepen, but she no longer tried to resist. 'But you...' she whispered, half-accusingly, her eyes wandering to his body which was still fully clothed, apart from coat and waistcoat.

Richard guided her hands to the buttons of his shirt. 'Will you help me then, love?' he asked softly.

A shiver ran through her body as she undid a button with clumsy fingers, touching the bare skin beneath. He looked at her in alarm, covering her hands with his so that she shivered again, more noticeably than before.

'Jamie, why are you still afraid of me? I swear to you there is no need.'

Jamie's heart turned over at the catch in his voice and the anxiety in his eyes. She smiled shyly up at him, dropping a tiny kiss on the back of his hand where it clasped hers. 'I am not afraid of you, Richard, nor have I ever been. It is just that, whenever I touch you, I...' She broke off, blushing fiercely again, and buried her face in his shirt front.

'Dear God, how could I have been so blind?' he moaned, as he began to kiss her deeply once more, pushing her on to her back so that he could tear off his own clothes without lifting his mouth from hers.

Then there were no more words, only the nerve-tingling excitement of touching and teasing, stroking and suckling. Her breasts seemed to swell to fill his ministering hands, the rosy peaks hardening beneath the expert touch of his fingers and his lips. The fluttering in her belly had become a churning, longing ache.

She moaned, pleadingly, as his fingers explored lower, discovering just how ready she was. That sound was almost his undoing as he parted her thighs and moved to enter her. She arched towards him, unconsciously raising her hips to meet him.

'Forgive me, my love,' he whispered hoarsely, covering her mouth with his as he thrust deeply into her soft warmth. He heard her gasp beneath him and saw her eyes fly open, wide with shock. He held himself totally still, wishing he could draw all her pain into himself, could see the return of desire to her eyes. 'Forgive me, darling,' he said again, achingly sad.

The pain quickly melted away as Jamie became more and more conscious of the beloved warmth within her and of her overpowering need to be closer to him. She tried to shake her head, to tell him there was nothing to forgive, but she was not given the chance to speak.

The moment he saw the love and passion returning to her eyes, he took her mouth again in fierce possession.

And then he began to move within her, in long slow strokes, stretching his control to breaking point as he strove to bring her to the fulfilment he longed to give her, ruthlessly suppressing his own needs as he concentrated on fuelling Jamie's rising passion.

She moaned again, writhing beneath him. 'Oh, Richard. Please,' she pleaded incoherently. The tension was mounting in her body, begging for release, driving her to undiscovered heights of awareness, until finally it exploded in spasms of kaleidoscopic ecstasy.

As the shudders of completion racked her, Richard's rigid control was shattered. He drove into her one last time to find his own release and collapsed on top of her. His selfless consideration for his virgin wife had brought him to a climax which fulfilled him in a way he had never known. He had not thought such paradise existed, this side of heaven.

After a moment, he rolled on to his side, bringing Jamie with him, waiting for the pounding of their hearts to slow. They lay together for a long time, intimately entwined, savouring the glowing aftermath of their lovemaking. Only the sound of their breathing broke the stillness. At last Richard stirred. He needed to hear her speak, to hear her words of love and reassurance, but still he could find no words of his own. So, softly, he kissed her bruised lips as if to ask forgiveness for her pain.

She looked at him in wide-eyed wonder. 'I never thought…' she began tremulously. 'Oh, Richard! Is it always like this?'

'Between us, it will always be so, I hope,' he vowed tenderly, stroking her cheek. 'Darling Jamie, my little love, forgive me for hurting you. That, at least, will never come again, I promise you.'

She was puzzled for a second. Then she smiled, radiantly, allowing her free hand to stray down the length of his back. 'It is already forgotten,' she said, daring to explore lower.

He rolled quickly on to his back to trap her wandering hand. 'Madam wife,' he grinned, 'I am sure that you will wish me to return you to your own bed before morning. But if you continue with such tantalising behaviour, you are like to be disappointed.'

She transferred her hand to his chest and began to walk her fingers down towards his flat stomach, an age-old smile on her face. 'Disappointed?' she repeated innocently. 'No. I don't think so.'

Chapter Nineteen

The house was already stirring when Richard carried Jamie back to her own bedchamber, tucking her lovingly beneath the covers. 'Sleep now, my love,' he insisted gently, smiling as he remembered just how much she needed it. 'I shall return later when you are rested.' He started to leave.

'Richard?' She sounded anxious. She should have no reason to be so.

'What is it, darling?' He turned quickly at her question and came to sit down on the edge of the bed, not touching her, though his gaze travelled lovingly over her face, seeking for the cause of her concern.

'What are you going to do?'

He looked suddenly grim. 'I am going to visit my agent again. He reports that he may have discovered who your father's London man is. I admit I am not very hopeful, but this is the only lead I have. Please understand, Jamie. I must do this alone. It might not be safe for you to come.'

'I do understand, Richard. But please take care.'

'I shall.' His gaze softened once more. She really

was an exceptional woman, in more ways than one. He grinned mischievously. 'Besides, I need my wife to be fully recovered before this evening, lest she…er…lack the energy for more enjoyable pursuits.' Ignoring her obvious confusion, he reached forward to pick up her hand for a gentle kiss, affectionate but with the promise of passion to come. Tonight, he would slip the Hardinge betrothal ring on to her hand. The diamond belonged there now, surely? 'Until this evening, then?'

'Yes,' she whispered. 'Until this evening.' She snuggled down contentedly and he left her to sleep the morning away.

It was early afternoon before she was wide awake, bathed and ready to face the world. But there was nothing pressing for her to do. Hardinge House ran perfectly smoothly without any intervention from her. Emma Fitzwilliam would not call again until the morrow, so there was no one but the servants for her to talk to. Richard's unpleasant errand would surely keep him occupied for hours.

Books and letter-writing held no attractions for her—this was no time for quiet pursuits. Jamie felt so vibrant, so full of life and love, that she wanted to sing and dance and shout from the rooftops. She longed for a good gallop, to feel the wind in her hair and the power of a horse beneath her. None of that was possible, not for a lady in mourning, so she decided to make do with fresh spring air and exercise— a good, brisk walk in the park. She would look for ideas for a spring garden at Harding.

* * *

An hour later, much invigorated and still bubbling with happiness, she was just about to cross the square to return to the house, when a closed carriage overtook her and drew up beside the flagway a little ahead. Her heart sank as she recognised it— Calderwood! Her glorious day was suddenly clouded.

'My lady, perhaps we should go back to the house?' urged Annie. But her warning words were too late. A white head was poking out of the window and calling to Jamie.

'Papa!' cried Jamie, shocked by the sudden encounter. Her mind was in a whirl.

'Come here, girl,' he commanded. 'You don't expect me to shout across the square, do you?'

Automatically obedient to her father's penetrating voice, Jamie approached the carriage, trying to read her father's stern expression. What was he doing here?

'That's better,' he said curtly, 'but it's cold with the glass down. Come, step inside for a moment, I need to speak to you.'

Jamie hesitated and then backed away a little.

'It's about your sisters,' he added, swinging open the door. Her father had drawn away from the door as he spoke, so that she could no longer see his face in the shadowy interior. 'Come, do as I bid you!'

His insistence made Jamie increasingly suspicious. 'Papa—'

As she turned round to look for Annie, she realised that the two grooms had climbed down from the back of the carriage and were almost upon her. She started to run, but they seized her by the arms and bundled

her through the open door before she had gone more
than a few steps. A sudden violent movement of the
carriage threw her back on to the seat. Her father
calmly leaned across her to pull the door closed while
the coach gathered speed out of the square.

'What are you doing, Papa?' she cried.

'What I should have done long ago,' he growled
fiercely. 'Making sure you do your duty by your family.'

'But I am married, Papa,' she pleaded desperately.
'You know that I am. My husband wrote to you.'

'Your marriage was illegal and will be annulled,'
he stated flatly. 'I gave my word that you would
marry Ralph Graves, and I intend to see my pledge
redeemed. You may forget your precious Lord
Hardinge. He is lost to you now.'

Jamie looked round anxiously for some means of
escape from the swaying vehicle. Anything was preferable to letting her father carry her off to Ralph
Graves! The only option would seem to be to throw
herself out of the carriage. She might be injured in
the process, but even that was preferable to what her
father intended for her. She began to edge towards
the door.

'You may be easy, my dear,' said her father sar-
castically. 'There will be no more escaping. My servants will foil any attempt you might dare to make.
There is no hope for you in that direction, you may
be certain. Who would dare to help a wilful girl
against the lawful claims of her father?'

There was no point in saying that the lawful claims
of her husband should come first. Her father was ob-

sessed with preventing her from thwarting his plans. Logic would never reach him, not from her.

Jamie forced herself to sit back in her seat, closed her eyes and tried to regain control of her thoughts. She must keep calm if she were to have any chance of escaping from this nightmare.

She took a deep breath, willing her pulse to slow. Annie had seen what happened, she told herself. Annie would tell Richard. Surely he would come to find her? She held tightly to that hope, a talisman and a shield against despair, as the Calderwood carriage sped out of London.

Annie stood petrified on the flagway, watching in disbelief as the Calderwood horses were whipped up and the carriage rattled off at top speed. She had recognised the white head, and now she knew the thin hand which reached out to pull the door shut. Sir John—and he was kidnapping Miss Jamie!

She tried to shout, but there was no one about to heed her cries. Besides, who would take the part of an abigail against a gentleman? Her only hope of finding help would be Hardinge House, so she picked up her skirts and ran as fast as she could round the square, banging urgently on the knocker of the front door.

The butler opened the door in the midst of her hammering. He looked more than a little taken aback to find only a servant standing there. It was a flagrant breach of etiquette. 'Whatever is the matter, Miss Smithers?' he asked, moving aside to let her enter. 'Where is her ladyship?'

'Is his lordship back yet?' gasped Annie, trying to master her distress.

'Why, no. He sent a message for her ladyship, just after you went out, to say he would be late. He was being taken to meet someone who had important information.'

'Oh, God!' moaned Annie. 'What are we to do?'

'I think you had better come and sit down, Miss Smithers,' said the butler kindly. 'Perhaps I can be of some assistance?'

It did not take her long to tell him what had happened. He was suitably concerned, but he had little practical help to offer for recovering Jamie, other than the obvious remedy of sending to ask for his lordship at his clubs.

No trace of Lord Hardinge was to be found. It was more than three interminable hours before he eventually returned.

'My lord,' began Annie, dropping a slight curtsy as she hurried across the hall, 'thank God you are come back!'

Richard recognised immediately that her words could mean nothing but trouble. 'Annie!' he cried, using his wife's mode of address for the first time, for it was his wife who was uppermost in his mind. 'What is the matter?'

'She is gone, my lord!' exclaimed Annie somewhat vaguely, preparing to launch into her tale of woe.

Richard raised a hand to stop her in mid-flow. 'Come into the library. Now, Annie,' he continued anxiously as he closed the door, 'tell me what has happened.'

As she explained, the colour drained from his face and his jaw clenched tight. His anguish was almost unbearable when he realised just how much time he had lost. The trail would be well-nigh cold by now. Pray God her father had taken her to Calderwood. If she were anywhere else, he might never find her.

'There is no chance that my wife went willingly, is there?'

'No, my lord, none,' answered Annie immediately. 'She was forced into the carriage, and her father drove off without even closing the carriage door. The coachman whipped up the horses as soon as her ladyship was inside. It was obviously pre-arranged.'

'But why on earth are they still pursuing her?' he cried angrily. 'There must be more to this than injured pride.'

Annie shook her head helplessly.

'No matter,' Richard continued, without giving Annie time to respond. 'We can resolve that later. There is no time to lose now. First we must find her, and get her out of her father's clutches. By God, if he…' He broke off abruptly, refusing to allow his emotions to rule him when there was so much to be done to rescue Jamie.

He then proceeded to issue precise and detailed instructions to his servants about his imminent departure. In barely twenty minutes, his carriage was on its way to Calderwood Hall.

Their progress was slow. The streets of London were thronged with traffic. It seemed to take hours to make their way out of the city, in spite of all the coachman's efforts. They would make only slow progress after darkness fell, especially if the sky did not clear.

Richard tried to make the time pass by imagining the worst possible punishments he could inflict on his father-in-law, but it did not serve. Jamie's pale face, with her eyes full of fear, could not be banished from his thoughts. He could not even pray.

It was almost three in the morning when they drew up at Calderwood. The journey had been accomplished remarkably quickly in the circumstances, thanks to the skill of the coachman and some welcome intervals of moonlight. The passengers inside had lapsed into silence long before. Anything they might say would simply intensify their fears.

Calderwood Hall stood dark and totally silent. Somewhere an owl hooted eerily. Inside the carriage, Annie shuddered.

Richard wasted no time. He leapt down from the carriage and ran up the steps to the main door. He lifted the heavy brass knocker and began to pound it, venting his frustration on the dark oak panelling. The sound echoed strangely in the darkness.

Eventually, a candle was seen at an upstairs window. Someone in the Hall was checking on the identity of the noisy arrivals. The candle disappeared again, but no one came to open the door.

Richard continued his pounding.

'Will you cease than infernal noise?' shouted a man's voice from an upstairs window. In the darkness, it was impossible to discern the owner of the voice.

'Not until this door is opened,' yelled Richard, attacking the knocker with increased ferocity.

'There is nothing for you here,' shouted the voice in reply. 'Go away.'

'I have come for my wife, and I shall not leave without her.'

The upstairs voice cackled nastily at that. 'Will you so? Will you indeed? You will be here a vastly long time, then, my impetuous young friend, for your wife, as you dare to call her, is not here. *My daughter* is safely tucked away where you will not find her and where she will remain until she has done her duty. You will never set eyes on her again. Now, begone! Before I set the dogs on you, you misbegotten abductor of children!'

Richard was suddenly very still. 'So you think to deprive me of my wife, do you, Sir John? I warned your crony of the risks of that. I now warn you. Unless you release her immediately, it will be the worse for you. You have my solemn word on that!'

Sir John's disembodied voice cackled again, louder this time. 'And now I warn *you*, my lord. She is *my daughter, not your wife*, not any more. You have no power and no rights.' His voice rose, almost to a scream. 'And in any case, it is too late!'

The window slammed shut, the sound echoing in the sudden silence.

Richard closed his eyes for a brief second, then turned sharply on his heel and covered the distance back to the coach in three strides. 'Drive to the nearest inn for fresh horses, William,' he commanded, flinging himself into the coach.

He opened a concealed flap in the carriage to withdraw a pair of wicked-looking pistols. He began methodically to check their priming, his lips set in a grim line. If he had to use them, he would make sure he did not miss—even if he were hanged for it.

'My lord?' Annie whispered apprehensively. 'What will you do?'

He looked quickly up at her, smiling mirthlessly. 'I am not about to murder my father-in-law, Annie, much though he may deserve it. No. In fact, I should thank him! He has been just a little too clever this time. He has told me where she is!'

He put the pistols back in their hiding place. 'Sir John can wait. I have a score to settle in another quarter now. Pray heaven we are in time!'

Chapter Twenty

Jamie awoke to total darkness. She had no idea where she was or how she had come there. All she knew was that she felt dreadful. Her head ached abominably, her mouth tasted foul, and her body was stiff and bruised.

She tried to move to ease the stiffness, but she could not. Her arms were bound beneath her. Even her ankles were tied. All she could do was to roll on to her side, to take the weight of her body off her hands and upper arms.

Memory began to return, haphazardly at first. She remembered the start of her journey quite clearly, from her total stupidity in going anywhere near that carriage in Hanover Square, until the point where they had reached the posting-inn for the first change. Her father—she could not think of him without being overcome with fury—her father had not permitted her to leave his carriage at the inn. He had merely condescended to order a cup of coffee for her, to keep out the cold, he had said. And she had drunk it, as the only shred of warmth being offered her.

After that, the memories were only fragments. She did not know how long they had travelled, nor the route they had taken. She had only a vague recollection of other changes of horses and of driving for many hours, sometimes on very poor roads. She had been asleep—drugged, she concluded bitterly, by her own father!

What a fool she had been. She should have run the moment she saw him. He did not care for her in the least—only for his own warped desires. But she refused to allow herself to dwell on what her father intended for her. More important to set about trying to escape! She forced her mind to sift methodically through the few facts she had about her perilous situation.

When the first light of dawn began to filter through the window of her prison, it revealed a small, unfamiliar room under the eaves of the house. From the look of the layers of cobwebs and dust, and the smell of damp, the room was not used. The bed on which she lay had no covering on the thin, lumpy mattress. Apart from the bed, there was a chair and a table. The stout door was bound to be locked.

Jamie swung her legs to the floor and pulled herself into a sitting position. Then, with an effort, she forced herself to stand, praying that her legs would not buckle under her. So far, so good! At least her legs were not totally numb.

She hopped across to the little window, trying to be as quiet as possible, and peered out through the grimy pane. Below her was a large park with fine trees, bordered on one side by dense woodland. In the distance, she could see cows grazing and smoke rising from cottage chimneys. It was an idyllic picture—which she had never seen before. She had not the least idea of where she was. So much for her hope that she was at Calderwood, where some of the servants might be persuaded to help her to escape. Here there would be no one. Her heart sank a little.

At the sound of heavy footsteps on the stairs, she hopped quickly back to the bed and flopped on to it, resuming her earlier position. The footsteps stopped outside the door. She held her breath, listening to the sound of the key turning in the lock. Then the door swung open to reveal a huge and menacing figure—Caleb!

In her shock at seeing him again, Jamie recoiled, her green eyes huge in her pale face.

'Well, so we're awake, are we, missy?' he sneered, advancing towards the bed to tower over her, clearly enjoying the sight of her panic. 'Never thought ter see me again, did yer, you an' yer precious lord?'

Jamie was not about to let this man believe he had the upper hand, no matter how hopeless her situation might be. But she was acutely conscious of his clenched fists and the veins standing out livid purple on his forehead. He was unpredictable—a very dangerous man. She must force herself to be calm.

'What is this place?' she asked quietly.

'Ye'll find out soon enough, missy,' he replied with a nasty laugh. 'Soon enough.'

'I need a drink, Caleb. Will you bring me one?'

He shook his head. 'Master'll see ter that. I ain't ter do anything fer ye, 'cept'n ter keep yer all right an' tight 'til he arrives. Nice little spot I've chosen fer yer, ain't it?' He looked round the miserable attic with a satisfied smirk. 'But this'll be like paradise ter yer *after*, once master's seen ter ye. Not long ter wait now.' His smirk had widened to a gloating grin.

He said no more. He was waiting for her to ask who the 'master' might be, but she knew he would merely continue to torment her if she did, so she said nothing. She gazed past him as though he were not there, refusing to betray her fear and loathing.

'Toffee-nosed little hussy!' he spat. 'But the master'll soon change all that, never you fear! Not long now!' he said again, with relish, and left the room, locking the door behind him.

Jamie heard him retreating down the wooden staircase. Silence descended once more.

She lay on her side, staring vacantly into the middle distance, trying to make sense of what was happening to her. Caleb again! Caleb, who had tried to kidnap her once already! But how could he be involved with her father? Unless…

She remembered again Richard's words on their wedding eve—a gentleman's servant had paid Caleb and his accomplice to kidnap her. Her father? She wished she could dismiss such wickedness in him, but, in truth, she could not. Her father seemed like a man obsessed, willing to go to any lengths to achieve his ends. He might even be mad. She shuddered involuntarily, before hauling her thoughts back to her immediate predicament.

Where on earth was she? She had never been to a house with a park like this one. Who might—?

The sound of returning footsteps on the stairs interrupted her fevered train of thought. The door was thrown open. Without a word, Caleb crossed to the bed. He reached his huge arms towards her and picked her up as though she weighed no more than a feather. 'Let's go,' he growled, tossing her so roughly over his shoulder that all the breath was forced out of her body.

Caleb carried her down the stairs, making light work of her attempts to struggle. The stairwell was dark and smelled of dust. Reaching the floor below, he flung open a door and carried Jamie into the room beyond, throwing her on to a large bed with a grunt of satisfaction. Then he took some cord from his pocket and tied her feet to the bedpost. 'Don't want yer ter go wanderin' about, do we?' he sneered. 'Master's decided my choice o' room ain't fitting, but he'd be mortal offended if yer was ter leave his.' As the door closed, his laugh echoed in the hallway.

Jamie lay helpless, desperately trying to control the fear which flooded through her at this new turn of events. 'Richard,' she whispered, over and over again, 'Richard, I love you. I know you will come.' The constant repetition slowed her racing pulse and her over-rapid breathing. She refused to believe he would not come. And she had to be ready to help him.

She found that this second room, though neglected, was a great improvement on her earlier prison. It was quite large and furnished with heavy old-fashioned pieces, dulled through lack of care. The bed on which she lay was soft and made up with linens. The bed hangings above and behind her were silk, sadly faded and torn, as were the curtains at the tall windows. It must once have been a fine chamber.

'How very pleasant to see you again, my dear,' said a voice from the door. 'I do apologise for the mistake about your earlier accommodation.'

Jamie gasped and then steeled herself as she turned towards the sound. The door had opened so quietly that she had not heard it. The voice, however, was the unmistakable high-pitched whine of Ralph Graves!

'I am sorry I was not present to do the honours myself when you arrived but, nevertheless, welcome to Bathinghurst, Jessamyne. I promised you a visit, did I not?'

'This is not quite what I had in mind,' retorted Jamie hotly, giving her anger full rein to prevent him from seeing how frightened she was.

'Ah, no, nor I, but it has its compensations, as you will soon find out. We shall enjoy getting to know one another better, my dear, I promise you.'

His lascivious smile made her skin crawl. 'My husband will kill you for this,' she hissed venomously through clenched teeth. 'But, if you let me go, you would have time to escape—'

Ralph Graves' cruel laugh echoed round the chamber. 'You have no husband, Jessamyne, not yet. Your so-called marriage was illegal and is to be annulled. Your father will already have set the wheels in motion, you may be sure.'

Jamie gripped her lower lip between her teeth to hide its trembling.

'Our wedding will take place in due course, my

dear, just as your father intended. In the meantime, you will remain here at Bathinghurst, learning the duties of a wife. You take my meaning?' he leered.

She lifted her chin proudly. 'I shall never submit to you,' she vowed. 'Never.'

'Never is a long time, Jessamyne. And there are ways of making you change your mind. You might like to think about that. Unfortunately, I have business to attend to today, so I cannot stay to…further our acquaintance. For the moment, I shall leave you to consider your position.' Then he was gone.

After the briefest moment of reflection, Jamie cursed her foolish pride. Antagonising him would not help her. He would keep her trussed up like a fowl for plucking. He would enjoy humbling her, depriving her of every last vestige of her will to resist. She must gull him into believing she had given up all hope of rescue—humour him a little. A shudder ran through her, at the thought that she might have to suffer his hands on her. But she refused to be ruled by her demons. She set about planning her tactics for their next encounter.

No one came near her for several hours but when, eventually, the door opened once more, she was ready for him.

'Cousin Ralph,' she pleaded through parched lips, 'may I have something to drink?' She had schooled her features to hide every trace of rebellion.

He gazed down at her, clearly gratified to see that his tactics were working. 'Very well, my dear, since you ask so prettily.' From somewhere behind one of the huge cupboards she heard the sound of liquid being poured. He approached the bed, carrying a half-full tumbler.

In spite of the numbness in her limbs, Jamie struggled into a sitting position before he could get near enough to touch her. 'Will you not free my hands, sir?' she pleaded, trying to make her submission appear complete. 'They are so very painful, tied as they are.'

He assessed her thoughtfully for several moments. 'You cannot escape from here in any case,' he concluded with evident satisfaction, 'since the door will be locked and there is no other way out of this room. I advise you not to try the window, by the bye. It is locked, naturally—and it is quite a long drop,' he added nastily, savouring the shock on her face. He placed the tumbler on the bedside table and then, taking a vicious-looking knife from his pocket, he cut her hands free.

She gasped as the blood rushed back into her fingers. The pain in her shoulders was excruciating as she moved her hands from behind her back. Automatically, she began to rub the red weals on her wrists, ignoring the gleeful smile on his face.

'A timely reminder, I suggest, my dear, that willing compliance with my wishes is advisable. For this is a mere token of what I *might* do.' He handed her the tumbler of water which she drank greedily, refusing to look at him.

'You will remain here for the present. This chamber is perfectly adequate for your needs. Caleb will be on guard outside the door, so do not attempt anything foolish or I might find a need to chastise you further. Caleb would welcome such an opportunity, I am sure. He abhors half-wits. And he hates you!'

Jamie continued to concentrate on rubbing her wrists.

'Caleb will bring your meals to you and anything else you need,' continued Graves. 'I shall join you here for dinner this evening, I think, and afterwards we can get to know each other a little better, hmm?'

Jamie would not allow herself to dwell on what lay behind his ominous words. She forced herself to smile up at him. 'I did not know Caleb was in your service. It was you, then, I suppose, who tried to carry me off from Harding?'

'A sadly botched business but, luckily, the man who was caught knew nothing of my part in it. And as for Caleb—well, he was the best I could find nearby at such short notice. It helped, of course, that he was so keen to take revenge on you, young lady. I should beware of giving him any opportunity, if I were you.'

She ignored his threat. 'But why go to such lengths?' she exclaimed. 'Is it simply because I slighted you? Let me go! Please! After all, I can bring you nothing.'

Graves went off into peals of laughter which almost doubled him up. 'How little you know, my dear, you and your precious Earl. What a pity I shall never be able to tell him, face to face!' He crossed to the door, still chortling at his private joke. 'I shall leave you to untie the rest of the knots yourself. It will help to bring the feeling back into your fingers!'

The door closed behind him with a thud, and the key was turned in the lock.

First things first! Jamie struggled to undo the cords which bound her. It took several minutes, for her fingers seemed to have lost all feeling and the knots were more than thorough. But at last she was free.

She put her feet to the floor to try her legs. It was very painful, but she could just about walk. She moved with difficulty at first, but soon she was pacing up and down the room, trying to get the strength back into her limbs again, while she reviewed her situation.

Most decidedly, it was not good. There was nothing in the room that she could use as a weapon. The water jug was not stout enough. Apart from that, the room and all the cupboards were empty. There was not even a set of fire irons by the grate.

An idea came to her, a mad, perilous notion. At first she pushed it aside because of the enormous risk. She continued to pace, seeking for some alternative solution. She found none.

If she were to have any chance of avoiding the attentions of Cousin Ralph, she must make do with what she had, whatever the risk. She had no choice. She went to the door, before she lost her nerve.

'Caleb,' she called through the thick wood, 'are you there?'

'Aye. What is it?'

'Your master said you would look to my needs. I am freezing in here. I need you to light a fire.' She heard a low grunt and then nothing more. She spoke his name again, but there was no answer. There was no way of knowing whether he would comply with her request.

Amazingly, he did. Some fifteen minutes later, he opened the door to bring in logs and kindling. Jamie retreated prudently to the furthest corner of the room, putting as much distance as possible between them. He seemed so unpredictable—and she doubted whether Graves would restrain his violence. Still, he seemed marginally less terrifying with his back to her, kneeling at the grate.

'I never suspected you worked for Mr Graves, Caleb,' she ventured, trying to keep her voice even.

'Lots o' things you don't know, ain't there, eh?' he replied nastily, without bothering to turn round.

Jamie allowed herself a tragic sigh. 'Yes, I have been a fool. But how was I to guess that a mere gardener could plan a kidnapping?' She noted with satisfaction how the muscles in his massive shoulders tensed at her biting sarcasm.

He turned his head for a moment to glare at her. 'This "mere gardener" can plan a deal more'n that, I'll have yer know, Miss High an' Mighty. Who do yer think made sure we got yer in London, eh? Yer father's plan wouldn't never have worked. I told him yer wouldn't get in his coach unless we forced yer.'

'I'll admit you have been very clever, Caleb. But why did you throw your lot in with Graves in the first place? If you're caught—'

'Won't be,' Caleb grunted, laying the final logs in the grate. 'His way, I gets my revenge and I gets paid as well.' He laughed. 'Followed ye all over London, I did, and yer never once suspected. Never once. A feeble pair y'are, ye and yer lordling. And now he's lost ye fer good. Or p'rhaps it's fer bad, eh? Eh?'

Jamie did not speak. She knew she would not be able to keep her voice steady.

Caleb turned back to the grate to light the fire, which was soon crackling merrily. 'Won't be leaving yer no extra logs, though,' he said, rising from the hearth. 'The master may think ye're tamed, but I knows better. Think ter hit me o'er the head wi' one o' these, did ye, dearie? Well—think again!' Gathering up all the unburnt logs, he left.

'No, Caleb,' she whispered softly as the key turned once more in the lock. 'I might have tried it, if you had given me a chance. But there are other options you have overlooked. I have a better plan than yours.'

It took the best part of an hour to make all her preparations. Everything she did had to be quiet and careful, lest she arouse Caleb's suspicions. Once, as a curtain tore suddenly under her desperate tugging, she thought he must hear and come in. But he did not.

She continued her painstaking work. She dared not rush, for her very life might depend on the care she took now.

When at last all was ready, she crossed to kneel by the grate, pulling a long brand from the flames. She could feel the searing heat from it on her face. She moved swiftly to the door and set the flame to the pile of torn hangings she had heaped there. Dry as dust, they caught immediately. Within seconds, there was a huge blaze licking at the door and the panelling around it.

Jamie did not stop to admire her handiwork, or the speed with which the flames were taking hold. She picked up the water jug and hurled it through the locked window with all her strength. Glass flew everywhere. If only the fire could hold Caleb for a few minutes!

She grabbed hold of the rope of twisted bedclothes which she had tied to the four-poster. It was nowhere near long enough to reach the ground. No matter! Anything was better than the fate which awaited her with Ralph Graves!

Hitching up her skirts, she climbed nimbly over the sill. She began to descend the rope, hand over hand. Halfway down, she thought she heard distant shouts from above. She needed to climb faster.

At last, she came to the end of the rope and looked down. It seemed a very long way to the ground—but perhaps the flower-bed would break her fall.

She had no choice now. She let go of the rope.

Chapter Twenty-One

Richard was on the box for the final stretch of the journey, allowing William a last, well-earned rest. As the carriage rounded the bend to enter the long driveway leading to Bathinghurst, Richard saw part of the house in the distance, half-hidden by the rise—and there were flames shooting out of the roof at one end!

Dear God, the house was on fire. Jamie… He whipped up his lathered team in a desperate attempt to gain a little more speed. If only he were in time…

Nobody seemed to be fighting the fire. A small knot of servants stood huddled together on the front lawn, shoulders slumped, watching helplessly. Of Jamie— and of Graves—there was absolutely no sign. Richard groaned aloud. The house seemed to be an inferno, apart from the few rooms on the ground floor by the entrance. If she were anywhere but there…

The horses were already snorting in fright at the smell of the fire, as he pulled them to a screeching halt, twenty yards short of the house. Leaping from the box, he sprinted to the partly-open main door and pushed his way inside. The hall was surprisingly smoke free.

For a moment he heard nothing, except the voracious sound of the fire, inexorably consuming the house. Then, a cracked voice spoke to him from somewhere above, its source indistinguishable. 'You have come then, Hardinge? Ah, but you are too late. Too late. Your precious *wife* set the fire herself, and now she has perished in it, damn her. I am glad you are here to see it. I may not have her, but neither will you. Neither will you!' A shout of hysterical laughter was followed by silence, and then the sound of something heavy being dragged across bare floorboards.

Richard refused to believe the evidence of his eyes and ears. Most of all, he refused to believe Graves. All through the journey from Calderwood, he had seemed to hear her voice, repeating his name, over and over, with the words 'I love you'. He thought he could hear them still. She could not be dead. Somehow he would have known if she were. He refused to believe it.

Heart pounding fit to burst, he raced out of the house. He must find something to shield him against the smoke and flames. Precious minutes ticked away as he and his companions searched for water. The few house servants were useless—they seemed to have been frozen into immobility.

At last a bucket of water was found by the stables. Pulling a dripping rug over his head, Richard ran back to the house. The eerie sound of scraping could still be heard, seemingly farther away now. The smoke was thicker than ever. Only by the doorway could he see his way at all.

He began to feel his way up the stairs, step by step. The acrid smoke was soon choking him. In his head he could still hear her voice calling 'Richard! Richard!' He must find her! He must save her!

Her voice seemed to be getting louder. He prayed that he was not imagining it. No. She must be here. She must be closer to the top of the stairs than he had dared to hope. He made his way along the landing, wondering desperately where to begin.

The first doorway was engulfed in flames. The door itself was long gone. The room beyond was a blazing furnace. He called her name, once, twice, in rising desperation. There was no response. He forced himself to go on to the next chamber.

There the fire had less of a hold, though the room was full of smoke. Dropping to his hands and knees, he crawled inside. Was there a corner where Jamie might have taken refuge? Again he called her name. Again there was silence.

Dear God, if he could not hear her any more, did that mean she was dead? It came to him then, like a bolt of lightning, that if she were lost to him, his life would be hollow and empty. Without her, life would be nothing. He must, *must* find her—even if he perished in the attempt.

He began to make his way farther along the landing. He was starting to lose his sense of direction in the dense smoke. It was beginning to affect his breathing. The dripping rug had almost dried. Parts of his clothes were beginning to singe as he crawled across the hot floorboards.

'Richard!' came that voice again. 'Richard! Please come back! Oh God, please don't let him die!'

The change in the now familiar litany brought him suddenly to his senses. It *was* her voice. Surely it was coming from down below, nearer the door? He began to feel light-headed. Was he dreaming? Was he already dead? Perhaps her voice was calling to him from beyond the grave? He shook himself out of his wandering thoughts. The smoke must be getting to his mind. It was certainly choking his lungs. He pushed himself even closer to the floor and began to edge painfully back towards the staircase.

The voice came again, more distinctly this time. 'Richard! Oh, Richard, where are you?'

Jamie! She *was* there! She was alive! 'I'm coming, my darling!' he croaked, through raw lips. It was barely audible. He reached the top of the stairs, gasping for air. He was exhausted. He had not the strength to move another inch. But if he remained where he was, he would surely die. With a silent prayer, he allowed himself to go limp and roll down the stairs.

The body which reached the bottom was senseless. 'Help me, William!' shrieked Jamie. 'He is here!' Together Jamie and the coachman dragged the inert body across the hall and into the blissfully fresh air outside. As they laid him on the cool grass, an enormous sheet of flame burst through the roof and the main timbers collapsed inwards on the floors below. What little had been left of the house was now completely engulfed by the fire. Bathinghurst was doomed.

Ignoring the tears streaking down her smoke-grimed cheeks, Jamie set about trying to revive her husband. 'Bring me some more water! Quickly, Annie! And you, William, the rugs from the carriage!'

She was cradling his poor blackened head in her arm while she bathed his face with cool water. 'Richard! Oh, Richard, I love you so. Don't leave me!' she cried in desperation, willing him to come back to her. Then pure, mutinous anger took possession of her. Nothing would be allowed to take him from her, not now. 'I won't let you die! I won't!' She repeated those stubborn words over and over as she gently tended her husband's hurts and tried to cool his over-heated body.

She was rewarded, at last, with a croaking attempt at a laugh as he came to himself again. 'It will take more than a little smoke to carry me off,' he whispered hoarsely. 'Especially now that I know I love you.'

Joy flooded through every fibre of Jamie's being. She was so overcome with emotion that she could not say a single word. She simply flung herself on to his chest, sobbing in relief.

His hand came up to touch her hair. 'Hush, my dear love. It's all over now. We are together. No one shall part us now.'

Jamie allowed herself the indulgence of tears for only a few moments before her practical side reasserted itself. Richard was hurt and exhausted. He must be taken at once to somewhere safe where his injuries might be tended.

'William! Help me bring his lordship into the carriage!' she commanded incisively.

Richard was now struggling to rise and would have collapsed again without the help of his wife and his coachman. Even as it was, Jamie was buckling under his weight, for he was too weak to support himself.

'You there!' cried William to one of the Bathinghurst servants watching open-mouthed. 'Get over here and make yourself useful!' The man hastened to obey, relieving Jamie just in time. His lordship's tall, athletic body was quite a burden, even for two men.

Jamie rushed to ready the carriage, but Annie was before her. She had spread the rugs and made a makeshift pillow with the clothes from his lordship's valise. It was no easy task to get Richard inside—he had lost consciousness once more—but eventually he was safely bestowed along the seat. Jamie took the seat opposite, anxiously chafing his hand and holding a damp cloth to his forehead to cool him.

William stood by the open door. 'Where to, milady?'

Jamie looked down at the faithful retainer, seeing his fatigue for the first time. How many hours had he been driving in search of her? 'There must be an inn hereabouts, William. Try if you can find it.' She forced herself to smile at him reassuringly. 'His lordship must be tended. And you must have some rest.'

William coloured slightly. 'Oh, no, milady. I'm

good for hours yet. But we'll need a change, if your ladyship wants to go any further. This team is spent.'

'The nearest inn will do very well for us all, William,' she repeated, with a calm she did not feel. 'Where is Annie? We must go!'

'She is travelling with me on the box, milady, all right and tight,' he replied with a grin and closed the door.

Although it seemed like an age to Jamie, anxiously watching over her husband's motionless body inside the carriage, it took William barely twenty minutes to make his way to the nearest inn. As the carriage turned into the yard, Richard stirred and opened his eyes.

Jamie breathed a sigh of relief. 'Thank God, you are come to yourself again. William has brought us to the nearest inn. You can be tended here.' She removed the damp cloth from his brow and made to pull back the rugs.

'Is that my neckcloth you have there?' croaked Richard.

'Oh!' For the first time, Jamie registered what she was holding. She looked hard at her husband. In spite of his pitiful state, he seemed to be amused. 'I fear it is,' she replied sternly, 'since there was nothing else to hand. And what is more, your head has been pillowed on the rest of your linen, so—'

Richard groaned theatrically and choked out a single word. 'Gregg!'

Jamie allowed herself the luxury of a giggle. If Richard could indulge in such levity, his hurts were not as serious as she had thought. 'Don't worry,' she added blithely. 'It was Annie's doing. I shall let them fight it out.' She paused. 'And my money will be on Annie!'

Richard grinned, rather weakly, which brought Jamie back to earth.

With help from William and the landlord, Richard was conveyed into the inn and taken upstairs to the best bedchamber. The landlord and his wife fussed about, bringing hot water, soap and towels for the high-born but dishevelled guests. And the gossip ran through the inn like wildfire.

Jamie's attention was fixed solely on her husband. She removed his ruined clothes and bathed his smoke-blackened body. He needed a shave too, but there was nothing she could do about that. 'You look a positive fright,' she said brightly, when he reached out to take her hand with his bandaged one.

Richard tried to speak but could not, even when he had sipped the water she handed to him. He pressed her hand.

'I'm sure you will be better soon,' she said encouragingly. 'There's no need to talk now. What matters is that you are safe.'

His eyes spoke for him. *And you*, they said.

'Shall I send for some brandy?'

He nodded.

'And some food too, I think,' she added, ringing the bell and ordering bowls of broth to be served to them. The look on Richard's face spoke volumes, but she pretended not to notice. As the little maid turned to leave, Jamie remembered her other responsibilities.

'My servants are to be given a hot meal and good beds, if you please.'

'Yes, milady. I'll tell the landlord, at once. Will there be anything else, milady?'

'Yes. I pray you ask the landlord if he can find a coat for my husband. His own was ruined in the fire and it will be some time before his valet arrives with another.'

'Oh, yes, milady, I'm sure he can.'

In no time she was back with the brandy and a black coat, no doubt the landlord's best. Since he was a burly man, the coat was broad enough for Richard's shoulders, though it fitted nowhere else.

Richard swallowed a gulp of brandy and turned to grin wickedly at Jamie. He could just about speak again now, thank goodness. 'You shall get your just deserts for this sacrilege, wife.' He rose unsteadily and made his way to the fireplace. One glance in the mirror there confirmed the worst. He shuddered. 'What a sight!'

Jamie joined him. 'Then we are a matched pair, my lord, are we not?' And indeed they were, for Jamie was still clad in the gown in which she had been kidnapped. It was now filthy, torn and crumpled, fit for nothing but the fire.

Richard smiled sweetly down at her. 'Perhaps the landlord's wife has a gown for you?'

Since the landlady's girth was at least twice Jamie's, that was more than a little unlikely, and he must know it. '*Touché*, my lord,' responded Jamie with a grin. 'I shall see if I can surpass you in...er...elegance!' She put a finger across his lips as he made to reply. 'Hush! Don't try to talk now. Wait till you have recovered a little more. We have plenty of time now.'

He nodded, gazing down at her with glowing eyes, and opened his arms to fold her against his broad chest. It was an embrace of comfort and of reassurance, of tender love but not of passion. He rested his cheek on her disordered curls and drew her ever more closely to him.

If Jamie had had any lingering doubts about whether he truly loved her, that embrace removed them all. With her arms wrapped around his waist, she leaned into his protective strength. Now was not the time for words. Later, when he had recovered a little and they could talk about the ordeal they had shared, then she would tell him how much she loved him. She smiled blissfully into his borrowed coat.

Richard and Jamie were sitting in companionable silence in front of the fire in the inn's private parlour. Both were still too exhausted to speak much, and Richard's throat was too raw. It was enough that they were together, and that the danger was over.

The little maid returned to report that her ladyship's instructions had been fulfilled—their servants had been well fed and had been provided with beds. Jamie nodded contentedly. For the present, she needed nothing more.

'Beg pardon, milady, but there is a visitor to see his lordship.'

Who would have the impudence to intrude on them

at such a time? Jamie raised an eyebrow, for all the world the great lady, in spite of her appearance.

The little maid continued bravely, 'It is Mr Peacock. The magistrate,' she added shyly. 'About the fire.'

Richard nodded wearily. The law must take its course.

Thomas Peacock, Esquire, seemed more than a little taken aback when he entered the private parlour to meet the Earl and his young Countess.

Richard hauled himself stiffly to his feet and extended his bandaged hand, pulling his ill-fitting coat together as best he could. 'Mr Peacock,' he said. 'I am afraid you find us in rather a sad way, for which I must ask you to accept my apologies. Will you not sit down?'

'Forgive me for disturbing you, my lord,' began the magistrate formally. 'You will understand that I have my duty to do.' He sat stiffly on the edge of the chair Richard had indicated. 'I understand you were involved in the fire at Bathinghurst, my lord?'

Richard nodded mutely and resumed his seat.

'Will you be so good as to tell me what happened?'

Jamie intervened quickly, before Richard could overtax himself. 'My husband was caught inside among the smoke and flames, sir, and can barely speak, but I was there when the fire started.'

The magistrate turned to her in surprise.

'Ralph Graves, the owner of Bathinghurst, is a distant relation of my family,' Jamie began crisply, keeping strictly to matters of fact, while watching out of the corner of her eye for any signal from Richard that she should not tell everything that had happened. None came. He was smiling slightly at her, which she took for encouragement. 'He...he had me abducted from London and was holding me against my will in that house.' Jamie had decided, almost without thinking about it, to omit any direct reference to her father.

'But this is unbelievable!' exclaimed the magistrate. 'What on earth could a man like Graves hope to gain from such a wicked act? Criminal, I should say, rather!'

Jamie looked towards Richard who nodded imperceptibly, still smiling warmly. 'Ralph Graves believed that my marriage to Lord Hardinge was not legal and could be set aside. He wished to marry me himself. He told me I would become his wife whether I willed it or no. That was the reason for my abduction.'

'Dear God,' breathed Mr Peacock, turning pale. He frowned, puzzled now. 'But what about the fire? I am afraid I fail to understand what that has to do with your abduction, my lady.'

'I started that deliberately,' she admitted immediately, with disarming candour. 'It was intended as a diversion, so that I could escape from the house without being seen by Graves and his people.'

Richard laughed throatily. 'Some diversion! I was wondering how you had managed to get away. I am still all agog to learn the way of it,' he added, reaching for the tumbler of water at his elbow.

'It was nothing so mysterious. As with the fire, there was really no other choice. I twisted a rope out of the bedcovers so that I could climb down from the

window. Since it was locked fast—as you would expect—I had to break it first.'

'I don't dare ask how you did that!' smiled
Richard.

Jamie shrugged. 'I flung the water jug through it.
There was nothing else to hand.'

'Of course! I should have known!' nodded Richard,
leaning back in his chair to admire his modest, courageous wife.

Mr Peacock coughed discreetly. He looked to be a
little embarrassed by the loving byplay in that
exchange. 'Forgive my plain speaking, my lord, but
you must understand this is a formal investigation,'
he said reprovingly. 'Pray continue, my lady.'

'I managed to reach the ground without being
hurt—the flower-beds under the window were quite
soft, considering how little they had been tended—
and I escaped into the woods which border the park.
Nobody saw me. At least, nobody followed me. I suppose they were too busy with the fire.'

'They thought you were still inside, my love,' in-
terposed Richard seriously. 'They did not know you
had escaped. Graves himself told me that you had set
the fire—and had died in it. He gloated over the fact
that he had taken you from me.' He reached out his
hand to cover hers.

The magistrate pricked up his ears at that. 'Graves
spoke to you, my lord? Where was he?'

'Upstairs somewhere. I thought at the time that he
was on the first floor, though when I reached there,
he still seemed to be some distance away. The mind
plays very strange tricks in the dark, I'm afraid, amid

all that smoke. I thought I heard my wife's voice too.'
He threw her a strange sidelong look, half-mocking,
half-serious.

'But you did!' exclaimed Jamie instantly.

Richard looked round sharply at her. 'What?'

'When I saw the carriage arriving, I shouted and
shouted, but apparently no one could hear me. I suppose I was too far away. So I started to run back to
the house. I tried to get to you before you went into
the fire, but it was such a long way from the woods
to the house that I was too late. You must have been
somewhere on the first floor by the time I reached the
main hall with William. You must have heard me
calling from there.'

'Yes,' he agreed slowly, fixing his eyes on her face,
'but not only from there. In my mind, I heard you all
the time, almost from the moment I knew you had
been taken.' The look which passed between them
then was filled with wonder, as they tried to come to
grips with what he seemed to have experienced. Was
it possible…?

Mr Peacock coughed again, more deliberately.
'Could Graves have been on the second floor, my
lord, on the landing above you?'

'Possibly. Why? Does it matter? Did he escape
from there?'

'He did not escape at all, my lord. That is to say,
we found two bodies after the fire. One was a great
bear of a man, scarcely recognisable. The other was
much smaller, and almost untouched. The servants
identified that as the body of Ralph Graves.'

Richard nodded. 'Yes, that makes sense. And the

other would have been his henchman, Caleb, who was acting as my wife's gaoler, I believe. What happened to him?'

'Trapped by a falling beam, my lord, and burned to death.'

Jamie shuddered and put her hand to her lips, picturing the scene. What a terrifying end, even for Caleb. And she was responsible! She had started the fire!

'And Graves?' asked Richard sharply, apparently unmoved by the deaths his wife had caused.

'We think he was on the second floor, trying to move a huge strongbox down the staircase. It must have meant more to him than the house or anything in it, even her ladyship. When the roof fell in, it took all the internal floors with it. Graves and his strongbox came down together and ended in the cellars, with Graves under his precious box. I'm afraid it killed him.'

'Justice,' said Richard harshly, without a moment's pause.

'I beg your pardon, my lord?' asked the magistrate, rather shocked.

'I said "justice", Mr Peacock,' repeated Richard deliberately. 'I learned yesterday that Ralph Graves was a blackmailer and a miser, who made his money by preying on the weak. He loaned money at exorbitant rates to people at their wits' end and, when the debtors could not repay, he sucked their lifeblood like a very leech. Many were totally ruined. I believe my wife's father was one of his victims. The man was an out-and-out villain. At least his death will give his victims back their peace of mind, if all his papers have been destroyed. I assume they have?'

Jamie had barely registered the end of Richard's recital. She was staring at her husband, wide-eyed with shock. Her father?

'I am most grateful for that information, m'lord,' said the magistrate. 'It explains a great deal. There can be no question of any action against Lady Hardinge, given the circumstances. The man Caleb was certainly an accomplice in Graves' criminal activity. And Graves was as culpable in the matter of his servant's death as in his own. The irony is that Graves risked his life to pull his strongbox out of the fire, but the box survived intact anyway. I may tell you—in confidence, of course—that it contains a great deal of money. It also contains documents, almost all of them undamaged.'

He cleared his throat. 'You might be interested in one of them,' he said, with a slight smile, the first he had ventured during the whole interview. 'It records a loan from your father to Sir John Calderwood, which was subsequently taken over by Graves. You should be able to recover the capital from the dead man's estate—once the formalities are completed, naturally.'

Richard nodded soberly, trying to conceal his surprise.

'One other thing, if I may,' said the magistrate, rising from his seat and turning to Jamie. 'You said Graves was related to your family, my lady. Would that be the Calderwoods?' Jamie nodded, bemused.

'And would you be Jessamyne Calderwood?' Jamie nodded again.

The magistrate smiled more broadly now, reaching into his pocket. 'Then, I see no need to retain these papers. They did not belong to Graves. I think these are your property, my lady,' he said, offering her a sheaf of legal documents.

Jamie was too astonished to move. Richard had to take them from the magistrate's hand.

'Your dowry, I believe, my lady,' continued the magistrate. 'You *are* married, I take it?'

Jamie began to protest at his question, but she was overtaken by a shout of hoarse laughter from her husband. 'Oh, yes, sir, I promise you, we are truly man and wife, though there was never any thought of a dowry when I proposed, I can assure you.' He laughed again, ignoring the strange looks from Mr Peacock, who probably thought the smoke had affected his lordship's mind.

'Come here, wife,' commanded Richard when they were alone once more. Jamie came to stand in front of him, still looking puzzled. With one swift move, he pulled her on to his lap and into his arms.

'Cease your frowning, my love. Those papers are the deeds to lands which were left you by your mother, to be under your control when you came of age, or on your earlier marriage. Although he had no right to do so, your father seems to have pledged them as security for his debts to Graves. I imagine he could not redeem them, so you were to be the means by which Graves would take possession of the forfeited land. There was no other legal way. It explains his illogical desire to marry you. It also explains the rush to tie the knot before you came of age and learned of your inheritance.'

Jamie stiffened in his arms. 'Illogical, is it, my lord, to wish to marry me? Why, you—'

'For him, since he already had you in his power. Not for me, you little vixen,' he admitted, silencing any further protests with a long, thorough kiss.

'And now, my love, my lady wife, I think it is time for bed, do not you?' She blushed delicately, but did not protest.

Much later, as they lay together in the intimacy of sated passion, Jamie voiced the question which had been on her mind since their arrival at the inn. 'You have told me you love me, Richard, but you have never asked me if I love you, or even given me a chance to say so. Why is that?'

'Because I already know, my love,' he announced, in tones of maddening certainty, beginning to stroke the lock of hair which lay across his shoulder.

Jamie dug a fingernail into his chest to regain his undivided attention. 'You are very sure of yourself,' she accused, 'considering I have said nothing.'

He picked up the offending finger and carried it to his lips, where he nibbled it gently. 'Wrong, my love. You told me over and over again, all through my journey from Calderwood to Bathinghurst. I could hear your voice calling my name and saying "I love you". Was it not so?'

'Yes...' she breathed in an awed whisper. 'It

helped me to keep my sanity. But I never really thought that I could reach you.'

'You have not enough faith in the power of love, my darling—which is strange, considering how much under my mother's influence you have come. And that reminds me...'

He reached across to the bedside table for the box that rested there. Then he took the Hardinge betrothal ring out of its velvet cushion and slid it on to her finger. 'Where this diamond is given and received in love, it brings blessings on both giver and receiver,' he said solemnly, his eyes locked with hers. 'I believe we have those blessings already. I love you, Jamie Hardinge.'

* * * * *

MILLS & BOON®

Makes any time special™

Mills & Boon publish 29 new titles every month. Select from...

Modern Romance™   Tender Romance™

Sensual Romance™

Medical Romance™   Historical Romance™

MAT2

FREE!

2 Books
and a surprise gift!

We would like to take this opportunity to thank you for reading this Mills & Boon® book by offering you the chance to take TWO more specially selected titles from the Historical Romance™ series absolutely FREE! We're also making this offer to introduce you to the benefits of the Reader Service™ —

- ★ FREE home delivery
- ★ FREE gifts and competitions
- ★ FREE monthly Newsletter
- ★ Books available before they're in the shops
- ★ Exclusive Reader Service discounts

Accepting these FREE books and gift places you under no obligation to buy; you may cancel at any time, even after receiving your free shipment. Simply complete your details below and return the entire page to the address below. *You don't even need a stamp!*

YES! Please send me 2 free Historical Romance books and a surprise gift. I understand that unless you hear from me, I will receive 4 superb new titles every month for just £2.99 each, postage and packing free. I am under no obligation to purchase any books and may cancel my subscription at any time. The free books and gift will be mine to keep in any case.

H1ZEB

Ms/Mrs/Miss/Mr ....Initials................................
BLOCK CAPITALS PLEASE

Surname..

Address..

....

....Postcode ....

Send this whole page to:
UK: The Reader Service, FREEPOST CN81, Croydon, CR9 3WZ
EIRE: The Reader Service, PO Box 4546, Kilcock, County Kildare (stamp required)